The
SCOLE
CONFESSION

Jacqueline Beard

The Lawrence Harpham Mysteries are published by Dornica Press

The author can be contacted on her website
https://jacquelinebeardwriter.com/

While there, why not sign up for her FREE newsletter.

ISBN: 978-1-9160506-2-4

ISBN-13: 978-1-91-605062-4

First Printing 2020

Dornica Press

Dedicated to:
Mum & Dad & Martin, Pat & Philip Dennis
with fond memories of happy times in Overstrand

Also by this author

Lawrence Harpham Murder Mysteries:

The Fressingfield Witch
The Ripper Deception

Novels:

Vote for Murder

Short Stories:

The Montpellier Mystery

PROLOGUE

Scole, January 1892

"Repent therefore and turn again that your sins may be blotted out."
Acts 2:19

My fingers tremble as I raise the hand mirror and regard my features through faded eyes. A murderess, clad in the guise of a harmless middle-aged woman, returns my gaze. She has one foot on the path to old age, but will never arrive. Death is close behind her and catching up fast.

She and I were once the same – selfish, greedy and without compassion. But I have changed. We are different people now. A fleeting moment of regret made its home in my heart and nested there, bringing with it a conscience. A conscience that crept like a vine, infiltrating my memories, nagging and whining like a spoiled child. It thrived on sickness, revelled in infirmity and grew like the disease that ravages my body.

I am not yet fifty, but my face bears the marks of old age and a life poorly lived. My hair, once a lustrous brown, is grey and patchy. Heavy bags nestle beneath my sunken eyes and wrinkles furrow my face. I try to smile, but my mouth lingers in a permanent scowl, as well it might. My worthless life is coming to a lonely end.

I blink as a sharp pain sears into my eyeball and peer into the mirror to locate the source of my discomfort. The pain is from a loose eyelash which I brush from my eye with a gnarled finger, then I lower the mirror, and it falls onto the bed. The looking glass is brass, with a tiny bevel the only nod to luxury. It is not elaborate, but I appreciate it, knowing that not every woman can afford a hand mirror. It was a treat to myself with the money I received when Fanny died. It must be fifteen years ago now, but I remember as if it were yesterday.

I shake my head to dislodge the memories, but they will not leave. I find myself wishing that the disease had taken hold of my sanity as it did with Mrs Peters, who lives in the room below. Her mind went long ago, and now she croons to herself with a vapid smile on her face as she rocks the day away staring from the window without a care in the world. Her life is easy and pointless, but unlike me, she was always a harmless old bird. In the end, the good Lord gives us the end we deserve.

He came into my life three or four years ago, the good Lord, that is. I hadn't known I needed him, hadn't reached the depths of despair that followed later. Hope still glimmered, if not burned. But back then, I thought nothing of death and was quite content to profit by doing nothing. I did not consider my silence unreasonable, but self-awareness wasn't far behind.

The Lord entered my life one warm August evening. I'd been walking down Mount Street towards the Market Place on my way to perform a chore. I can't remember what it was. As I passed the Kings Head Hotel, I noticed there were boards propped up against a brick wall on the opposite side of the road. The printed boards announced an address by an American evangelist. He was due to speak at half past seven, and a small crowd had gathered to watch. I hastened along with no intention of listening, but entirely by chance, I found myself returning down Mount Street at a quarter to eight. The evangelist was in full flow, and the crowd had increased in size. They gazed at him with rapt attention. I found myself stopping and without giving it any further thought, I settled on a step and began to listen. I continued watching, fascinated by his words, and he held my full concentration. The preacher was not American at all but spoke with a distinct East Anglian twang. He could almost be a native of Diss, though his deep voice bore traces of another accent and some of the words he used sounded foreign. Not American, though – somewhere more exotic.

The evangelist was tall with high cheekbones and a full head of white hair. He wore a grizzled, un-trimmed beard that reached the top button of his threadbare waistcoat and he spoke confidently. Impassioned, honeyed words dripped from his mouth, leaving me spellbound. I hardly noticed the minutes pass by, and he finished in no time. One by one, the crowd departed until I was the only one left still sitting on the step and with no inclination to move. He approached me and held out a weather-beaten hand. His leathery skin was the colour of burnt wood and smooth to the touch. He smiled as he pulled me to my feet and asked me what was wrong. I remember wondering what he saw in me that made him ask. "I have sinned," I whispered as a torrent of feelings I had never acknowledged raced to escape.

He didn't ask questions or attempt to pry, but with a notable lack of curiosity, said, "Shall we pray?" and I nodded. We knelt together on the dirty pavement, and he spoke to God with fervour and faith. When he finished, he smiled at me, and I brushed my skirts and stood before him. But our reverent silence was disturbed by a rattle of stones, and I glanced across the street. Two boys, the Scott twins, were standing there pointing with percipient smirks on their faces. They were laughing at me, and my face reddened as I considered their interpretation of my actions. There was I, older than forty summers kneeling on a dirty pavement with a stranger. I had made myself a figure of ridicule. And it was at that moment that I realised what I had always known. All the secrets I had kept and the lies I had told, would never bring love or happiness or peace. My loyalty was misplaced.

The preacher watched as I wiped a tear away. Then, he turned and reached into a cardboard box tucked behind one of the boards and took out a Bible. He wrote in the front then handed it to me. Clasping my hands around the holy book, he quoted, "The love that lasts longest, is the love that is never returned." He watched me through weary, knowing eyes and I recognised a kindred spirit.

I stammered my gratitude and left for my home in Scole, barely remembering the journey back. The same night, I placed the Bible in a drawer where it remained for many months. But from that day, my conscience grew increasingly troubled. Time spent alone gave me opportunities to contemplate the unrequited love that had justified my silence. And as my health failed, and the object of my passion remained indifferent to my suffering, I burned with shame for the part I had played.

I reach for the hand mirror again and hold it to my chest. I cannot bear to see my reflection a second time, but the weight of the cold metal gives a strange, familiar comfort. Doctor Brown says that it won't be long now. My time is approaching, and my strength fails. I touch the brass to my lips and think of the man whose face I loved and the crimes I concealed on his behalf, though he never loved me. I should tell Sergeant Hannant and let him know what has lain undiscovered for so long, but old habits die hard. I cannot betray my love though I can and must salve my conscience before I die. The mirror slips onto the floor, and I leave it there, reaching instead for the Bible on my bedside table. I pick up the stubby pencil lying beside it, lick the point and write on a flimsy blank page at the end of the book. It takes an hour to get the words down – an hour of concentration and despair. But I finish it while I still can.

The words are clumsy, untidy, but written from the heart. They form my confession though I doubt anyone will ever read it. At least I can go to God with peace in my heart. I tear the page from the Bible, and it rips with an untidy, jagged edge. Then I fold it twice and roll it until it curls. It fits easily into the spine of the Bible, and I push until it is out of sight before using my last reserves of strength to place the book back on the table. I wonder if it is enough to save my soul, but it is all I have left in me. I sink back into my bed covers and wait.

CHAPTER ONE

An Overstrand Holiday

Overstrand, April 22, 1895

"Well, that's awkward," said Lawrence. "You might have told me."

Francis Farrow put down his knife and fork and dropped a napkin onto his empty breakfast plate. Lawrence winced as a fishbone drifted onto the white table linen and wondered how long it would take before he felt compelled to move it.

"I don't see what the problem is," Francis replied. "Have you quarrelled with Myers?"

Lawrence sighed as he remembered the last time he saw Frederick Myers, a man he distrusted and feared. A man who had tried to kill him and afterwards had the nerve to ask for his discretion to cover a terrible crime. Lawrence had acquiesced, not from fear, but compassion. And because telling the story would benefit no one. It had been easy to conclude that the truth was not only unnecessary but vastly overrated. Which was all well and good, but it meant that only Violet and Michael ever knew the full story. Violet, never comfortable with concealing information, refused to discuss it at all. Michael, being a clergyman, was bound by the restrictions of his profession. So, although Francis was a close friend, Lawrence hadn't told him about the events in London that resulted in his incapacitation for the best part of two years. Had he done so, he might not now be sitting in the breakfast room of a man who turned out to be an intimate friend of Frederick Myers, and more if certain rumours were true.

"Not a quarrel, exactly," said Lawrence, moving his hand towards the plate. He picked up the fishbone and deposited it in a cup while making a split-second decision to lie. "Myers and I had some business dealings, which didn't work out."

"I doubt he's mentioned that to Cyril," said Francis. "They will have far more important matters to discuss."

"Perhaps," said Lawrence, distracted by the fishbone floating in the coffee grounds at the bottom of the cup. He stood and walked to the window where he placed his hands on the sill and leaned towards the garden. "They all know each other, though, don't they?"

"Who?"

"Our host, Cyril Flower – sorry, Lord Battersea as he is now known. He was a friend of Edmund Gurney too."

"Ah, the chap who died in Brighton. I see. Didn't he form part of one of your investigations? Something suspicious, if I remember rightly? I hope you don't think Cyril was involved."

"Not at all. Cyril dined with Gurney the night before he died, but there is no question of any wrong-doing. He is a good man as far as I know."

"A decent man," said Francis. "An alumni of Trinity College. That's where we met."

"So, I gathered. It's good of Lord Battersea to extend the invitation to the four of us. I only wish he wasn't so well acquainted with Myers."

"That's the sort of generous fellow he is," said Francis Farrow. "As soon as I told him why I had declined his invitation, he said I must bring you all if that's what it took to get me here. A fine fellow."

"And when do we get to meet him?" asked Lawrence turning from the window. He scowled at the coffee cup and dropped a napkin over it. The fishbone was finally satisfactorily hidden from view.

"At dinner tonight. The Batterseas are in Norwich today. Constance has a long-standing engagement at the prison."

Lawrence raised an eyebrow. "Sounds serious?"

"Not at all. Lady Battersea is an advocate for women prisoners' rights and is seeing the board of governors to campaign for better conditions in gaol."

Lawrence grimaced and wondered how wise it had been to accept the hospitality of a liberal politician. While far from sympathising with the 'hang 'em and flog 'em brigade', he had seen enough appalling crimes committed by both sexes to be unconcerned about the conditions in which they found themselves incarcerated.

"Talking of Lady Battersea--"

The door opened before Francis could finish, and a young housemaid appeared carrying a large silver tray.

"Excuse me, sirs," she said, bobbing a curtsy. She placed the tray on the sideboard and began to clear the table.

"Oh dear."

Lawrence watched as she knocked the coffee cup that he had hidden from sight under the napkin. A line of coffee grounds seeped into the white linen table cloth and dripped onto the carpet.

Lawrence bit his lip. "Sorry," he mouthed.

"I'll fetch a damp cloth," said the housemaid.

"What were you going to say about Lady Battersea?" asked Lawrence once the maid had left the room.

"Ah, yes. I didn't mention this before because I didn't want you to feel uncomfortable. After all, Cyril is much more down to earth. He knows men from all walks of life and status is less important to him."

Lawrence turned around. "Why do I get the feeling that I'm not going to like what you are trying to tell me?"

Francis walked towards the mirror opposite the sideboard and straightened his tie. "Lady Battersea comes from a prestigious family. She was a Rothschild before she married."

"Not the daughter of Sir Anthony, the merchant banker?"

"Yes."

"I didn't know."

"No reason why you should, old man. The point is that although she is passionately concerned for the welfare of the poor and needy, her natural companions are among the aristocracy. Lord and Lady Battersea entertain all manner of people from statesmen to royalty." Francis turned to face Lawrence before continuing. "As you know I am acquainted with Cyril from Trinity College. My father is a knighted high court judge; God rest his soul, so Michael and I have the right background..." His voice trailed away.

"I may not have advanced to your level in the police force," said Lawrence pursing his lips, "but my family have money and connections."

"You are not the problem," said Francis looking at his feet.

"I see. You are referring to Violet, aren't you?"

"She was a governess, Lawrence. She is from a different class."

"She is more of a lady than many I have known from the upper classes. And if it is such a problem, why did you invite us?"

"Please don't take offence. I have nothing but admiration for Violet. She is a friend and is welcome in my house at any time. The invitation was extended to both of you because I chose to honour our existing arrangements. I wanted to enjoy some time together, which is why Lord Battersea insisted that you come too. It's because I don't want Violet to feel embarrassed that I told Cyril that she was the daughter of a Scottish baronet."

"Please tell me you didn't. Violet hates deceit of any kind."

"Well, she's in the wrong job, then. Isn't that how you find things out?"

"Of course. Violet understands that it is necessary from a business point of view, but expects absolute honesty outside of that."

"I'm afraid she will need to treat this visit as if she was undercover. It will be easier for us all."

Lawrence shook his head. "I wish you hadn't misled Lord Battersea, Francis. Violet won't believe I didn't know."

Francis Farrow sighed. "It is done now. You had better find her and tell her the plan."

"Isn't this splendid, Cyril." Lady Constance Battersea beamed as she surveyed the dining room table, which was, as usual, beautifully laid out. Taking pride of place in the centre, was a whole salmon arranged upon a silver salver and surrounded by slices of cucumber. Caviar topped each slice, and the addition of giant king prawns and dressed crabs made a mouth-watering presentation.

"Yes, my dear. Cook has excelled herself. Please sit down." Cyril Flower gestured to his guests.

Lawrence Harpham took Violet's arm and guided her to a chair. When she was comfortably seated, he took his place beside her.

"Thank you," she said, biting her lip.

He patted her hand. "My pleasure."

"Well," said Lord Battersea. "It's good to see you at last, Francis. It's been far too long. What kept you away from us?"

"The Masonic lodge takes up most of my time these days," said Francis. "And I am on the board of Guardians for the Mill Lane workhouse, of course."

"Very commendable," said Lady Battersea nodding approvingly. "We also take a keen interest in the welfare of the needy. Cyril was in the village last week helping out with the Riseborough boy. So very sad."

"What was wrong with the poor lad?" asked Michael, ducking out of the way of the footman who was trying to fill his tumbler with water.

"He is dying from consumption." Lord Battersea shook his head sadly. "I delivered a box of food to his family. They are poor and in great want – but it is not enough to save him. A sad situation. His mother is widowed, and he is the eldest son and provides for the family."

Michael bowed his head. "God bless him," he said. Violet reached to her right and squeezed his hand.

"Your gardens are magnificent," said Francis trying to alleviate the gloom that had settled upon the room. He scooped the contents of one of the crab shells on to his dinner plate and ate it with relish. "Delicious."

"Overstrand crabs are the sweetest in the country," agreed Lady Battersea. "These are fresh from the sea today. As for the gardens, the credit is due entirely to Cyril. They are far from finished, but I love the view of the poppy garden from the veranda".

"You love it now, my dear. It wasn't always so."

"But you have made so many improvements since we first came to Norfolk. That awful, draughty cottage. I was never so cold in all my life. And now we are about to join the two villas into one grand house."

"Really? That sounds like a lot of work," said Francis.

"And it will take a long time to finish," Lord Battersea replied. "But I have employed the services of Edwin Lutyens. His architectural plans are almost ready. It will be a grand residence when it is complete."

"And you can entertain as many people as you wish," said Constance. "Which will make you very happy, I am sure. Now, tell me about yourself, Miss Smith. I understand you hail from Scotland."

Violet lowered her fork. "There isn't much to tell," she said softly.

Lawrence watched her with concern. It was unlike Violet to be quiet. She had barely spoken during the meal and was showing signs of nervousness in the presence of Lord and Lady Battersea. Lawrence worried that the ordeal of masquerading as someone else had quelled her natural enthusiasm for being in company. Knowing Violet, she would feel

9

like the worse kind of imposter. Under normal circumstances, Violet fitted into any social situation. Tonight, she should have shone, dressed in a royal blue dress with a delicate neckline and looking every inch a lady. Violet Smith was no beauty. The kindest description would cast her as homely, but being in her early forties suited her. Clear unlined skin and delicate laughter lines enhanced her features. She had recently lost weight, but not too much. Her cheekbones now appeared sharper and her jawline firmer. Lawrence realised that he had been staring and took a sip from his tumbler of water wondering why the wine hadn't arrived yet.

"How do you know dear Francis?" asked Lady Constance, trying to put Violet at ease.

"Oh, we met in Bury Saint Edmunds. I--"

The dining-room door opened, and the butler appeared. "Excuse me, your Lordship, Lady Battersea. Mr Morley has arrived."

"Do show him in," said Lady Constance.

John Morley followed behind the butler. Cyril Flower stood, and Francis followed his lead.

"No, please sit," said Morley. "Carry on eating. It looks splendid."

"We have saved you a seat," smiled Lady Battersea.

Morley pulled out a chair at the foot of the table and sat down. "Please forgive me. I was delayed in London unexpectedly."

"Don't give it another thought," said Lord Battersea. "Francis, this is my good friend and colleague, John Morley. John, meet Francis and Michael Farrow, Mr Harpham and Miss Smith."

"Pleased to meet you," said Morley nodding his head. He sat down and helped himself to a plate of food while the footman poured water into his glass.

"How are matters in Ireland?" asked Lady Battersea.

"Complicated," replied Morley. "And not helped by the interminable disagreements within our party."

"Lord Rosebery again?" asked Lady Battersea.

Lawrence loaded his plate with another slice of salmon while Morley nodded in agreement. He wasn't especially hungry, but Lawrence had no interest in politics, and it created a distraction to disguise his evident apathy.

"We'll talk about it later," said Cyril. "The internecine disputes within the Liberal party are not an aid to a convivial conversation. How are you finding retirement, Francis?"

"Very agreeable. I don't know how I found time to work." Francis continued to regale them with stories of his last year as a senior ranking officer in the Suffolk constabulary. Meanwhile, footmen cleared the salvers away and replaced them with an array of mouth-watering desserts.

"And I still see my old colleagues at the Masonic lodge, of course," Francis continued. "And last week brought a nice surprise. The Social Design lodge invited me to join as an honorary member. They want me to assist in the organisation of a banquet in honour of the first Suffolk Grandmaster."

"Can you be in two lodges at once?" asked Michael.

"I won't be. The honorary position is for the Oddfellows, not the Freemasons. They are a friendly society composed, in the main, of town tradesmen."

"I am sure you will be able to offer valuable advice," said Lady Battersea eating a spoonful of cherries and cream.

"I hope so," said Francis. "Representatives will be arriving from Liverpool and Manchester next week. The planning has to be meticulous for an event of this magnitude."

"Ah, Liverpool. I wish you were going there rather than them coming to you," said Lawrence. "I have promised to visit Uncle Frederick next week and would have enjoyed some company on the train. And your Brougham is very comfortable for travelling to the station."

"I will be leaving Norfolk in two days," said John Morley, "and going straight to Liverpool. "If you decide to visit early for any reason, it is only a short journey to Cromer railway station. We could travel together."

"My uncle is expecting me next week," said Lawrence. "He is a creature of habit and not given to changes of plan. But thank you anyway."

"I understand. Let me know if you change your mind."

"Would you like to join me in the music room?" Lady Battersea finished her dessert and dropped her napkin on the table.

"I will, thank you," said Violet looking anxious.

"Are you quite well, Miss Smith?"

"I am well," she replied. "Just a little tired."

"Then you must retire to your room and rest. I will find something else with which to occupy myself while the men talk."

"Thank you, your ladyship. You are very kind."

She waited for Lady Battersea to leave the room, then followed behind.

Lawrence flashed her a smile as she rose, but she did not catch his eye and left the room with her head bowed.

As soon as the ladies had departed, Cyril Flowers got to his feet. "Gentlemen?" he said, gesturing towards the door.

Lawrence discovered why there had been no wine at dinner as soon as they retired to the smoking room. Lord and Lady Battersea were enthusiastic members of the Temperance Society and enforced the prohibition of alcohol after one of their staff committed an unmentionable act while under the influence. Though Lord Battersea alluded to it, the exact nature of the misdemeanour remained a mystery. Lawrence probed him on the matter, but Cyril was tight-lipped. John Morley was evidently in the know but loyally tried to explain the move to temperance in political terms. The Liberal party encouraged abstinence and its many members now embraced it.

Nevertheless, once in the safety of the smoking room, Cyril produced a decanter of whisky and offered it to his guests. Lawrence and Francis both accepted a glass while the others declined. The ensuing conversation was informative and free-flowing, despite the lack of alcohol for one half of the party. But after an hour, Lord Battersea suggested that they regroup on the veranda. By then Lawrence had consumed his third glass of whisky. One look at Cyril's anxious face and he concluded that Lady Battersea was unaware of the alcohol concealed in her husband's private room. It was clear that he was hastening a rapid departure before they drank enough to give the game away.

The tactic was well-judged. Lady Constance had not retired and was sitting on the veranda gazing into the distance with a contented smile on her face. It was approaching nine thirty, yet the evening temperature was still warm. Lady Battersea greeted them cordially and beckoned them to join her in the well-furnished outdoor space. After a few moments of small talk, Morley asked Lord Battersea to join him in a stroll around the garden. They meandered past the poppy beds and were soon out of sight.

"I expect they have party business to attend to," said Lady Battersea, by way of explanation. "Now," she said, turning to Lawrence. "What is wrong with your companion?"

"Nothing that I know of," Lawrence replied. "The journey might have overtired her."

"Yes, that is very likely. It is a pity that Miss Smith retired early. Now I must make conversation with three old bachelors." She continued, "What a shame that you have all missed out on the pleasures of married life. My dear Cyril is the most beautiful of men and such an amiable companion. I cannot imagine life without him."

"I'm not sure Michael qualifies as old," said Francis, "and Lawrence is not a bachelor."

Lady Battersea raised an eyebrow. "I am sorry. I did not realise that you were married," she said. "Francis failed to mention Mrs Harpham."

Lawrence drew a deep breath, unsure of how to reply without causing embarrassment, but Francis seized the initiative. "Lawrence is a widower," he said.

"I am sorry," replied Lady Constance.

Lawrence sighed. "Please don't apologise. You were not to know."

Francis diverted the conversation towards the arts and found himself arguing with Michael about the relative virtues of Byron and the American poet Emily Dickinson.

Lady Constance had been fidgeting throughout their conversation. With the brothers fully occupied in their debate, she turned to Lawrence again. "I have loved Cyril since the day I first set eyes upon him," she said. "And I know the pain of loss when I see it. I am sorry that I upset you."

Lawrence leaned back in his chair and observed his hostess. Her eyes shone with genuine concern. Talking about Catherine was never easy, but it was unavoidable without appearing rude.

"You are not the cause of any distress," he said. "But Catherine died on May Day, and it is rapidly approaching. It will be the eighth anniversary of my wife's death – and also that of my daughter."

"You lost a child?" Lady Battersea's eyes widened, and she leaned forward. "I am so very sorry for you. What a tragedy."

"They died in a fire," said Lawrence, offering the information before she asked. "Catherine, my wife and Lily. She was only four years old. A beautiful little thing..." his voice trailed away, and he swallowed a lump. The pain of their loss had abated during the last few years, yet here tonight, it was raw again. He tried to speak, but the words stuck in his throat.

13

Lady Constance touched his hand. "In difficult times, we turn to our friends," she said. "It is so important to have loyal and compassionate companions." She smiled towards Michael and Francis.

Lawrence nodded. "I have known them most of my life," he said. "They are excellent men. Violet has also been a great comfort, although I have not known her nearly so long. But her kindness is inestimable."

Lady Battersea arched a brow, and Lawrence wondered whether she had misinterpreted his meaning. But there was no time to correct her as Francis had given up trying to persuade Michael about the superiority of Lord Byron's poetry.

"What's that about Violet?" he asked.

"Mr Harpham has been telling me about her many virtues," said Lady Battersea. "Ah, Mr Morley and my husband, have finished, it would seem. Hello, my dear," she said, rising to greet Lord Battersea who had emerged from behind the shrubbery.

"Come inside, it is getting cold," said Cyril, ushering them back into the house.

But Lawrence remained seated, in no mood for company. He stared into the darkness of the garden, brooding as he listened to the churning swell of the North Sea. It had been many years since the thought of Catherine had wrenched at his heart as it had tonight. Though he would always love her, he had become accustomed to her absence. His work as a private investigator had given his life meaning again. And because he was rarely alone, he seldom grew introspective and moody. Violet's influence had saved him from the worst of himself. Violet. She would know what to say to make the pain go away, though words were not what he needed. Being in her presence was enough and would take the edge off his misery. Damn Lady Battersea, for all her kindness. Without her interference tonight, the anniversary of Catherine's death might have passed without notice. Now, he was as afflicted by the yearly dread of May Day as he had ever been.

He looked at his pocket watch. It was a quarter to eleven. Violet's room was down the corridor from his own, and he must walk past it to get to bed. Lawrence entered the double doors in the dining room and slipped into the entrance hall bypassing the drawing room where his dinner companions were still talking. He climbed the stairs, then navigated to the west wing landing. Taking a deep breath, he knocked on Violet's door.

CHAPTER TWO

A Tragedy

April 23, 1895

Lawrence woke to the shriek of gulls. Cold air enveloped him as he pushed back the bedspread and rubbed his eyes. The wind must have unhooked the latched window in the night, and it was now splayed open and showing signs of damage. He pulled on his dressing gown and slammed it shut, watching the trees tremble and bend in the blustery wind.

Lawrence perched on the side of the bed and poured himself a glass of water, then contemplated the previous night. His despair at the memories of Catherine had lifted, as he knew they would once he was in Violet's presence. She had a calming effect, and dark thoughts never intruded when she was near. But he shouldn't have gone to her – shouldn't have compromised her position. And now today, he had a new set of problems.

He decided to walk off his worries before breakfast. The weather was unusually cold for April, and dry but with squally winds. A solitary walk on the Overstand cliffs with the sea breeze whipping at his face would make him feel alert and alive. He would know what to do by the time he returned.

Lawrence dressed and descended the grand staircase into the spacious entrance hall. He removed his coat and hat from the stand by the door and made for the side entrance. A murmur of voices alerted his attention to someone in the morning room, and he craned his neck to see who it was. Violet and Francis Farrow were exchanging pleasantries across the table.

"You're up early," he said, popping his head through the door.

Violet was stirring a cup of tea pensively. "I couldn't sleep," she said.

"Nor I," said Francis. "I must have eaten something that interfered with my digestion. Damned dyspepsia. I didn't catch a wink last night."

"I am going to take a stroll," said Lawrence. "Would either of you care to join me?"

Violet looked up and nodded. "I'll get my coat."

"I'll walk part of the way with you," said Francis, wincing as he stood. "I don't think I can manage much of a distance, though."

When they were suitably attired, they strolled through the water gardens and into Gunton Terrace. A right turn at the bottom took them to the promenade where steep stone steps descended to the beach. The tide was out, and rock pools draped in seaweed covered the sand flats. They walked across the beach barely speaking, while gusty winds whipped past their ears ruling out any attempt at small talk. It was just as well. Both Lawrence and Violet were deep in thought, and Francis was grimacing in pain. At the end of the promenade, they climbed a further set of steps reaching the cliff top without uttering a word.

"That's enough for me, old man," Francis yelled against the wind as soon as they reached the coast road. "Are you coming back now?"

Lawrence shook his head. "No, I want to walk a little longer."

Francis raised his hand as they parted, and he set off towards the centre of the village. Lawrence and Violet continued in silence until they reached the Mundesley Road. Then, Violet stopped and took a deep breath. "Are we going to talk about it?" she asked.

"Violet. I'm sorry, I..."

Whatever Lawrence was sorry about remained unspoken. As he was talking, a man dressed in a white shirt and dusty work apron, tore up the road towards them. "Help me," he cried.

"What is it, man?" asked Lawrence. "What on earth is the matter."

The man stopped, caught his breath and put his hands over his face. "I think he's dead; God help him," he said. "Give me a hand cutting him down."

"Who?" asked Lawrence, but the man was already racing back the way he had come.

"Hurry," he called over his shoulder.

Lawrence and Violet exchanged glances, then ran after him, catching him up in a large yard about fifty feet away.

"In there," he spluttered, pointing to a large shed.

"I'll go first," said Lawrence stepping inside.

As Lawrence's eyes grew accustomed to the dark shed, a shape hanging from the rafter in the middle of the room swam into view. It was the body of a man with his head tipped forward, and snow-white hair covered his eyes. The early morning sun had dappled his dark apparel as it filtered through holes in the dilapidated shed. Stack after stack of neatly piled bricks surrounded the corpse, each one standing over six foot high. Closer to the body lay a set of smaller piles. Each block was staggered and fashioned into a rudimentary staircase giving access to the rafters.

"Don't come in," said Lawrence gruffly, but it was too late. Violet was beside him, staring at the hanging man in horror.

"Help me cut him down," said Lawrence, bounding up the brick staircase. He reached the top and touched the man's neck.

"He's still warm," he yelled. "Get me a blade."

The man in the work apron fumbled in his pocket, then pulled out a wooden-handled pocket knife. He held it towards Lawrence who began hacking at the rope. After a few strokes, the frayed rope split and the body fell crashing to the ground. Violet ran towards the man and cradled his head. His face was deathly pale beneath greying stubble, and small patches of blood had formed on his lips and eyelids. She gripped his wrists and felt for a pulse.

"Well?" asked Lawrence.

Violet shook her head. "He is beyond our help."

The man who had raised the alarm let out a strangled cry.

"Do you know him?" asked Violet.

"He's my father-in-law," said the man. "His name is Edward Bowden."

"I'm sorry," said Lawrence. "I wish we could have saved him. Can you fetch a doctor, Mr...?"

"Cotton, George Cotton," said the man who was now sitting on a packing crate looking shocked and pale.

"I don't know. I'm--"

They were interrupted by the arrival of another man. "Oh, no," he said, clutching his chest. "Poor old boy. Have you told Mr Riches?"

George Cotton shook his head. "I've not long found him."

"Then I'll fetch him," said the young man, rushing away.

"Get the doctor, too," shouted Lawrence.

George Cotton scrambled to his feet, still pallid. "Wait for me," he said, stumbling from the shed.

"How are you feeling, Violet?" asked Lawrence, squatting on his haunches beside her. She was still holding the dead man's head.

Her voice trembled. "He looks peaceful," she said, "but I can't bear to think of anyone feeling so unhappy that this is their only option." She touched the rope still tied around his neck. "Should I undo it?"

Lawrence shook his head. "No, wait until the doctor arrives. Look, old girl," he continued, touching her arm. "You can't stay like this. Put him down."

"I can't leave him on the cold floor," she said.

"You must," said Lawrence firmly. He stood up and walked towards the door where he had seen a burlap sack earlier. Lawrence returned to Violet, moved Edward Bowden's head away from her lap and placed it gently on the sacking. "There is nothing more you can do," he said before holding out his hand. Violet grasped it, and he helped her to her feet.

"What's that," she asked, pointing to a second packing crate by the right of the brick staircase. Lawrence approached it to find a threadbare handkerchief, a few coins and a Bible.

"They must belong to him," said Lawrence. "He placed them there before..." Lawrence could not finish and stared mutely at Violet.

She bit her lip. "Poor, poor, man."

Without thinking, Lawrence picked up the Bible and opened the cover. "Another Edward," he said. "It's stamped inside. Edward Moyse, The English and Foreign Bible stall, Mann Island. Funny, that name seems familiar."

"What are you talking about."

"The inscription in the Bible. There's a verse inside, and the bookseller has signed it. He's from Mann Island. I know that name, but I can't remember where it is."

"Hmm," Violet half listened as she watched over the dead man, still reluctant to leave him.

"That's it," exclaimed Lawrence, clicking his fingers. "I jolly well ought to know. Mann Island is in Liverpool. It's not far from my uncle. Are you listening, Violet?"

"Yes," she snapped. "What does it matter. A man is lying dead, and all you can think about is the provenance of his Bible. Why are you so interested? And who is this other Edward?"

"Who indeed?" said Lawrence. He paced for a few moments, then returned to the packing crate and opened the Bible again.

"I knew it," he cried. "I must be getting old, Violet. Of course, the name is familiar. It's been all over the newspapers."

"What has?"

"The murder of Edward Moyse earlier this year in Liverpool."

"It can't be that Edward Moyse?"

"It must be. Moyse was a bookseller in Mann Island."

Lawrence clutched his forehead. "Honestly, Violet. I'm losing my faculties."

Two men rushed into the shed before Violet had time to respond.

"George Riches," said the shorter man reaching out his hand. "I own the brickyard. Mr Bowden was one of my men. This gentleman is the coroner."

"I am Lawrence Harpham, and this is Violet. We are very sorry for your loss."

The coroner knelt and inspected the body. "I can confirm that life is extinct. He's probably been dead for a few hours. Did you find him?"

"No, it was George Cotton – his son-in-law.

"Thank you. There's nothing else you can do," said the coroner. "Leave us to it."

Lawrence nodded and guided Violet towards the door, passing by the packing crate. He waited until both men were facing the body, then discreetly lifted the Bible and placed it in his breast pocket.

CHAPTER THREE

The Bible

"If you'd told me it would be this damp, I would have changed my shoes," said Violet, struggling to keep up with Lawrence's rangy pace.

"Sorry, you should have said. I'll slow down so you can avoid the wet grass," Lawrence replied.

"What's the rush, anyway?"

"There isn't one. I'd just rather be doing something than nothing."

Violet sighed. They had returned to the Battersea residence straight after their unfortunate encounter with what remained of Edward Bowden. By the time they reached the villa, Lady Battersea had left for an engagement at the Belfry school while Lord Battersea and the Farrow brothers had gone for a round of golf at the Cromer golf course.

"He made a quick recovery," said Lawrence after the housemaid informed him that Francis was much improved.

"There's not much that Doctor Morses' compound syrup doesn't fix," she'd replied. "Now, can I offer you tea or coffee?"

Lawrence declined, opting to meet the men at the golf course instead. "It's not far," he had told Violet, and they set off at a brisk pace down Paul's Lane. They considered walking past the ruined church and along the main Cromer Road but settled for a walk across the cliffs.

The grass was still damp from the early morning dew. As Violet's shoes grew wetter, she became more irritable and struggled to disguise it. Lawrence was eager to discuss the Bible that they had found near the hanging body, but Violet was reluctant. She always found death unsettling, but this time was worse than usual. Lawrence became increasingly concerned over her mood, as it veered between sadness and anger. The longer they walked, the more distressed Violet became. Eventually, she turned to Lawrence and asked him to make a solemn promise never to suffer in silence if he was feeling low. Understanding at once that her fears came from witnessing the suicide, he reached for her hand and brushed it against his lips.

"You know I always seek you out if I am worried," he said. "Like I did last night."

She smiled, expecting him to drop her hand, but he did not. They were still walking hand in hand when they approached the Royal Cromer Golf Club.

"Look," said Violet, pointing to a group of men in the distance.

"There they are," said Lawrence. "Michael is wearing his dog collar."

Lawrence raised a hand as they approached while Lord Battersea stepped forward and removed a golfing iron from his bag. Lawrence placed his finger to his lips and whispered. "Wait." They stood in silence until Battersea had taken his shot which whistled down the course and onto the dogleg.

"Well done," said his partner approvingly.

"Hello. Good to see you've caught us up," said Francis Farrow, patting Lawrence on the back.

"Who is Lord Battersea playing with?" asked Lawrence.

"None other than the great Willie Aveston," said Francis.

"Is that supposed to mean something?"

"Not to a philistine like you, with no love for the noble game. He is a professional golfer and very well regarded," said Francis.

Lawrence shrugged.

"Shall we go, then?" asked Michael, watching Lord Battersea and Willie Aveston walking down the course to take their next shots.

Lawrence put his hand out. "It feels like rain," he said.

"Nonsense," said Francis Farrow, but within moments the heavens opened.

"They're not going to stay out in this?" asked Michael striding towards the clubhouse.

"I expect so," replied Francis. "Anyway, it will soon be over."

They settled inside watching from the window. Michael and Violet cupped mugs of tea while Lawrence and Francis nursed brandies.

"Where did you two go after I left you this morning?" asked Francis.

Lawrence and Violet exchanged glances. "You tell him," said Lawrence as Violet recounted their experience.

"But that's not all," said Lawrence, interrupting her as she described the mean little pile of coins and the handkerchief on the packing crate.

"He left a Bible from a bookstall run by none other than Edward Moyse."

"The murder victim?" asked Michael.

"The very same."

"Dashed odd," said Francis. "Still, there's a Bible seller in every town."

"Fascinating, don't you think?" asked Lawrence.

Francis grunted.

"I've still got the Bible," said Lawrence. "I suppose I ought to take it back. I had better find out where the family live."

"Who are they?" asked Michael.

Lawrence screwed up his eyes in concentration. "The dead man is called Bowden, and his son-in-law is George Cotton."

"Gunton Terrace, then," said Michael.

"How the devil do you know that?"

"Lady Battersea and I spoke at length about their charitable work yesterday," he replied. "Lord Battersea was unduly modest when he mentioned the Riseborough boy at dinner. He often takes gifts of fruit and food items to the poor and sick. The eldest Cotton lad broke his leg last year and was unable to walk for several months. Lord Battersea visited the family on several occasions."

"Where is Gunton Terrace?"

"Close to the villa, opposite the Water Gardens."

"Excellent. We'll go now. Are you coming, Violet?"

Violet sighed as she looked at her wet shoes before pushing her half-finished mug of tea away.

"Yes, for all the good it will do," she muttered beneath her breath.

Number four Gunton Terrace was a red brick house in a terrace of similar properties. Located opposite the flint wall surrounding the Battersea residence, it was a tidy property. Cheerful curtains adorned the front windows, and a pretty window box full of daffodils complemented the brickwork. Lawrence knocked on the door to be met by a slender young woman dressed head to toe in black. Her eyes were swollen and red-rimmed, and a young child squirmed in her arms.

"What do you want?" she asked defensively.

Lawrence hesitated.

"We would like to give our condolences." Violet stepped in before Lawrence said something insensitive. "We found Mr Bowden in the shed this morning."

The woman's features softened. "My husband said there were other people there," she replied. "Thank you for trying to help him."

"Who is it, Amelia." A quavering voice emanated from the back room of the property.

"Visitors, Mother. They have come to pay their respects."

"Show them through."

Lawrence and Violet stepped into the hallway and through a door to the front parlour immediately on their right. Inside, were six wooden chairs arranged around a fireplace above which hung a large oil painting of a fishing boat. Heavy net curtains blocked the light bringing a sombre quality to the room.

"Take a seat," said the young woman releasing the wriggling child from her arms. She left the room, and the child stood in the doorway, watching them balefully. Violet reached her hand towards the little girl, but she shrank away, then toddled down the hallway towards her mother. They sat in silence for a few moments until Amelia Cotton returned, accompanied by a stout, grey-haired woman, also dressed in black.

"This is my mother," she said.

Lawrence stood and bowed his head. "I'm pleased to make your acquaintance. I wish it were under happier circumstances."

"Thank you," she replied, offering her hand. "Do take a seat."

Lawrence perched on the chair, wondering how to proceed, but Jane Bowden spoke again.

"Amelia said that you tried to help my husband."

"We attempted to, but he was beyond our aid."

"I did not hear him leave the house this morning," she said, pausing as she tried to control the tremor in her voice. "I have been unwell, and he let me lie abed. Had I risen with him, he might not have..." Her voice broke, and a single tear slid down her soft cheek.

Amelia Cotton knelt beside her mother and held her hand. "Please don't blame yourself," she whispered. "Father has not been right for a while."

"Did he ail?" asked Violet.

"Not physically. My father was sick in his head," Amelia replied.

"Edward's spirits never recovered after he lost the foreman's job," said Jane Bowden.

"He did not lose it." Amelia corrected her mother. "Times were hard, and there was not enough work for everyone. My father was a good man, unassuming and loyal, and couldn't bear to let his men down, but there was no choice. Circumstances forced him to let some of them go – men with families and mouths to feed. He never forgave himself and never recovered his spirits. He couldn't work for a long time, but Mr Riches was kind to him, more than most employers would be. He talked to my father, and they came to an arrangement. Mr Riches would replace him with a younger man who would become the new foreman and father could stay on at the yard. A lesser man than Mr Riches would not have cared, and we might have starved."

"I have only met him once, but he struck me as a decent chap," said Lawrence.

"The very best," agreed Jane Bowden, dabbing her cheeks with a black lace handkerchief.

"How will you manage now?" asked Violet

"We are lucky. Edward was a member of the Oddfellows. They will provide for us."

"Oddfellows?"

"A friendly society, I believe," said Lawrence.

"Yes, a burial club. Edward paid tuppence a week to the Loyal Albion lodge in Cromer. They helped us when he couldn't work a few years ago, and they will pay out now that he has died." Mrs Bowden put her head in her hands and sobbed silently.

Lawrence rubbed his chin, feeling uncomfortable at her distress, then remembered his reason for being there.

"This belonged to your husband, I believe," he said, producing the Bible. He passed it to the grieving widow.

She smiled through her tears. "Yes, this belongs to Edward. This little book was one of his few pleasures in the end."

"I noticed the mark on the front," said Lawrence. "The Bible came from Liverpool."

"It was a gift from his friends in the lodge," said Jane Bowden. She opened the book and pointed to an inscription.

Lawrence read it aloud, "Do not call to mind the former things, or ponder things of the past. Isaiah 43:18."

"Was that a favourite Bible verse?"

"No," said Mrs Bowden, "but some of the Norfolk Oddfellows arranged a fraternity visit to Liverpool at the end of last year. It was a big event with many lodges talking part. Edward was too unwell to go and was very disappointed. His friends in the Loyal Albion visited the Albert Docks and passed a Bible stall on Mann Island. The English and Foreign Bible stall, I think. Anyway, John Dennis and a few of the other men saw the inscription in the Bible, thought of Edward and his troubles, and purchased it for him. It was a source of great comfort, and I am grateful for its return."

Lawrence smiled weakly. His conscience was beginning to get the better of him at her gratitude for returning something he shouldn't have taken in the first place.

"We should leave now," said Violet. "We have taken up enough of your time."

Mrs Bowden smiled graciously, and Amelia showed them to the door.

"Our condolences once again," said Lawrence, tipping his hat as they left.

Violet chatted as they walked the short distance to the Battersea residence, but Lawrence was monosyllabic.

"What are you thinking?" she asked while they walked up the driveway.

"Odd business, this Liverpool killing," he said.

"Not really. Hasn't the murderer been caught?"

"Well, yes."

"Then it's all over, bar the hanging."

"Hmmm."

"Lawrence. I know that look. There is nothing about this crime that requires our attention."

"I know," he said. "I know." He retired to his room and settled on the end of the bed deep in thought, watching the gulls circle round the cliff. He was still watching them two hours later.

CHAPTER FOUR

Last Dinner at The Cottage

"I jolly nearly thrashed him," said Lord Battersea, carving a slice of beef from the magnificent joint taking pride of place on the dinner table. "A spot of bad luck at the last hole put the kybosh on it, but it was a close-run thing."

"Well done, Cyril, old chap," said Francis tucking into his evening meal with relish, the earlier attack of dyspepsia a distant memory.

"It was good practice ahead of my game with Lord Suffield at the weekend."

"Does Suffield play well?" asked John Morley.

"He's won the majority of our games so far, but he won't win this one," said Lord Battersea, nodding his head confidently.

Lady Battersea smiled at her husband. "Have you recovered from your ordeal this morning?" she asked, turning to Violet who cocked her head solicitously.

"Yes, thank you," Violet replied.

"And you called upon Mrs Bowden?"

"We did. She was very distressed as I am sure you can imagine. It had only been a few hours since her husband passed away."

"I will drop in on the family tomorrow," said Lady Battersea. "It is the least I can do. Dear Mother instilled in us a great sense of duty. There is much pleasure to be had from helping others to lead full and happy lives."

Michael smiled. "I am sure they will appreciate your attention," he said. "I fear I may have a visit of my own to make when I reach my parish tomorrow."

"Really?" Lady Battersea looked at Michael with concern.

"Yes. Suzanne Hardy, the coachman's wife. She's been suffering from tuberculosis and can hardly rise from her bed. I happened upon her husband in our little church the day before I left. The poor chap was knelt on the floor and praying to God with such concentration that he did not hear me enter. I placed my hand on his shoulder, and he started in shock, so I joined him, and we prayed together and asked that God might spare her. I can only hope that he answers our prayers, but I fear she was too far gone to hold out much hope."

"Life is but fleeting," murmured Lady Battersea.

"Hmmm." Lord Battersea smiled at his wife. "Let us speak of happier things, my dear," he said.

"Like your golf game," laughed Francis.

"I could talk about that all night, but my head will grow big," said Lord Battersea. "I say, Mr Harpham, did you get to the post office in time?"

"Post office?" echoed Violet.

Lawrence coughed. "Yes, I did," he replied, turning away from Violet's gaze.

"Ah, so you are going to join me tomorrow?" asked Morley.

"Yes, if it is still convenient. Thank you again for your kind offer."

"What offer?" Violet did not attempt to conceal her suspicions.

"Mr Harpham has agreed to join me on my trip to Liverpool, and Lord Battersea has kindly arranged a carriage to the station."

"You are going to Liverpool tomorrow?" asked Violet angrily.

"Yes. I sent a telegraph to Uncle Frederick this afternoon, and he replied just before dinner. Fortunately, he has no other engagements, and it suits him to see me this week instead of next."

Violet did not answer. She stopped eating, put her cutlery down and glared at him with ill-disguised annoyance.

"Francis and Michael will accompany you to Bury Saint Edmunds. It will be no different from our original plan except that there will be three travelling instead of four."

27

"How long will you be?" Violet watched him through reproachful eyes, her anger already turning to disappointment.

"A few days, at most," said Lawrence. "I will catch a train at the end of the week."

Violet opened her mouth to ask how she was supposed to manage their office alone again. Then thought the better of it, remembering that she was acting as the daughter of a Scottish baronet during this visit. She recovered herself and politely asked Lady Battersea about her earlier visit to the Belfry school.

Lawrence let out a deep breath. He had escaped Violet's wrath for now, but would no doubt have to face the consequences in the not too distant future.

CHAPTER FIVE

Mann Island

April 24, 1895

Lawrence and John Morley parted ways by the Albert Docks. Morley was due to resume his post in Ireland the following day and had taken rooms at his usual hotel. Lawrence had declined the offer of a drink on the pretext of going straight to his uncle's house in Derby Square. He would go there, eventually, but not before he visited the bookseller's stall in Mann Island. The murder of Edward Moyse fascinated Lawrence for reasons that he didn't fully understand. Ordinarily, he would not have rushed to Liverpool at the risk of upsetting Violet. She had taken the dominant role in the business part of their occupation since Lawrence's injury and after being incapacitated for the best part of two years, Lawrence had stopped acting on impulse and did not take unnecessary risks. He was calmer and more measured in his approach towards investigations. Violet had been right, and the business had recently become profitable due to her more cautionary nature. Lawrence no longer dreaded paying the rent and keeping on the right side of Violet was a price he was happy to pay. But, he told himself, he was only bringing a planned visit forward by a week because the transport arrangements were better. And he might as well visit the scene of the murder while staying in

Liverpool. After all, he was a private investigator, and it was perfectly reasonable to take an interest.

Lawrence alighted from the railway carriage to heavy rain which continued for half an hour before petering into a drizzle. He walked along the greying pavements, not bothering to open his umbrella. The dockyard buildings brought a pang of familiarity as he thought of happy childhood visits. Lawrence inhaled a lungful of salty sea air and gazed towards the sea. Sleek-backed gulls swooped low across the sky, buffeted by sea winds. The younger birds, now independent of their mothers, picked at the detritus on the pavements. Circling above, the adult gulls shrieked and mewled their disapproval.

Lawrence closed his eyes and tried to visualise the last time he had been in Liverpool. Aunt Clara had still been alive, and Catherine was with them so it must have been a short time after they married. Had it really been that long since he had visited Uncle Fred? He felt a momentary pang of guilt, quickly forgotten as he approached a pavement opposite a terrace of red brick houses. His attention had wandered to a row of stalls where street vendors were trading their wares. Lawrence hadn't known where to find the Bible seller, but his knowledge of Liverpool was good and he'd thought he could still remember where to find the Mann Island stalls. Sure enough, he located the bookseller's stand close to the Liverpool landing stage. Behind it was a young boy with deep brown eyes and skin the colour of polished ebony. He smiled as Lawrence drew close.

"Can I help you, sir?" His voice was deep and resonant with an unfamiliar but pleasing accent.

"Do you sell Bibles?"

"Uh, huh."

"That's a good start, but I am looking for a particular stall." Lawrence retrieved a notebook from his coat pocket and scanned the pages. "The British and Foreign Bible Society stand, to be precise."

"This is it," said the young man, gesturing to a poster immediately behind him.

"Ah, yes," said Lawrence, relieved. "Do you usually look after the stall?"

"I only been on it 'bout half an hour," smiled the young man. "I've been keeping watch for Mister Patterson while he's gone on an errand."

"When will he be back?"

The boy shrugged. "An hour, maybe two."

"Thank you." Lawrence reached for a red leather Bible and opened the cover. The bookseller's mark, familiar from the Bowden Bible, was on the flyleaf, stamped but without an inscription. "Did you know Mr Edward Moyse?" asked Lawrence.

"I knew him by sight," said the boy. "I never spoke to him an' now I never will."

"But Mr Patterson knew Moyse?"

"Might have. I don't know. Mister Patterson knew the murderer though, and that's for sure."

"How do you know?"

"Because he told me. William Miller was the man's name. I only met Miller once, but he called me names and kicked me out of the way. Mister Patterson took over the stall after Moyse died. When it got busy, he'd ask me to look after it while he did other things. One day, he picked up a newspaper and said he was surprised about Miller's arrest as he never knew him to be violent. I told him that the man was guilty fo' sure. He kicked me when all he had to do was ask me to move."

"Do you think he killed Moyse?" asked Lawrence.

"Everyone thinks so," said the boy, nodding his head. "He was not a nice man."

"Well, thank you for your time," said Lawrence, smiling. "I'll be on my way now."

"You don't want to buy a Bible?"

Lawrence shook his head and retraced his steps, walking the pavements until he reached Derby Square. From there, it was only moments to his uncle's house in Lord Street. He knocked on Uncle Fred's front door, and without waiting for a reply, he stepped inside.

"Lawrence," how lovely to see you. Uncle Fred shuffled down the stairs as Lawrence stepped into the hallway. They shook hands warmly.

"Did you have a good journey?"

"I did," said Lawrence. "Thank you for accommodating the new date of my visit."

"It was no trouble," said the old man, gripping a wooden stick which he'd propped up against the stair post. He gestured ahead to a door on the right.

Lawrence obliged and entered the drawing room where a large photograph of his aunt Clara took pride of place above the marble fire surround. Lawrence smiled at her likeness in fond remembrance. The rest of the room was largely unchanged since his last visit and evoked an unexpected nostalgia.

"Sit down," said his uncle.

Lawrence waited for Frederick Harpham to settle. The older man limped towards a wing-backed armchair and carefully lowered himself onto the seat.

"Gout," said Uncle Fred, by way of explanation before Lawrence had the opportunity to ask.

"How are you keeping, Uncle."

"Tolerably well, for a weak and feeble pensioner."

"And Harriet?" Lawrence had not seen his cousin for at least a decade.

"She is back." His uncle beamed. "She has had enough of Devon and will not return."

"Excellent," said Lawrence. "My father sends his regards," he continued disingenuously. His father would have extended his regards, had he known Lawrence would be in Liverpool a week earlier than planned.

"Good. And how is Lionel?"

"Very well and often calls in on Uncle Max."

"Ah, is Max still spending every waking hour whittling wood?"

"Probably more than is good for him, so Aunt Myrtle says."

They carried on chatting about family until Uncle Frederick took out a pocket watch and checked the time. "What about a spot of tea?" he asked.

"That would be nice."

His uncle lifted a bell tucked away to the side of his chair and rang it vigorously. Moments later, a woman in her sixties, attired in a pinafore dress and white apron, appeared in the doorway.

"Connie, my dear. Would you fetch some tea and cake?"

"Yes, Frederick," she smiled.

Uncle Frederick leaned forward. "This is Connie, my housekeeper," he said, smiling at the woman.

"Pleased to meet you." Lawrence nodded his head, wondering if he ought to stand and offer his hand. He wouldn't ordinarily shake hands with a domestic, but the relationship between his uncle and the housekeeper seemed oddly informal.

Connie left the room before he could decide, and the two men continued talking. Before long, she re-appeared with a wooden tray containing a teapot, cups and a china plate piled high with gingerbread.

"I made it myself," she said proudly.

"Capital," beamed his uncle, stretching forward to take a piece. "Delicious," he continued as crumbs spilt down his waistcoat. "You have excelled yourself."

Connie's face turned pink, and she left the room, beaming.

"A good cook," said Lawrence, eating his cake. It was palatable but no more than that. Still, it wouldn't harm to flatter the housekeeper, as it seemed to matter to his uncle."

"She's a treasure," said Uncle Frederick. "I do not know what I would do without her."

"Has she been with you long?"

"About a year," he said. "I grew tired of managing my domestic affairs after Clara died. And it was lonely with Harriet away. Connie is both housekeeper and companion."

Lawrence nodded, understanding all too well the absence of a loved one. His reaction had been different from his uncle's when he became a widower, and he had chosen a more solitary path. Lawrence had attended to his chores alone, feeding himself only when strictly necessary. It was different now, of course, with time having passed and the torrent of grief trickling to only brief moments of pain. Lawrence would not wish any hurt upon Uncle Fred and what harm could it do if his housekeeper was something more? Good for him.

"I was in Mann Island earlier," he said, changing the subject.

"Whatever were you doing there? There isn't much to see."

"Re-visiting childhood haunts," said Lawrence.

"Of course," chuckled his uncle.

"And I happened upon a Bible stall."

"Oh?"

"Edward Moyse used to own it."

"Moyse, you say. Wasn't he the chap that got himself killed?"

"Yes, he was."

"Rum affair," continued Frederick Harpham. "They've caught him, you know."

"The murderer?"

"Yes. William Miller."

"Guilty as charged?"

"No doubt whatsoever, though he continues to deny it. Too many witnesses, though. He will hang."

"Was it a robbery?"

"Well, it seems that way. Though according to the newspapers, he left a purse of money in the house."

Lawrence leaned forward. "Is that what you meant when you said 'a rum affair'?"

"Partly," said his uncle.

Lawrence waited for Frederick to continue, but he looked fixedly towards the window and stayed silent.

"Did you know him?"

"Who?"

"Moyse."

"No. Not at all."

"Was the murder discussed at your club?"

"Not really. When it first happened, it was all anyone spoke of, of course. But not for long. Why don't you go and see young Strettell, if you want to know more? He was at the heart of it."

"Tom Strettell? Is he still in the police force?"

"Yes, why shouldn't he be?"

"We worked together about eight years ago," said Lawrence." A case of fraud crossing several counties. He didn't come out of it well as I recollect and I haven't seen him since. I could try, I suppose."

"I thought you wanted a break from investigating," said Frederick.

"This is a break," Lawrence smiled. "And if you have the time to spare, you can show me the sights. But I might see Tom while I am here too, for interest's sake. You don't mind, do you?"

"Not at all." His uncle helped himself to another slice of ginger cake. "I am getting old, Lawrence, and spend too much time in this chair asleep, much more than I care to mention. You must come and go as you please."

"Then I'll drop in on Tom tomorrow."

Lawrence sipped his tea and watched as, true to his word, Uncle Frederick drifted off to sleep.

"A rum affair," his uncle had said, without expounding on what he meant. The more Lawrence considered it, the more he felt that his uncle had skilfully evaded a pertinent question. Any murder was unnatural by definition, but there was something nebulous lurking in the background of this one. Something his uncle hadn't felt able to say. The hairs on the back of Lawrence's neck prickled in anticipation. Something was wrong with the Moyse murder, and Violet wasn't here to stop him looking into it. Tomorrow, he would investigate as if the case was officially his.

CHAPTER SIX

Redcross Street

April 25, 1895

"Detective Strettell is outside," said the young police constable. The sallow-faced policeman was sitting at the front desk with his feet on a stool wearing rolled-up sleeves. A half-eaten sandwich lay in full sight. Lawrence regarded him with disappointment. Standards in the police force had dropped over the last few years.

"Where exactly?" asked Lawrence.

"In the yard, around the back."

"Don't get up. I'll find him myself," said Lawrence sarcastically as the constable continued to stare vacuously at the facing wall.

Lawrence walked towards the rear of the police station manoeuvring past a row of cycles propped up against the dirty exterior of the building. He noticed Tom Strettell immediately. Strettell had hardly changed and was ageing well with barely a wrinkle and only a smattering of grey at the temples. He stood in front of an odd-looking vehicle with his arms crossed. Lawrence walked towards him and held out a hand.

Tom Strettell looked up with a puzzled expression that gradually altered as recognition dawned.

"I know you, don't I?" he said, with a hint of an accent.

"Lawrence Harpham, former Suffolk Constabulary. We worked on the Croxteth case.

Strettell's face darkened. "I remember," he said. "What do you want?"

Lawrence rubbed his left palm as he considered his response. It was a habit he had almost lost since discarding his trademark leather gloves the previous year. His brush with death in '91 had encouraged him to scrutinise the less than perfect parts of his life. His obsession with concealing the scars on his damaged left hand suddenly seemed like an unwarranted indulgence. He'd elected to discard the gloves along with some other bad habits feeling an immediate relief akin to shedding an uncomfortable skin.

"I want to ask you something, but first, tell me about this carriage? I have never seen anything quite like it."

Lawrence gestured towards the contraption in the middle of the yard.

"She's a beauty, isn't she?" said Tom Strettell smoothing his hand across the polished wooden carcass.

"Yes," agreed Lawrence, tactfully. "Though not dissimilar to a large perambulator."

Strettell scowled. "It's a horseless carriage," he hissed. "Three horsepower with a tube ignition."

"Is it yours?"

"No. It's a prototype belonging to a friend of mine. He was going to test her up a hill."

"Then, what is it doing here?"

"Waiting for a mechanic," said Strettell.

"Ah. It's broken then?"

"Never you mind. What do you want?"

"You remember my uncle?"

"Vaguely."

"I'm staying with him. He happened to mention the murder case you are working on."

"Did he?" Strettell raised an eyebrow.

"Well, yes. And as I'm in the area and uncle is otherwise occupied, I decided to come and ask you about it."

"Why would I want to discuss my cases with you? The last time I made that mistake, I got a dressing-down, and you got a commendation."

"That was hardly my fault."

"It certainly wasn't mine," said Strettell bitterly, flushing a deep red.

"I'm sorry," said Lawrence. "I can't re-write history, and anyway, they wouldn't listen to me. I did try."

Strettell pursed his lips. "The Moyse case is cut and dried, anyway," he conceded. "We captured his killer within a week of the murder and the boy Needham has made an identification."

"There was a witness?"

"Yes, who was also a victim. That animal Miller damn near killed the boy in Redcross Street. God alone knows how he survived so many blows from a poker."

Lawrence grimaced.

"I hear it was theft."

Strettell didn't answer.

"Was anything taken?"

"I've got nothing else to say, Harpham. The case hasn't even gone to trial yet. If you want to know more, you can read about it in the newspapers."

"Just one more thing?"

"What?" Strettell glared as he spat the word out.

"Uncle Fred said there was something rum about the case. I wondered what he meant."

Strettell laughed. "Yes, there's something rum, alright. More about the man than the murder." He turned away from Lawrence and stalked off towards the front of the police station. Moments later, Lawrence could still hear him chuckling.

Thomas Strettell was a good detective. The Croxteth fraud case might have damaged the professional relationship between Lawrence and the Lancashire policeman, not that it was ever close, but Lawrence still admired Strettell's tenacity and drive. Though unlucky on that one occasion eight years ago, Strettell had enjoyed an otherwise impressive career. But if Lawrence could think of one flaw in the man, it was that he never knew when to stop talking. Like a few moments ago when Strettell had inadvertently given Lawrence the address of the crime scene in Redcross Street. And Lawrence knew exactly how to find it.

He traversed the streets in the direction of Mann Island, striding confidently towards familiar haunts. And before long, he arrived on the corner of Redcross Street, a mean little terrace of buildings that had seen better days.

Lawrence walked up and down the road, trying to find any obvious clues that might lead him to the correct property. Nothing stood out, so he doubled back to a barbershop that he had passed at number twenty-six Redcross Street. Lawrence peered through the curved, multi-paned window to see if anyone was inside. The windows were in dire need of a clean, but he could make out a slight movement. He pushed the door, and it opened to the clang of a bell.

The barber was midway through a wet shave when Lawrence stepped inside. He grimaced at the disturbance, narrowly avoiding nicking his customer's ear as the jangle of the bell disrupted his concentration. "Sit down," he said, pointing to a row of wooden chairs peppered with woodworm. "I'll be with you shortly."

Lawrence perched on the sturdiest chair and examined the room, which was small, untidy, and liberally coated with dust. He rubbed an imaginary stain from his jacket and watched the barber drip foam onto the floor. Lawrence considered the wisdom of using a cut-throat razor in such insalubrious surroundings. He waited as the barber continued his work, using the blade with great dexterity. When he had finished, the barber suggested a trim which the man duly accepted. A clock ticked loudly in the background and Lawrence watched while the barber worked in silence. After a few moments, the occupant of the chair rose, reached into his pocket and grunted a thank you as he paid.

"What can I do for you, sir?" The barber sighed as if he was about to perform an arduous chore.

"A shave, please," said Lawrence. He didn't particularly need one, but finding a customer in the shop had put him off course. He no longer felt able to ask what he wanted without availing himself of the services.

He positioned himself in the chair and waited while the barber sharpened his razor from a long strop that dangled from the wall.

"You from around here?" asked the barber, lathering soap onto Lawrence's face.

"No. I am visiting."

"Thought I didn't recognize the accent."

"I'm staying with my uncle."

"Very nice, I'm sure."

"He said there had been a death in Redcross Street."

"There was, right above this shop," said the barber puffing out his chest as if proud of the connection.

39

"Here?" Lawrence could not hide his surprise. He had unknowingly stumbled on the crime scene. "Did you know him?"

"Of course. The dead man rented out the upstairs rooms, and now my landlord needs to find a new lodger – not easy with all Moyse's effects still lying around."

"Has nobody been to collect his possessions?"

"His nephew came and said he would pack them up and take them away this weekend, but he didn't show up."

"I may be looking for rooms."

"I thought you said you were staying with your uncle."

"Temporarily," said Lawrence as the barber dried his newly shaved face with a brown stained towel.

The bell jangled again, and an elderly man hobbled into the room and heaved himself onto a chair.

"Morning, Charlie."

"I'll be right with you."

"Can I see them?" asked Lawrence.

"See what?"

"The rooms. I need to know if they are large enough."

The barber looked at him. "Are you serious about renting a room?"

"Very," said Lawrence, handing the man a few coins.

"Here." The barber reached inside an earthenware jar on the counter near the door and pulled out a set of keys. "Go through the yard and up the passage. The door is on your right."

Lawrence took the keys and made his way outside while the barber started work on his next customer.

The heavy wooden door led into a narrow hallway with a door off to the side. Lawrence opened it to find a small parlour with a sofa and two wooden chairs. A coal scuttle lay on its side by the fireplace, and a pair of fire tongs hung from one side of a poker set, the other side unbalanced and empty.

A flight of steps rose from the end of the hallway, finishing in a scullery situated above stairs. The planks groaned under Lawrence's weight as he tiptoed upstairs trying not to look at the brown stains smudged along the bottom of the wall. A wooden table, chairs and a stove dominated the dimly lit scullery, and a film of dust lay across the table upon which two blackened pans rested, still containing the remnants of

Moyse's final meal. Lawrence passed through the room and into an inner hallway leading off to two bedrooms. A set of wooden steps lay directly beneath an open loft hatch. Lawrence climbed the steps and peered inside. It was pitch black, so he retreated, and reached for a small tin that he habitually carried containing fire lighting material. Lawrence retrieved a match and lit the stump of a candle. Holding it aloft, he examined the space. Bloody handprints surrounded the interior of the loft hatch and dust had been disturbed. It appeared as if someone had been feeling around inside. The tiny light was too dim to see much further, so he climbed down and opened the smaller of the two doors. The room was in disarray, coated with dried blood and buzzing with flies. Lawrence held his hand over his mouth, trying to keep the contents of his stomach in place. Someone had made a token effort to tidy the contents of the room with no thought given to the filthy floor which had lain uncleaned and bloody since the slaying. Lawrence wondered whether the barber's landlord knew how unsanitary the conditions were.

The bigger room was in better shape with a stripped-down bed and floorboards bearing evidence of a cursory clean. At one end of the room, an empty wardrobe hung open, and at the other, boxes of possessions stood haphazardly by the side of a large trunk. Lawrence picked his way across the room, approached the trunk, and heaved it open. Inside were stacks of books on top of which was a bundle of letters affixed with antipodean postage stamps. Lawrence removed a thick piece of paper and read a paragraph from one of the missives. "I joined brother Maguire at Table Cape, and we had glorious meetings in the church. In six weeks, nearly sixty souls were brought before Christ," he read.

Lawrence flicked through the remaining letters, all written in a similar vein. "Must have been an evangelist," he muttered beneath his breath. He placed the letters to one side and removed a handful of books. There were vast numbers of prayer books, Bibles and other religious texts, most likely intended for the Bible stall. Lawrence was about to replace them when he noticed two small journals which he picked up and opened. The first was an address book written in the same neat hand. The majority of the addresses were from settlements in Australia and New Zealand. He placed it back in the trunk and opened the second journal which, on closer inspection, proved to be a diary. It was a dull journal containing details of appointments and a smattering of Bible verses. There were occasional entries journaling Moyse's thoughts about the day or future pursuits. He had recorded one or two meetings, and there was a reminder to buy lamp oil. But Lawrence was drawn to an intriguing entry in January. It read, *Has Jackson replied re the Scole confession? Ask about Fanny Nunn.*

Lawrence walked to the bedstead and sat down, reading and re-reading the entry. Who were Jackson and Fanny Nunn? What was the Scole confession? Could it be the title of a novel? Surely not. As Lawrence mulled it over, he remembered the address book and recovered it again from the trunk. He flicked to the letter 'N' reading entries for Newman, Naylor and 'New Zealand – Hobart, Brethren', but there was no sign of Fanny Nunn. He licked his thumb and turned the pages back again until he reached the letter 'J'. There, written in tidy italics, was an address – Mr William and Mrs Amelia Jackson, Scole Street, Thorpe Parva, Scole, Norfolk. That was Lawrence's home territory. Scole was only twenty miles or so from his office in Bury Saint Edmunds. And if memory served him well, Michael's new parish in the tiny hamlet of Frenze was close to Scole. He could ask the Jacksons about Edward Moyse, and while he was about it, enquire after Fanny Nunn. He scribbled the Scole address in his notebook, closed the trunk and left the room.

Lawrence returned to the barber's shop and found Charlie talking earnestly. The conversation was one-sided, with the barber struggling to get a word in. It suited Lawrence's circumstances. With the men distracted, he deposited the key on the counter and mouthed a 'thank you', quickly exiting without having to explain himself.

It was a short walk to his uncle's home in Lord Street, but Lawrence used every second to contemplate the diary entry. The murderer of Edward Moyse was, without doubt, William Miller. There was no logical reason for him to get involved, and Violet would not approve at all. Yet, every instinct Lawrence possessed was on alert, triggered by the innocuous diary entry. One way or another, he needed to find out what had happened in Scole.

CHAPTER SEVEN

Lord Street

"Hello, young Lawrence." Uncle Frederick beamed as Lawrence opened the drawing room door. "You are just in time for a sherry." Uncle Frederick was sitting in his customary chair with a silver salver containing a decanter and glasses by his side.

"I don't mind if I do," said Lawrence perching on the arm of a nearby chair. He waited for his uncle to finish pouring, then reached for the sherry glass, crossed the room and relaxed into the comfortable sofa. "I'm glad to be back," he said. "You will never guess where I was this afternoon?"

"Involving yourself in a case that doesn't concern you, I should think," said his uncle, raising an eyebrow.

"How well you know me," said Lawrence dryly. "Still, it's been interesting."

"In what way?"

"The crime scene, for one thing," said Lawrence.

"Ahh, so Tom Strettell was happy to accept your help? Good of him to let you in."

"Tom Strettell doesn't know. He hasn't forgiven me for the last time we worked together."

"I see. So how did you get inside? I presume that's what you mean?"

"A little subterfuge," said Lawrence. "It doesn't matter. It was pretty revolting in the property. It's been several months since the murder, and the place is still covered in blood."

Frederick Harpham pulled a face. "They have had more than enough time to clean up."

"Yes. Anyway, the downstairs was in disarray, but some of Moyse's possessions were stacked upstairs. He kept a diary, and there was something odd about one of January's entries."

Uncle Frederick sipped his sherry and licked his lips. "What was wrong with it?"

"Something about a Scole confession. Does that mean anything to you?"

"No. Not a thing."

"Scole is a village in Norfolk."

"So it is. Near Diss, if I remember."

"Hmmm. Is that all you know about Scole?"

Frederick nodded.

"Have you ever heard of Fanny Nunn?"

Uncle Frederick stroked his chin. "I don't think so. Did she come from Scole?"

"I have no idea," said Lawrence. "She may not even be a real person. I thought you might remember something from your time in Suffolk."

"That was nearly forty years ago, now," said his uncle. "The name is vaguely familiar, but I'm blowed if I know why. Anyway, I can't see how it makes a difference."

"Neither can I," Lawrence admitted. "But it feels like it should."

He took a sip of sherry and continued. "My search of Redcross Street was not a pleasant experience. There are bloody handprints all over the loft space, and it looks like someone made a thorough search yet Miller left a purse of money behind."

"Perhaps he couldn't find it. Don't the papers make mention of it being under the mattress?"

"Isn't that the first place he would have looked?"

"If he was thinking rationally, but he had just killed a man. Perhaps he panicked."

"There is no doubt that he was searching for something," said Lawrence. "There's evidence all over the house."

"We will probably never know. I say, Lawrence. I forgot to tell you. A telegram arrived earlier. It's on the mantlepiece behind the clock."

Frederick gestured towards the fireplace.

"I'm not expecting anything," said Lawrence, knocking back his sherry in one gulp. He set the glass down, reached for the telegram and slit it open. "It's from Violet."

CHAPTER EIGHT

A Telegram Arrives

Thursday, April 25, 1895 – 3:30 pm
From: Smith, Bury Saint Edmunds
To: Harpham, Lord Street, Liverpool

Hope all is well. Letter has arrived marked 'urgent' for your attention. Love to Frederick. V.

Thursday, April 25, 1895 – 4:45 pm
From: Harpham, Liverpool
To: Smith, Butter Market , Bury Saint Edmunds

Something odd about the Moyse murder. Go to Scole as soon as possible. Speak to William Jackson, Scole Street, Thorpe Parva. Ask about Edward Moyse and Scole confession. What letter? L.H.

Friday, April 26, 1895 – 9:00 am
From: Smith, Bury Saint Edmunds
To: Harpham, Lord Street, Liverpool

Would ordinarily refuse, but Michael at Frenze, and will join him for weekend then speak to Jackson in Scole. Assume no hostility to questioning? Shall I open it? V.

Friday, April 26, 1895 – 10:08 am
From: Harpham, Liverpool
To: Smith, Butter Market, Bury Saint Edmunds

Also, ask Jackson about Fanny Nunn. No hostility anticipated. Yes, open the letter. L.H.

Friday, April 26, 1895 – 10:52 am
From: Smith, Bury Saint Edmunds
To: Harpham, Lord Street, Liverpool

Who is Fanny Nunn? The envelope contains a drawing of a family crest. No note. V.

Friday, April 26, 1895 – 11:17 am
From: Harpham, Liverpool
To: Smith, Butter Market, Bury Saint Edmunds

Describe crest. L.H.

Friday, April 26, 1895 – 12:15 pm
From: Smith, Bury Saint Edmunds
To: Harpham, Lord Street, Liverpool

Silver with a red stripe and Celtic crosses left to right. Blue dolphins either side. Will leave for Scole this evening. V.

Friday, April 26, 1895 – 12:58 pm
From: Harpham, Liverpool
To: Smith, Butter Market, Bury Saint Edmunds
A cruel hoax. Catherine's family crest. Destroy. L.H.

.

CHAPTER NINE

Toxteth

Saturday, April 27, 1895

Lawrence stared at the bowl of porridge then stirred it for the fourth time. His appetite had deserted him since reading Violet's last telegram. But Uncle Frederick was insistent that he join him for breakfast and the thought of eating anything more substantial made him feel ill.

"Is there something wrong?" Uncle Frederick watched Lawrence anxiously. "You look tired, dear boy. Did you sleep well?"

"Very," he lied. Lawrence had barely slept at all. His anxious mind would not settle while he pondered the identity of the person who had posted a copy of his dead wife's family coat of arms – and why? From the moment Violet mentioned a crest, he had known. A wave of foreboding had passed through him. Part of him wanted to know more, but mostly he dreaded finding out. Even so, he had hastened to the post office to ask Violet the question that would provoke the inevitable response.

Catherine had been immensely proud of her heritage. The two dolphins naiant in her crest represented a fusion of her Blennerhessett Suffolk roots with those of Clan Kennedy in Scotland. The family had traced their lineage to the time of Richard II, documenting their genealogy and commissioning a crest. Catherine received an ornate carving of the heraldic shield on the occasion of her engagement, and it took pride of place over the mantlepiece in their dining room. Lawrence had seen it so often that he knew every detail of the crest. The fire that took Catherine's life also took the wooden coat of arms and most of his household furniture and possessions. It would have been a small price to pay, had Catherine and Lily survived, but that night, he lost everything he held dear. It was only now, almost eight years later, that he was finally able to find peace again. Posting Catherine's crest was an act of utter spite made worse by the cowardice of anonymity. Whoever sent it must have understood the consequences, showing a clear intention to drag up memories of the past with all the devastation that accompanied them.

The chiming from a grandfather clock roused Lawrence from his thoughts. It ticked noisily beside the table, accentuating the silence between the two men. Lawrence fought for composure. Somehow, he had made an enemy, and that enemy knew precisely how to hurt him. Lawrence pushed the porridge away as another wave of nausea enveloped him.

"I have a headache, Uncle," he said, pre-empting Frederick's inevitable concern. "I can't eat. I need to go out and walk it off."

"Where are you going?"

"I don't know. To do something useful, I suppose."

"Connected with this murder?"

"Perhaps."

"You should lie down. You might be coming down with a cold. I'll ask Connie for a cough linctus."

"Please don't trouble her. I don't have a cough."

"Then don't spend too long outdoors. You will catch something nasty and end up in the hospital."

"That's a thought," said Lawrence. "I wonder if the Needham boy is still under medical care. Perhaps I'll visit him."

"He's long gone," said Frederick. "The boy was discharged back in February. Made a swift recovery, by all accounts, and is now living with his sister."

"I thought you said you didn't know anything about the murder?"

"I don't. Needham's sister, Mary Fagan, chars for Cornelius Sullivan. He's a friend of mine, and we were speaking of it only recently."

"Were you?"

"Yes. I had intended to ask Mary to do a bit of cleaning a few times a week. But young Needham came home and was under her care so she couldn't oblige."

"Why do you need a cleaner when you have a housekeeper?"

"Connie prefers to cook," said Uncle Fred. "She is not a char."

Lawrence sighed, torn between loyalty to his uncle and fears about Connie. He was glad that Uncle Frederick had found a companion but concerned that she was taking advantage of his good nature.

"Where does Mary live?" he asked.

"Close to the church on the edge of Toxteth – about a mile away."

Lawrence placed his napkin on the table and stood. "Then that's where I'm going," he said.

"It's raining, Lawrence. You'll get wet. The boy may not be there. You're not well, and it may be a wasted journey. You'd be better off in bed."

"Don't worry, Uncle," said Lawrence placing his hand reassuringly on the old man's shoulders. "It doesn't matter. It's the walk that I need." He collected his coat and an umbrella from the coat stand and walked into the drizzly street.

Lawrence had never been to Toxteth and doubted that he would re-visit. The walk along The Strand opposite the dock was, if not exactly pleasant, then at least familiar. But as he strolled past the warehouses and along Sefton Street, the buildings grew smaller and closer together. Many were in varying states of disrepair, and some were empty. The terraces of houses crammed together added a claustrophobic tension to the swirl of emotions in Lawrence's chest. He half hoped that Mary Fagan wasn't at home. The thought of communicating with a stranger was far from desirable, but better, he supposed, than being alone with his thoughts.

Lawrence approached the corner of Hill Street near to the anchor works. A group of navvies smoking coarse pipes clustered around a lamppost and glared suspiciously at Lawrence's neat attire as he attempted to pass. A thickset man stepped forward and blocked his way. "What's a gentleman like you doing here?" he asked in a heavy Irish brogue. Lawrence ignored him, in no mood for a confrontation while his mind still churned with thoughts of crests and Catherine. Then he reconsidered. Lawrence's geographical knowledge of Toxteth was limited. Uncle Fred's was better, but his directions to Mary Fagan's house amounted to 'somewhere near St Thomas Church'. Lawrence realised he would need help, and he might as well take the opportunity that had presented itself.

"Do you know where Mary Fagan lives?" he asked.

"Which Mary Fagan?"

Lawrence shook his head. He had not anticipated there being more than one.

"She has a brother, a young man called Needham."

"That will be flaming Poll," said a tall, dark-haired man, spitting a jet of chewing tobacco to his right. He approached Lawrence. "What do you want with her?" Traces of saliva clung to his swarthy face as he eyed Lawrence keenly.

Lawrence recoiled at the smell of the man's hard labour as he intruded too close for comfort. He considered the safest response. "It's the boy I need to speak to," he said.

"You had better not bring any trouble to his door," said the first man. "He's had enough of that."

Lawrence nodded. "I know. There will be no trouble, I swear."

"Henderson Street," said the dark-haired man pointing ahead. Number thirty-seven. Tell her Padraig sends his regards."

"I will." Lawrence nodded his head as he crossed the road and made his way in the indicated direction.

He arrived outside Mary's house, having found it by process of elimination. As many houses lacked door numbers as those that possessed them and Lawrence narrowed it down to the most likely by guesswork alone. The front door was open, and a bucket and scrubbing brush lay beside the wet front doorstep. He raised his hand to tap on the door as a woman with copper coloured hair appeared in the doorway. She was clad in a dark brown dress with fraying sleeves and clutched a squirming kitten in her hands, which she deposited by the doorstep.

"Off with you, now," she said as the kitten skittered across the road.

"Yours?" asked Lawrence, trying to start a conversation.

"Kate Harrington's, I shouldn't wonder. Her cat is always in the family way. I don't want the dirty thing in my house with George only recently recovered."

"George Needham?"

"Yes. Why?" Mary's eyes narrowed.

"I'm a detective. I want to speak to him if I may?"

"You may not." Her mouth set in a thin line. "He has told you what happened over and over again. He has nothing more to say until it goes to court."

"I won't trouble him long."

"You won't trouble him at all. Now be off with you."

Lawrence turned to go, then remembered the navvy. "Padraig sends his compliments," he said. A pink flush spread across her freckled face. "That man is wicked, so he is," she exclaimed. "And me a married woman." Then she softened. "Look, I'll ask George if he will speak to you, but if he says no, then let him be. He still gets upset whenever he talks about it."

Lawrence nodded and loitered by the doorstep while Mary retreated inside. He was still waiting five minutes later when he felt a warm body press against his trouser leg and heard soft mewls and purrs. He looked down to see the little kitten rubbing herself against his ankles and knelt to tickle her furry ears. She returned his stare through round blue eyes set into a tabby face. Lawrence did not like cats as a rule, but this one was rather appealing. He rubbed it under the chin again, then flinched as a black object landed on the back of his hand. He moved to brush it away, but the creature leapt out of reach. Lawrence stood up and shooed the kitten away. The last thing he needed was an armful of flea bites to add to his other problems.

"I told you it was dirty," said Mary Fagan re-appearing in the doorway. "This is George," she continued, ushering a scrawny dark-haired boy forward. "He has agreed to speak to you. Do you want to come inside?"

"No, sister," said George, in a thin, reedy voice. "I would rather walk. This way," he said, pointing southwards down the terrace. They made their way to the end of the street in silence, then George turned right onto Warwick Street and continued towards the docks.

"I don't want to say anything else in front of Mary," said George. "She gets so upset, feels responsible somehow. I don't know why."

"Maybe it's because she is a good deal older than you?" offered Lawrence.

"Perhaps," George agreed. "This way."

He stopped in front of the Brunswick docks, and they walked across rows of cobbles captivated by the crowded port. Ships, sailboats and flat-bottomed barges jostled for space in the busy docks. Ahead of them, groups of men dressed in hard-wearing work attire hauled planks from freight vessels into a giant warehouse. Two enormous cranes stood idly in the distance, their operators waiting for orders to continue the dock expansion work. The air was warm and salty, and the sea calm and blue.

"Here," said George, gesturing to a quiet area on the dockside. He lowered himself onto the edge and leaned back, swinging his legs against the sea wall. Lawrence removed his jacket, placed it on the ground and sat beside him.

"Thank you for speaking to me."

"Are you a real copper?" George came straight to the point.

"I am a detective," said Lawrence.

"But not from round here. You don't sound right."

"I'm not from here," Lawrence admitted. "I'm visiting my family."

George seemed content with the inadequate explanation. "Did you know him?" he asked.

"Who?"

"Old man Moyse."

"No."

"He was a good sort." George picked up a stone and sent it skimming into the sea. "Good and kind. He treated me well. He treated us all well."

"There were others?"

"Before me, yes. And sometimes Mr Moyse needed more help when it was busy. He gave me food, shelter and employment. He did not deserve it..." His voice trailed away, and he bowed his head.

Lawrence waited for him to continue.

"I suppose you want to know what happened?"

Lawrence nodded.

"Is this part of the trial?"

"No. I visited twenty-six Redcross Street yesterday. The house is still in disarray. I would like to know a little more about what happened that day if you are up to telling me."

"Why?"

"I can't help feeling that there's more to the murder than money alone."

"I'll tell you what I know, as long as I don't have to go back there. I never want to see the place again." George Needham shuddered.

"Of course not," said Lawrence softly. "Tell me what you can remember."

Needham stared at the sea for a long time, then swept back his hair with dirty fingers, exposing a vivid welt down the side of his neck.

"It was a normal evening," he said. "We must have returned about five thirty, six o'clock as usual. I began to prepare our evening meal, and Mr Moyse went to Myrtle Street to pick up some books. He can't have been gone for more than five minutes when there was knock at the door, and I saw a man standing there."

"Miller?" asked Lawrence.

The boy nodded. "Miller," he said. "I had never seen him before, and I didn't much like what I saw. He had a queer twitch to his face whenever he spoke. The first time he came, he asked after Moyse, and I told him he wouldn't be back until later and carried on making tea."

"And Miller returned?"

"Yes. The second time I could not put him off. He insisted on waiting while I carried on cooking. I set the old man's meal aside for later and ate mine at the table while Miller watched. And all the while I was eating, he kept asking where Moyse kept his money and valuables. He said it was wrong that I didn't know in case something happened."

"Like what?"

"He didn't say. Only that friends and family would never know where his things were."

"What things?"

"Money, mostly. But he kept asking about personal papers, books and records. I don't know where Mr Moyse kept those things. I didn't need to know."

"No, of course not." Lawrence smiled encouragingly as George Needham's voice rose. "What happened next?"

"Mr Moyse returned," he said, picking at a hangnail on his thumb. "He recognised Miller and greeted him warmly, like a friend. He said that Miller was an old lodger of his and could stay if he wished."

"He had no home to go to?"

"I don't know. I don't know anything about Miller, and I had gone downstairs to the passageway while they were talking. When I returned, Mr Moyse asked me to make up the bed in the best room for Miller to sleep in the following night and he would have to make do with the sofa that night."

"He wasn't expected, then?"

"No. Mr Moyse would have told me. He shared his supper with Miller that evening, but he was always hospitable. He would have told me if he had known Miller was coming so he could be sure there was enough food to go round."

"What did they talk about?"

"I don't know. I went upstairs to bed and rose again at five in the morning. It was still dark so I lit a candle and I made my way to the scullery in my nightclothes as usual. Miller was there." George Needham closed his eyes and put his forehead on clasped hands. His body rocked involuntarily as the memories flooded back. "Oh, that wicked man," he breathed.

Lawrence waited for the boy to regain his composure.

"He was half-dressed," said Needham, lowering his hands, "in a blue serge jacket and trousers. He hadn't yet put his boots on, and he had thrown his coat and hat upon a chair. I wished him good morning, and he looked at me with that odd twitch in his face and said, 'I can't waken the master, and there is no coal to light the fire.' So, I showed him the coal hole and gave him a bucket and a hatchet for breaking the coal. Then I went back to my bedroom to finish dressing."

"Where was Moyse?"

"In his room, I suppose. I never saw him again after supper the last evening."

"And Miller?"

"He must have followed me," George whispered gazing into the distance. "I remember a puff of wind and the candle went out, then something struck me, and I fell to the floor. I must have passed out for a while, but I woke up and saw Miller coming out of the master's room with a poker in his hand. I pleaded for my life, but he raised it over his head and hit me again and again. I lay upon the floorboards, too injured to move, and then Miller stood over me as if trying to make his mind up whether to finish me off. He told me to not to move, or he would kill me, and I stayed as still and quiet as a body can be. Blood dripped into my eyes from my broken head, and I thought I would pass out at any moment and die there on the floor. But then I heard him go downstairs and the door slammed shut. I waited for a long time, then pulled myself downstairs and somehow stood up and staggered into the street. I cannot remember much more until I woke in the infirmary."

"That's quite an ordeal," said Lawrence. "I am sorry to dredge up such difficult memories."

"The trial is in a few weeks," said Needham. "I am due to give evidence. He must lose his freedom, and I must tell the court everything they need to know. It will not be easy."

"Is that why you agreed to talk to me?" asked Lawrence.

The boy nodded. "If I can talk to you, a stranger, then I can do my duty in court."

"Will you answer one final question?"

"Yes."

"Is there any doubt that Miller was your attacker?"

"Not the smallest," said George Needham. "I could be mistaken about his voice, or even about his appearance. But that twitch of his, that mannerism – it will stay with me until my dying day."

CHAPTER TEN

Scole

Sunday, April 28, 1895

"Violet, how lovely to see you. It's been at least four days." Michael Farrow smiled as he took Violet's hand and helped her from the coach.

"Thank you for coming to meet me," she replied, reaching for her chatelaine bag which had become detached from her belt during the journey. She clipped it back together and fastened the ribbon tight.

"Wait a minute," said Michael, approaching the driver. They talked for a few moments while Michael pointed to a waiting pony and trap. The driver dismounted and hauled Violet's carpetbag over to the cart, returned to his carriage, and wiped his brow with a large, red handkerchief.

"Would you like to stay at my lodgings tonight, Violet? The spare room is free today, but not tomorrow. I have spoken to George Panks at The Crown in Diss, and you can have a room there. Then, you can get on with whatever brings you to Scole today."

"Hopefully," said Violet.

"Hopefully?" Michael raised an eyebrow.

"I need to speak to a man called Jackson," she said. "But there has been no time to find out whether or not he is at home. I know nothing about him save for an address in Scole Street."

"It's nearby," said Michael. "We can walk. What do you want with Jackson?"

"I am not altogether sure."

"That sounds like something Lawrence would say."

"Or something that he would ask someone else to do."

"Ah. It's like that. Are you here under sufferance?"

Violet sighed. "Yes and no. On the one hand, Lawrence has gone to Liverpool on a whim, as you know. Another case that isn't a case, masquerading as a visit to his uncle".

"His uncle is in Liverpool."

"I know. I have met Frederick. But you know very well that he left prematurely when we happened upon a murder that supposedly needs his urgent attention."

"And you have agreed to help him?"

"Only because I get to visit you," she said. "And because I have quite a soft spot for Diss. One of my aunts lived here, and we often visited. Just as well as the other lives in Cornwall."

"Dreadful journey," said Michael. "Best avoided."

"I have always thought so. But there is another reason why I wanted to humour Lawrence. Something odd has occurred, and it has upset him greatly."

"What?"

"A print of Catherine's family coat of arms turned up in an envelope at our office. I opened it, and there was nothing inside except the crest, no note."

"Oh, dear. Poor Lawrence. That must have hit him hard."

"It has. And it's nearly May Day."

Michael was about to respond when a sign above a shop on the street ahead caught his eye.

"You are in luck," he said, pointing to the wooden banner over the shop front. "William Jackson Coal and Grocery supplies."

The door was ajar, propped open by a sack of flour. Michael and Violet negotiated their way around it and entered the establishment.

The grocer's shop was in a large, airy room fronting the road and appeared to form a substantial part of the ground floor of the property. The neatly organised shop was well furnished. Rows of symmetrical shelving ran from floor to ceiling on the back walls, and a small counter ran along the middle of the room. There was an abundant stock of groceries, but no sign of the proprietor.

"Perhaps he's through there?" Michael suggested, pointing to a thick wooden door with an iron lock and bolt.

"You can try it?" said Violet doubtfully. "It looks as though it's locked."

But it wasn't. The door opened into a walled garden planted with a surprising array of brightly coloured spring flowers. Two large vegetable beds contained the first signs of young plant growth.

A crash of metal against stone disturbed the tranquillity and drew their attention to a further area behind a trellis leading to a large yard. Sacks of coal and wooden pallets occupied one side, and a woman dressed in black knelt upon the floor.

"Allow me," said Michael squatting beside her as he collected a set of cast iron shelf brackets from the yard floor.

"Do excuse me," said the woman, standing up and brushing her dress. "I was trying to carry too much. Thank you for your help. Now, what can I do for you? Groceries or coal?"

"I rather fancy some tinned peaches and custard for my supper tonight," said Michael.

"Come this way, then," replied the woman as she led them back into the shop front. She grabbed the tin and gestured towards an upper shelf. "Bird's or Green's?" she asked.

"Either," said Michael reaching into his pocket for coins.

"Where is Mr Jackson today?" asked Violet.

"William? My husband is in Diss." She looked towards the clock by the door. "Or perhaps he is on his way back, by now. He didn't intend to stay long. Can I help?"

"That depends whether you know anything about the Scole confession," said Violet.

The woman regarded Violet quizzically. "I'm sorry. I don't know what you mean by that."

Violet sighed. "I thought that might be the case. I'm not sure whether Mr Jackson will know any better, but I would like to ask him, all the same."

The woman put her elbow on the counter and rested her chin on her hand, peering at Violet with curiosity. "Is it important?"

"It might be," said Violet. It could pertain to a man called Edward Moyse."

The woman gasped and covered her mouth. Her eyes were wide with shock, and she spoke with a trembling voice. "Edward was my brother. Amelia Jackson is my married name. I was Amelia Moyse before I wed. What has this confession got to do with Edward?"

"I am so sorry to have upset you," said Violet. "The truth is that I don't know. I am a private investigator, and my partner is helping the Liverpool police with their investigation into your brother's death. Lawrence contacted me yesterday and asked if I could find out about a confession mentioned in Edward's journal." Violet reached into her bag and extracted a sheaf of papers. She selected a telegram and passed it over the counter to Mrs Jackson.

"Here."

"Ask about Edward Moyse and the Scole confession." Amelia mouthed the words as she read the telegram. "I see. Oh, dear. How difficult."

"I'm sure it must be a dreadful time," said Michael, misunderstanding her meaning.

"No. Not that. It is upsetting, of course, but the greater problem is William. He is due back at any moment and will not brook any mention of Edward's name under his roof."

"Why? Edward is your brother," said Violet, offering what she hoped was a safe level of sympathy.

"Was my brother," said Amelia sadly. "Our family parted on bad terms, yet we lived in harmony to start with."

"As children?" asked Michael.

"Of course, but more recently than that. Edward lodged with us when he returned from New Zealand. He was a missionary," she said. "A godly man. He travelled to the other end of the world, bringing salvation to all who would listen." Her eyes shone with pride.

"That is a long way to go," said Violet.

"Yes. My brother was away from our shores for almost two decades," said Amelia. "From Hobart in Tasmania to Christchurch in New Zealand and many other places besides. His passion for the Lord's work was all that mattered to him. He suffered illness and scorn, but nothing could dissuade him from evangelising. That it should come to this." She shook her head.

"Yet your husband disliked Edward?" asked Violet gently.

"Not always. There was a time when Edward and William got on well. One moment they were friendly and the next William said he must leave. It was sudden and unexpected."

"What precipitated the announcement from your husband?"

"It was either the stranger or the..." she stuttered, tripping over her words, then recovered her composure. "The incident."

"What incident?"

"It doesn't matter. The police have caught Edward's killer, and there is nothing to gain."

"Perhaps," said Violet uncertainly. She was going to have to think on her feet. Lawrence had given her no useful information with which to work. "They have caught the murderer," she repeated, "but they need more information to secure a conviction when he goes to trial." She crossed her fingers behind her back, hating herself for the lie.

Amelia accepted her story without further questioning. "If you think it will help, I will tell you. Sit down, but we must be quick. If William returns, you must leave immediately."

"We will," said Violet. "I promise."

Amelia Jackson cleared her throat. "Two things occurred in quick succession. I think the man came first, but it all happened within a week, and could have been the other way around."

"Go on," said Violet.

"One morning in January, I was in the parlour, and William was writing out the ledger beside me. There was a knock at the door, and I opened it to find a stranger on the doorstep. He was about my age with white hair and skin the colour of burnt ochre, weathered and tanned."

"A foreigner?" asked Michael.

"I don't believe so," said Amelia, squinting as she recalled the scene. "He might have been English, though his accent sounded Australian. Edward's accent had changed during his time abroad, and the man spoke similarly. He did not strike me as having been born with dark skin – it must have come from spending a long time in the sun. Anyway, he knocked on the door and asked if Edward was available. I said that he wasn't and the stranger said that suited him because he had a private matter to discuss with the man of the house. I showed him into the parlour and left him talking with William. Ten minutes later, my husband showed him to the door and came into the kitchen with a face like thunder."

"Did he say why?"

"No. William said that Edward was not welcome in his house and he would be asking him to move out at once. I pleaded with him not to be so unkind. Edward had nowhere to go, and few friends due to his time abroad, but William was adamant that he must leave."

"Did he put him out?"

"He gave him a fortnight to pack his things and find another place to stay, but events took a different turn, and the situation worsened."

"How?"

"A policeman turned up at our house accompanied by a shopkeeper from Norwich. A certain Mr Roy from Messrs Bunting and Co. I don't know if you have heard of them, but they are drapers on St Stephen's corner. I have often used them. Their goods are of excellent quality."

"I am sure," said Violet.

"Well, Police Constable Slaughter insisted on inspecting the contents of my house."

"Whatever for?"

"You might well ask," said Amelia Jackson, standing with her hands on her hips. She bristled with indignation, even though the encounter had been several years before. "The very thought of it," she continued. "Well, of course, William said no, but the constable said it was not a request. William must stand back and allow him to get on with it, or he would make more than one arrest that day."

"Did he want to check the entire house?"

"Not at first. The constable asked where Edward slept, and we showed him to the room. He looked and found nothing then decided to search the shop instead. He opened a cupboard under the counter and pulled out two rugs and a coloured tablecloth that I had never seen before. Mr Roy examined them and said they were the stolen items. William was furious and accused Roy of putting the items in the cupboard. I thought they might come to blows, but at that moment, Edward returned. As soon as he saw the constable, he burst into tears and admitted the offence. He said that he stole the rugs from Bunting and Co in full view of the shop assistants. It was not the first time. He said he had stolen flannel cloth and some boots on a prior occasion."

"Did he want for money?"

"No. If Edward needed money, he had only to ask."

"It must have been a terrible shock," said Violet, gently.

"It was." Amelia's eyes welled up at the memory. A tear slid down her cheek, and she wiped it away. "Edward was older than me, and I'd always looked up to him. He was honest and good. I cannot imagine what drove him to it."

"Did he ever tell you?"

"He refused to discuss it. Not with me, anyway."

"What happened to him?"

"The magistrates treated him well. Reverend Savory appealed for clemency. He visited the magistrates and told them about Edward's work in the colonies. They viewed his case with compassion, but he still went to gaol and endured two months of hard labour."

"Could he have been unwell? It is not unknown for behaviour to change during sickness."

Amelia nodded. "It must have been something of that nature. Edward was a changed man when he returned to Norfolk. He suffered severe sunstroke in the outback, and it damaged his constitution and altered his mind. He suffered an enduring melancholy as if he was broken-hearted. He often said that he missed the Antipodes, but I think there was more to it."

"Why did he leave?"

"That's another mystery," Amelia sighed. "Edward said that he came back to England because he had no choice, but he would not say why."

"I am sorry," said Violet. "He sounds like an honourable man."

"He was. I am glad that you don't think the worst of him having heard the account of his trial. Now, I don't want to be rude, but William is due to return at any moment, and you must go."

"Of course," said Violet. "Just one more question. How did your brother end up in Liverpool?"

"It was due to the kindness of my cousin Albert," she replied. "Albert is a bookseller in Liverpool. With nowhere to live and a reputation damaged beyond repair, it was clear that Edward must leave Norfolk. He set off for Liverpool to make a new life there and leave the shame and disgrace behind. He wrote to me saying that he made a reasonable living from the bookstall and was happy. It suited him. How wicked of that man to take his life away when he'd finally found peace."

"God bless his soul," said Michael, who had stayed quietly in the background. "And thank you for your time." He ushered Violet from the shop.

"What do you make of that?" asked Michael when they got outside. Violet was about to reply when she noticed a cart outside the front of the grocer's store. A man was walking away from it towards a fenced enclosure on the other side of the road. He carried a heavy sack over his shoulder which he heaved to the ground before slitting the top with a knife. He scooped the contents into a trough and leaned over the fence, watching something on the other side.

"That will be Jackson," whispered Violet. "He's not going to want to discuss anything."

"No," Michael agreed. "It's bound to be tricky."

"Stand still," said Violet, opening her bag and removing a retractable silver pencil. She rummaged inside and located a cream coloured envelope which she placed against Michael's back."

"What are you doing?"

"I'm writing a note to Edward Moyse."

"Why?"

"You will see."

She slipped one of the telegrams into the envelope and tucked the flap inside having first addressed it to Mr Moyse of Scole Street, Diss.

Turning to Michael, she took a deep breath. "Come on then."

CHAPTER ELEVEN

No Love Lost

William Jackson stared at the chickens in the enclosure, oblivious to Violet's approach. He watched the birds vacantly as if he was not really looking at all. Michael and Violet loitered for a moment, then Michael coughed, and Jackson turned around.

"Mr Jackson?" asked Violet.

"Yes. What do you want?"

"I'm here to deliver a letter," she continued. "With instructions to bring it by hand. It is for your lodger."

"I don't have a lodger."

"Oh." Violet looked crestfallen. "Here," she said, thrusting the letter under his nose. "Mr Moyse, Scole Street."

Jackson scanned the note, then passed it back. "Moyse is dead," he said curtly. "You had better return the note to whoever sent it."

"Oh, dear," said Violet. "My friend wanted to ask him a question – a matter of some importance. Mr Moyse had alluded to it, but never fully explained."

"That won't be possible."

"Perhaps you can help?" she asked.

Jackson closed his eyes and gritted his teeth. He looked Violet full in the face before moving towards her. She tried not to react as she felt the warmth of his breath against her cheek. "I have nothing to say about that filthy sinner," he growled. "The man was a disgrace."

Violet tried to mask her surprise. "I thought he was a man of God," she said.

"So did I, but he deceived us all."

Violet considered eliciting more detail, but thought better of it and changed tack. "My friend was going to ask him about a confession," she said. "The Scole confession."

William Jackson stared mutely for a moment as if torn between helping or sending her packing with a flea in her ear. He chose the former.

"The confession was nonsense," he said. "Moyse was deluded. Had he not been part of the temperance movement, I would have thought him under the influence of alcohol when he wrote the letter."

"What did he tell you?" asked Violet.

"None of your business," Jackson replied. "What's it to you, anyway?"

"Nothing. I am helping out a friend. This is rather awkward. He would prefer to ask you himself, but unfortunately, it falls to me."

"What Violet is trying to say," said Michael, stepping in, "is that the presence of this confession is complicating your brother-in-law's murder investigation. But you imply that their interest is unnecessary."

"Indeed." William Jackson softened. "Edward Moyse was not right in the head. His exposure to constant sunshine and godless heathens affected his sanity. I cannot imagine why he thought I would be sympathetic to his fancies. He would have received a better reception had he sent the letter to my wife. For reasons best known to himself, he chose to waste my time. Now, tell me what you want to know and be quick about it."

"Thank you." Violet smiled at Michael, grateful for the intervention, then turned to William Jackson. "What exactly what was in the confession?"

"I cannot remember," said Jackson. "Moyse was vague in his language and sent a rambling letter expressing concern about a dead woman's Bible. He found it in a box of second-hand books, purchased from Henry Garrod at the auction house in Diss, days before he left for Liverpool. I expect he intended to sell them. He took the books away and later while sorting through the box, he found a Bible that he recognised."

"How?"

"Because there was an inscription inside written in his hand."

"Who did the Bible belong to?" asked Violet.

"A woman he'd encountered while preaching, which was hardly remarkable. He continued evangelising on his return to England and many, especially those who knew him, were sympathetic to his cause. According to the letter, this woman was memorable due to her burden of guilt. He had prayed with her and given her a Bible upon which she had subsequently written a confession. He expected me to believe that in defiance of reasonable coincidence, he had found it again in the box."

"You don't believe him?"

"I doubt it is an outright lie. There is likely is an element of truth in this half-baked story, but not much of one."

"What did the confession say?" Violet's eyes were wide with anticipation.

"Moyse did not go into detail. He said that it was a serious matter and had begun with the murder of Fanny Nunn."

"Fanny Nunn? I was about to ask if you knew the name. Who is she?"

"She died," said Jackson. "But it was almost twenty years ago, so how this has any bearing today, I do not know."

"How did she die?"

"She drowned in the mere."

"Was it an accident?"

"I don't wish to discuss it further. It is irrelevant. The alleged confession is fanciful. I do not believe there was anything to it. More likely, Moyse was trying to use it in an attempt to inveigle himself back into my favour."

"Did he name the woman?"

"No, he did not. Which is another reason why I suspect much of this is a product of his imagination."

"Do you still have the letter?" Violet asked, hopefully.

"No." Jackson snorted. "It was a source of irritation. If memory serves me correctly, I screwed it up and threw it into the crates. It will be long gone by now and good riddance to it. Now, have you finished?"

Violet unable to think of anything else to ask, thanked him and turned to leave.

"Lawrence has struck gold again," said Michael when they were out of earshot.

Violet sighed. "Perhaps," she said. "Though it does sound like Moyse was a man with an overactive imagination. And I cannot see how this confession connects to his tragic end."

"Yet the note refers to a death, and Fanny Nunn drowned."

"I was likely an accident and nothing untoward."

"But Jackson didn't answer your question. It would have been much easier to confirm that she came to a natural end."

"It is curious," said Violet. "But I will ask Lawrence what he thinks. Is there a post office nearby? I will telegraph him first thing tomorrow morning."

Michael nodded. "I'll show you where it is on the way back to my lodgings. Peaches and custard for supper," he said, shaking the can.

CHAPTER TWELVE

Dear Amy

January 1895

Dear Amy,

I wonder if you ever understood the thrill of drowning? It's a beguiling sensation sparking the senses alive. The splutter and gurgle of a dying breath; the splash of water during the fight for life, a sudden silence – all blend into an exquisite and sensual symphony. The sound of drowning resonates bone deep; cocoons and soothes the soul, evoking all senses. It is intense and satisfying.

The first time I took a boy's life, I was unaware of the pleasure it would bring. How could I know without trying? How could anybody? The second time, I set off with purpose, to persuade, not threaten, hoping to resolve a conflict without violence. I met my aggressor with the best of intentions. But an opportunity arose, and a split-second reaction changed the course of my destiny. I killed him, and though some questioned the manner of his death, I was never suspected. There were no consequences, and the matter rested. An insignificant life snuffed out early, with memories petering away so quickly that he might never have existed at all.

But today brings a problem, Amy. My luck may have finally run out.

You, of all people, know that the Crown Hotel is a focal point in Diss. People come, and people go all day long. Everyone passes through the doors sooner or later. They come for a drink, a chat, or a meeting. Or to make a delivery, as happened today.

But here am I, claiming my luck has run out, when of course, it cannot have. If so, I wouldn't have seen the letter. Somebody else would have picked it up. Though it lacks enough information to give me away, it could lead back to Moyse. And his account could lead to far worse. No, luck was with me. Fate placed me in the right place at the right time to protect my interests. And protect them, I will.

I was thinking of you earlier today when standing at the counter drinking with my companions. Your demise has not entirely removed you from my memory, and from time to time, I recall our haunts. Anyway, Jackson's delivery boy turned up and hauled a crate through the passageway where he unknowingly deposited a ball of paper in his wake. I picked it up, intending to hand it back, but he walked on ahead, and I unfurled the note. Imagine my horror as I read the second paragraph – Find out about Fanny Nunn.

I knew she would return to haunt me one day, greedy little piglet that she was; plump, homely Fanny Nunn and her meddling ways. The note gave me quite a start, and I hastened into the street to calm myself down. I found a quiet alleyway and re-read the letter, identifying by the end of it, two significant problems.

Do you recall a man called Moyse? Well, Amy dear, he is the writer of the note. Moyse, you will remember, is a bearded preacher always trying and usually failing to convert the gullible to godliness. I never understood his motivation. Why would anyone waste their life persuading men into actions contrary to their selfish nature? He is an interfering busybody, and though I have always believed him harmless, this is no longer the case.

The second problem is the note. It refers to a confession that Moyse possesses, of which you are aware. It has the potential to threaten my comfortable life. Somebody, possibly Jackson, crumpled it into a ball and discarded it. The act suggests a disregard for Moyse's claims and implies that time is on my side. Anyone who knows Jackson, also knows that he has argued with his brother-in-law – hardly surprising after the shame the prison sentence brought upon the family. There was a great deal of sympathy within Diss for the Antipodean felon, but not from me and most definitely not from Jackson. I have even less sympathy now.

Jackson may have discarded the note, but further interference from Moyse might yet draw unwanted attention. It is a pity, as things are going rather well. Business is good, and so the Moyse problem must be addressed. But the thought of confronting a full-grown, able-bodied man does not appeal. It is not my way. The note provides a contact address at twenty-six Redcross Street in Liverpool. I am going there now, Amy, as soon as possible. I have some clearing up to do.

CHAPTER THIRTEEN

More Telegrams

Monday April 29, 1895 – 9:05 am
From: Smith, Bungay Road, Scole
To: Harpham, Lord Street, Liverpool

Met Jackson. He thinks Moyse irrational & doubts credibility of confession. Fanny Nunn drowned twenty years ago. When will you be back?

Monday April 29, 1895 – 9:36 am
From: Harpham, Lord Street, Liverpool
To: Smith, Bungay Road, Scole

Re Jackson – why? Re Nunn – how? Not yet – will seek interview with Miller first. Who wrote confession?

Monday April 29, 1895 – 10:16 am
From: Smith, Bungay Road, Scole
To: Harpham, Lord Street, Liverpool

No love lost between Moyse and Jackson. Imprisonment probable cause of resentment – also presence of stranger. No details re Nunn drowning. Proceeding to Crown Hotel, Diss shortly. I do not know.

Monday April 29, 1895 – 10:49 am
From: Harpham, Lord Street, Liverpool
To: Smith, Bungay Road, Scole.

What stranger? Find out circumstances of drowning. Re confession – find parish register & note female deaths for last decade. Who was imprisoned?

Monday April 29, 1895 – 1:17 pm
From Smith, Bungay Road, Scole
To: Harpham, Lord Street, Liverpool

Seeing Michael later. Will search parish records tomorrow then return to Bury. No more details by telegram. Come back soonest.

Monday April 29, 1895 – 2:50 pm
From: Harpham, Lord Street, Liverpool
To: Smith, Crown Hotel, Diss

Dash it all, Violet. Give details of imprisonment. Cannot work without facts. Back when finished.

CHAPTER FOURTEEN

The Haven of Success

"Can I help you?"

Violet had arrived at the Crown Hotel and was standing in the foyer admiring a painting of a windmill. An attractive young woman popped her head up from beneath the counter, where she had been cleaning.

"Oh, you startled me," said Violet, clutching her chest. "I was somewhere in that scene," she explained, gesturing towards the picture.

"Lovely, isn't it?" said the girl. "Father bought it from the auction house only last month, and everybody seems pleased with it. It cheers the place up, don't you think?"

"Much more than the item in the cabinet below." Violet moved her hand across the glass-topped cupboard and peered at the rifle inside. The highly polished wooden gun bore the inscription 'H. Holland."

"It's a paradox," said the girl. "My father's pride and joy."

"Paradox?"

"It fires both shot and solid projectile. But don't ask Father about it unless you have a lot of free time."

Violet nodded and moved closer to the counter. "I have reserved a room," she said.

The girl turned a page in the hotel register. "Name?" she asked.

"Violet Smith."

"Yes, here it is. How many nights are you staying?"

"I'm not sure yet," said Violet. "One, possibly two."

"Have you eaten yet?" asked the girl.

"Not since breakfast and I'm famished." Violet had struggled to sleep in Michael's unfamiliar lodgings and had risen early, breakfasting before seven o'clock. Between the journey and sending Lawrence's telegrams, she hadn't found time for lunch.

"Would you like an evening meal? We've got mutton pie on the menu tonight. It's my favourite dish."

Violet's stomach rumbled in anticipation. "Yes. Dinner would be lovely."

"Here's your key. You're in room number five on the first floor. I will make your table up for six o'clock. Oh, and there's a telegram for you."

Violet raised her eyes heavenwards as she took the telegram and noted the sender. She tucked it into her pocket and climbed the staircase to the first floor of the building. Room number five was on the right-hand side of the corridor at the far end. She dropped her carpetbag and inserted the heavy iron key into the lock. It turned, and she entered a small room containing a single bed, a narrow wardrobe and a dressing table. Dark velvet curtains framed a square window overlooking Saint Nicholas Street. Violet sat on the end of the bed, reached into her pocket, and withdrew the telegram. She slit it open and frowned. "No, I won't give you any more information by telegram, Lawrence," she said aloud. "It is too much." She put the telegram on the dressing table, unpacked her few possessions, and hung her spare dress in the wardrobe. Then, she watched the busy street from the window for a few moments, yawned loudly and lay on the bed for a short rest before dinner.

Violet woke at a quarter after six, taking a few moments to remember where she was, and what she ought to be doing. She freshened up and bolted downstairs, arriving in the dining room just before half past six. Violet located a small table in the corner of the room. She was barely seated when a young woman clad in a black dress and white apron arrived carrying a notebook and a pencil.

"Dinner or cold cuts?" she asked.

"Dinner, please," said Violet.

"You can have beef stew or mutton pie, with treacle tart or rice pudding to follow," said the girl.

Violet made her selection, and the waitress licked her pencil and scribbled on the notepad in a spidery hand.

"It won't be long," she said cheerfully, looking over her shoulder as she bustled towards the kitchen.

Violet picked up her book and opened it at the page marked with a red ribbon. She was just getting lost in the story again when a buzz of noise preceded a procession of colourfully dressed men. They were walking past the dining room on their way to their meeting next door. Violet tried not to stare at their insignia and brightly coloured sashes and aprons. One man, who seemed to be the leader, wore a bright blue sash and a chain around his collar. The others sported silk tassels in shades of red and yellow which hung from double curved flaps on their white aprons bearing an open hand atop a golden ball.

The rumble of noise dissipated from the corridor and passed into the next room as the men walked by. Violet tried to resume her reading, but the noise was so loud that it disturbed her concentration. Violet's chair was immediately next to the adjoining room, and the monotonous tones of what sounded like a treasurer's report rumbled through the wall. She debated moving tables, but closed her book with a sigh and waited for dinner to arrive.

The waitress was as good as her word and delivered Violet's mutton pie quickly.

"Noisy lot, aren't they?" she said, placing the hot plate on the table cloth.

"Freemasons, I suppose," asked Violet, thinking of Francis and his regalia.

"Oddfellows," said the waitress. "It's different."

"Oh. I've heard the name Oddfellows recently," said Violet. "I think there is a lodge in Bury Saint Edmunds."

"There are lodges everywhere," said the waitress. "We have two in Diss – the Loyal Nelson lodge and this one." She waved her hand towards the wall. "These gentlemen are members of the Loyal Haven of Success."

"I love the unusual names. What do they do?"

"They are a friendly society, miss. They look after each other."

"A charitable organisation?"

"Yes, that too. But the Oddfellows see each other right when times are hard, or when someone dies."

"Oh, I see. Like a burial club."

"Yes, miss. Similar to the Freemasons. Lots of secrecy and strange ceremonies, so I hear. Have you met my father, Mr Panks?"

"Not yet."

"He's a Mason," she said, crossing her arms and nodding her head as if to make a point.

"But not an Oddfellow."

"No. Anyway, eat your dinner, miss, before it goes cold."

The mutton pie was every bit as good as Minnie had said. Violet was full and sleepy by the time she'd devoured the treacle tart but had arranged to meet Michael after dinner and waited for him in the lounge.

The room was empty when Violet arrived, and she tried to read again before another interruption stopped her. It was not to be. A heavyset man bowled into the room, panting with exertion. He pulled a handkerchief from his pocket, wiped his brow and placed a large leather satchel onto the table. It knocked against an ashtray which clattered to the floor.

"Damn and blast it," said the man, not appearing to notice Violet, who was sitting quietly by the window. He pulled out a fob watch, checked the time and tutted loudly.

Violet gave a gentle cough, hoping to head off another outburst, and he looked up with a start. "Sorry, I didn't see you there. What must you think of me?"

Violet smiled. "Please don't worry."

"Bad language," he said, collapsing onto the chair, "is unforgivable. Especially in front of a lady."

"Well, I do forgive you," she said. "So there is nothing to worry about."

He peered at his watch again. "There is," he said. "I'm late. Very late. Now, where is it?" He rifled through the bag and pulled out a shiny medallion on a blue silk fob. "There's my beauty," he said, holding it aloft.

"What is it?"

"A Member's jewel for the Oddfellows East Anglia Unity. There is a presentation here tonight," he said, closing the bag and depositing it in the corner of the room. "And muggins here forgot to bring the most important thing. I've run a mile and back again to fetch it."

"They were still making speeches when I came in here a few moments ago," said Violet. "You should have plenty of time."

"Yes, good." He gave his florid complexion one more wipe with the handkerchief, put two fingers to his head in an informal salute and left the room."

Violet smiled. The man must have been in his early fifties. Too young to be senile, but undoubtedly eccentric. His manner was endearing, and his membership of an organisation that went by the name of the Oddfellows entirely befitted his character.

She finally managed to finish a chapter of her book before Michael arrived.

"Sorry I'm late," he said. "The Reverend John has taken ill. Some unexpected paperwork to finish."

"It's no trouble," said Violet. "I've had quite an entertaining evening so far."

"You must tell me about it," said Michael. "But first, I need a drink. Would you like one?"

Michael's return from the bar coincided with the mass exodus of the Oddfellows from the second dining room. By the time he joined her, the lounge was full, and he could barely see her through the crowd of brightly dressed men. With typical foresight, Violet had placed her book on the adjoining seat, saving it for Michael. He squeezed through the throng and sat beside her.

"Sorry," she said. "It will be hard to talk with all this noise. Perhaps we should find somewhere quieter."

Michael was about to answer when a man approached them and thrust his hand out. "Reverend Farrow. How are you?" he boomed.

"Very well, Harry. How's that young son of yours?"

"Happy now his little horse has been returned."

"Sorry, Harry. Where are my manners? Let me introduce you to Miss Smith. Violet is an old friend of mine. She is staying at The Crown tonight. Violet, this is Harry Aldrich, proprietor of the auction house and father of little William."

Violet offered her hand. "And your little lad likes horses?"

"What did you say?" Harry struggled to hear over the chatter in the small room.

"Your little boy. Does he like horses?"

"A particular horse," said Harry with a twinkle. A wooden one. He left it in the butcher's shop. Michael found it and asked around until he discovered who owned it, then he returned it to my youngest."

"How kind," said Violet.

"It's noisy in here," said Harry. "And will get worse, no doubt." He nodded towards a group of men in the corner, each clasping a jug of ale with a spare one set aside on the table. "We're sitting in a quieter area in the other room. Would you care to join us?"

Michael looked towards Violet and raised an eyebrow. She nodded. "Thank you," he shouted towards Harry.

They rose and followed Harry Aldrich into the second, more substantial, dining room where three men sat around a square table near an open door leading to the rear yard. An elderly collie dog snuffled beside one of the men who Violet recognised from earlier.

"Ah," he said, "my nemesis returns to haunt me over my careless words."

"Not at all," she said.

"You've met Joseph, then?" asked Harry. "Once met, never forgotten."

Joseph bowed his head with a satisfied smile.

"Miss Smith, Michael, this is George Fairweather, you've met Joseph, and you know Arthur, don't you?"

Michael offered his hand to the wiry, dark-haired man seated by the door who returned the gesture.

"Good to see you again," he said, "in happier circumstances. We were talking about Tom earlier."

"Yes, poor chap. Violet, do you remember me mentioning the coachman with the ill wife when we were in Overstrand? Unfortunately, Tom's wife succumbed to the effects of consumption despite our prayers.

"We will see him right," said Arthur." He is one of us."

"The money won't heal his heart, brother," said Harry.

"But it will feed his children."

"There are not enough funds in the society to feed all yours, eh, George?" quipped Joseph, lightening the mood.

"Do you have many children?" asked Violet.

"Only eighteen," said Joseph before George could reply.

"That is a lot of mouths to feed."

"Arthur is halfway to catching me," George Fairweather growled as he gulped his pint. He was the only one at the table drinking alcohol.

"Nine and one on the way," said Arthur proudly. "I'll name him after you if it's a boy."

George scowled. "Don't bother."

"Or Grace for a girl."

"That's pretty," said Violet.

"Steady on," said Harry Aldrich as George knocked back the last of his pint.

"This obsession with temperance is making you boring," George replied, slamming the tankard onto the wooden tabletop.

"And closer to God," said Harry.

"Are you all in the temperance league?" Violet asked.

"I'm not," said Arthur. "But I don't drink at unity meetings out of respect ."

"It is not compulsory," said Harry. "Most of the men in the bar like a few drinks. I don't mind being around drinkers although I don't indulge myself."

"He's a Methodist, you see," said Joseph as if the two things went hand in hand.

"Tell me about the Oddfellows," said Violet.

Michael grimaced. "That might not be possible," he said.

"We are not so secretive now," laughed Harry. "Once upon a time, a response to that question would be strictly forbidden. Some friendly societies were banned. The Oddfellows survived, but the movement was riven apart with factional splits and secessions. We are more modern now, and although we don't discuss our oaths and rituals outside the organisation, we acknowledge their existence. And we have recently opened a ladies lodge."

Violet nodded approvingly.

"What brings you to Diss?" asked Arthur Thompson.

"I'm visiting Michael," she said.

"You've come a long way to go to church," said Joseph, tickling the dog behind his ears.

"But not to see a friend," said Violet. "Michael is not only a man of God. I have another purpose in Diss. I am looking for someone," she continued.

"Well, you've come to the right place," said Joseph. "We know everything about everyone. Harry's family have been here since Noah built the ark."

"Good," she said. "Though the person I seek may be dead, so forgive me if my enquiries sound insensitive. And what I need to ask about happened a long time ago, so I am led to believe."

"What was that?"

"A woman called Fanny Nunn. I think she may have drowned. I wondered if it was by accident?"

The table fell silent. Only the soft pant of the dog was audible as the men glanced uneasily towards Violet.

She bit her lip. "Sorry. Have I spoken out of turn? Please forgive me."

Harry Aldrich picked up his glass and sipped the water, then licked his lips as he considered his reply.

"You are right. It happened a long time ago, but Fanny's death has bothered me for many years. She did not die naturally. Somebody killed her, and I heard her drown. My father and I, we listened to those terrible screams as we tried to help her. But we couldn't save her. Even now, after all this time, her pitiful cries still haunt me."

CHAPTER FIFTEEN

Inside Walton Gaol

From the moment Lawrence decided to visit William Miller, he agonised over how he was going to access the gaol. Neither Tom Strettell nor any of the other policemen were likely to help. Quite the contrary. And he couldn't go wandering in and expect a welcome. There were strict rules in place about visiting prisoners. And notorious inmates accused of murder were even more closely monitored. Lawrence considered arriving at the prison unannounced and bribing the guard. It wouldn't be the first time he had used that tactic, but it was fraught with risk. It wasn't until he returned to his uncle's house having posted the third telegram to Violet, that an idea presented itself. It was a plausible plan, coming as the result of his uncle's latest obsession.

"What do you think of this, my boy?" Uncle Frederick had asked, as Lawrence entered the drawing room. Frederick was standing in front of a teak stand holding the ugliest looking black box that Lawrence had ever seen.

"What is it?" he asked, staring at the glass lens set into a hole in the centre of the box.

"It's a Kodak," said his uncle, proudly.

"I am still none the wiser."

"A camera, my boy. For taking photographs."

Lawrence examined the box doubtfully, noting a red string that dangled from a brass-coloured fitting. The contraption looked more like a decorated bird box than a mechanism designed to produce an image.

"Stand there," said his uncle, directing Lawrence towards the window where Connie was posing in an evening gown. "Now squeeze together."

Lawrence complied, trying to produce a smile that did not look artificial and forced. Uncle Frederick pulled a string then tripped a button on the left-hand side of the device. A mechanism inside emitted a gentle whir.

"Can I see it?" asked Lawrence.

"You can pick it up if you like."

"Not the camera," said Lawrence. "I meant the picture."

"Oh, my dear boy, no. That is not how it works. Not at all. Once the film is full, I send the box to Kodak. Then they print the photographs and return the camera. It's jolly clever."

"How long does it take?"

"That depends. This film has the capacity for a hundred photographs. It will take a good few months to use them and another three weeks for processing."

"How many photographs do you take a week?" Lawrence asked.

"One or two."

"Then, it will take most of the year before you see the fruits of your efforts. You will have forgotten what was on the film."

Uncle Frederick pursed his lips. "I expect that will be half the fun of it," he said. "Don't you approve?"

"It's not for me to have an opinion," said Lawrence, hoping he had not offended. "As long as you enjoy your photography."

"Look what it does," said his uncle, hobbling towards an armchair. He knelt, pushed his walking cane under one side of the chair and gave it a push. A large box emerged from the other side. Uncle Frederick retrieved it, opened the lid and pulled out a clutch of black and white images which he passed to Lawrence. The round images were grainy, but a clear representation of Uncle Frederick and Lawrence's father.

"When were these taken?" asked Lawrence, surprised. "I have never seen them."

"Back in 1888 when Lionel last visited. We had them done by a professional photographer. I was so impressed that I bought a camera myself."

"If these devices become readily available, photographers will go out of business," said Lawrence.

"I am surprised you don't make use of a camera yourself, given your occupation."

"How could I? They are cumbersome and slow to operate."

"Not all. Handheld cameras have been around for over a decade, and Stirn's patent concealed vest camera is now available in England."

Lawrence considered the value of purchasing one. "I can see how it might be useful," he admitted. "It would have helped Violet with her cuckolded husband case. She got there in the end, but a photograph would have provided compelling evidence. I will give it further thought."

"Good," said his uncle jovially, patting Lawrence on the back. "By all means, try the camera yourself, if you wish. This model is too conspicuous to be useful to you, but it's fascinating to operate."

Lawrence decided to humour his uncle and took up a position behind the tripod. He lined up a few practice shots using the 'V' shape on the leather to frame his Uncle Frederick and what would no doubt become his Aunt Connie. Once Lawrence was sure of his technique, he pulled the string and committed the moment to print. Turning a key on top of the box, Lawrence advanced the film as the germ of an idea formed in his head.

Tuesday, April 30, 1895

The hackney cab slowed to a halt outside Walton Gaol. Lawrence emerged carrying a tripod and a box containing the camera. He paid the bemused looking cabman and walked towards the turreted gaol. It was a handsome brick structure with stone dressings and round-headed windows, too grand to house the degenerate underbelly of Liverpool's criminal fraternity. Lawrence stopped for a moment to consider his options. There was no easy way to see William Miller and subterfuge was his only choice. Even then, he would need to approach the deception with a bold disregard for the rules. Having racked his brain for a more simple option, Lawrence had ruled out everything else. All that remained was the course of action upon which he was about to embark. He would masquerade as a prison photographer.

There were several reasons why he doubted the efficacy of this plan. Aside from the fact that there may already be a photographer, there was an equal chance of there never having been one. Some prisons routinely catalogued their offenders but by no means all. Worse still, Lawrence might walk in to find an appointed photographer already at work in the gaol. Either way, he would have to negotiate around this and any other problems that he might not have considered. It was essential to locate William Miller and find out how he had managed to conduct a burglary quite so unsuccessfully.

Taking a deep breath, Lawrence walked towards the gate and past the low railings that surrounded the building. He strolled beyond the towers to a large wooden door and rang a brass bell conveniently placed to the side. Moments later, a square window opened, and the deep-voiced guard responded.

"Yes?"

"I've come to photograph the prisoner, Miller."

"Which one?"

"William Miller. He's not been here long."

"I know the one," said the guard. "Shifty little weasel, but aren't they all. Wait a minute."

Lawrence peered through the open hatch as the prison guard removed a sheet of carefully ruled paper from a clip on the wall. He lifted his glasses and squinted.

"Nothing here," he said. "Didn't you come last week?"

"Yes," said Lawrence gruffly. "This is a special request."

"Who from?"

"The chief constable to your guv'nor," he said.

"It's not on my list."

"I can't help that. I've got my orders. Why don't you ask someone in authority?"

Lawrence waited with bated breath, hoping that the guard did not have easy access to the prison warden. With a heavy camera and a cumbersome tripod, Lawrence was in no position to make a quick getaway should the need arise.

"I can't," said the guard. "Just hand me the paperwork, will you?"

Lawrence fished into his jacket for a note of authority from the police station, which he had forged earlier in the day.

"Inspector Strettell," said the guard, as he recognised the signature block. "Seems in order. I'll hang on to this."

"As you wish," said Lawrence.

The door swung open, and Lawrence passed through it and into an inner courtyard. The guard nodded to a pair of younger men who were playing cards on a trestle table outside the guardhouse.

"One of you show him to 'D' block,"

"I'll do it." The fair-haired warder tossed his cards onto the table and picked up a packet of Woodbines and a box of matches. He led the way across the quadrangle in front of the entrance to the towered building dominating the prison complex.

"This way," he said, turning left into a long corridor. They had almost reached the other end when he turned right at a double door and into a seating area, beyond which was a barred door. "You can photograph him in there," said the guard, pointing to a large room on the left with a window facing into the courtyard. "I'll go and fetch him."

Lawrence was too nervous to sit down and tried the door of the side room, hoping to see the view from the inner courtyard. The door would not budge, so he wandered towards a pin board and read the few dog eared notices. Lawrence raised an eyebrow at a flyer from the Primitive Methodists appealing for temperance, hoping they had aimed it at the guards. Traditionally, prisoners lacked access to alcohol, but who knew what might come about from the constant prison reforms. His musings were soon interrupted by the arrival of the fair-haired guard and a man of about five foot six, with a thick brown moustache and chains around his wrists, who accompanied him. At about thirty years old, William Miller was younger than Lawrence had anticipated.

The guard stepped forward, unlocked the side room and ushered Lawrence through. "Set up over there," he commanded before retreating to the next room where he stood quietly next to the prisoner.

Lawrence opened the tripod and attached the camera, hoping that he looked authentic. The Kodak remained steady on the stand, which came as something of a relief. He raised a hand to the guard, who nodded before pushing the prisoner through the door. Then he selected a key from a large chain around his waist and unlocked the fetters. Miller rubbed his wrists and jerked his head while his eye twitched uncontrollably.

"I'll be outside having a cigarette," said the warden, closing the door. Lawrence watched the guard loiter next to a low window running the length of the side room. He lit a cigarette and stared at Lawrence intently.

Lawrence stood behind the camera and, as soon as it was clear that the guard was out of earshot, began to speak.

"I've been to Redcross Street," he said. "You left a mess."

Miller stared at him, and the corner of his mouth began to twitch in time with his right eye.

"People I know, influential people, think you may be innocent," Lawrence lied.

"How would they know?" growled Miller.

"Are you?" asked Lawrence pulling the red cord on the Kodak.

"What's it to you?"

"There isn't much time," said Lawrence. "If you are innocent, I can help."

"And if I'm not?"

Lawrence pressed the button which, in the hands of an expert, would produce an image. Nobody would see the finished article, so he only needed to look the part. The guard continued to smoke, and he assumed that the ruse was working.

"Then I can't do very much. Now, what were you looking for?"

"Where?"

"In the attic of Redcross Street."

"How do you know?" Miller stepped backwards in surprise.

"Never mind that. You missed every valuable item in the property. Nobody is that careless."

"I've got nothing to say."

"Fine. But have you got a good memory?"

Miller nodded.

"My name is Harpham. Lawrence Harpham. My offices are at the Butter Market in Bury Saint Edmunds. I am a private investigator, and I will try to help you."

"I don't need your help," hissed Miller.

The guard tossed his cigarette to the floor, stubbed it out, retrieved it, then dropped it in a waste bin. He glared at Lawrence suspiciously and entered the room.

"Finished?"

"All done," said Lawrence.

The guard repositioned Miller and locked his shackles. "Oy, Jessop." He bellowed to a man further down the corridor.

"Show him out, will you?" he asked, pointing to Lawrence, then without another word he unlocked the barred gate and marched Miller back to his cell.

Minutes later Lawrence emerged into the sunlight, wondering whether the experience had been worth it. He had gained no further information from Miller and, had he been a cat, would be several lives lighter. It might have been worthwhile had Lawrence felt a strong leaning towards Miller's guilt or innocence. Instead, he was ambivalent. His instinct had deserted him. Lawrence hailed a cab conveniently parked down Hornby Road. He would return the camera to his uncle and board the next train to Bury.

CHAPTER SIXTEEN

Message from the Past

It was a quarter past seven in the evening when Lawrence finally opened the doors of thirty-three Butter Market. He settled at his desk, feeling tired and irritable, recalling unpleasant memories of his train journey home. Lawrence had chosen an empty carriage and was reading a book when two innocent-looking children had invaded his space. At first, he was untroubled and eyed them with benign amusement. But as the journey progressed, they started asking a series of increasingly inane questions and his patience began to falter. He tolerated them until the younger boy started asking why cows slept standing up. Lawrence said he did not know. The boy tried again, and Lawrence gave the same answer. Finally, the boy dissolved in tears and kicked Lawrence on the leg. Lawrence scowled at the mother, waiting for her intervention, but her eyes remained shut. He spent the rest of the journey acting as an unpaid babysitter, glowering resentfully and convinced that she was feigning sleep.

Lawrence had arrived in Bury after what seemed like an eternity. He deposited his luggage at home without bothering to unpack and proceeded to his office. It was clean and tidy, as usual, and he was glad that he had listened to Violet when she insisted on employing a cleaner. Though initially reluctant, it had turned out to be a wise decision. Annie Hutchinson was hard-working and intelligent. Adept at dealing with general enquiries as well as cleaning, she was a safe pair of hands and more than capable of minding the office in their absence. But Lawrence suspected there was trouble ahead with the recent arrival of a young admirer. Annie's sister had introduced her to a young man, Robert Hicks. He had been hanging around far too often for Lawrence's liking. Not that he had anything against Robert, but because he lived in Norwich, he represented a threat. Lawrence had no wish for his reliable domestic to leave and settle elsewhere.

The ever-efficient Annie had piled his post in the centre of the desk. Three sealed letters rested on top of an open envelope, but only one of them held his interest. Lawrence had come to the office with the sole intention of locating the letter containing Catherine's crest. He'd asked Violet to destroy it but knew very well that she wouldn't. Now that it was possible, he felt an overwhelming urge to procrastinate. He ignored the open envelope and turned to another, addressed in the familiar hand of his Uncle Max. It contained an invitation for a luncheon engagement which Lawrence marked on the calendar. He filed the message in his bottom drawer, wondering why Uncle Max had chosen to post it to the office. Generally, mail found its way to his apartment unless it was business-related, but Uncle Max was getting on a bit. Perhaps it was a sign of things to come.

Lawrence picked up the second envelope. It was brown and most likely contained a bill. Under normal circumstances, Lawrence would have put it straight on Violet's desk, unopened. But such was his need to postpone the inevitable, that he opened it and read it, groaning aloud at the contents. The invoice was from the coal merchant who Lawrence should have paid two weeks ago. Violet had entrusted him with visiting the shop and settling the bill. He'd left with the best of intentions, but something had distracted him, though he could not remember what. In any case, Violet would be cross. He shoved the invoice into his jacket pocket intending to settle it another day. Then Violet wouldn't need to know.

Lawrence dealt with the third letter about a missing necklace and the fourth about a poisoned guard dog by making appointments in his diary. He wasted even more time scribbling quick replies to each enquirer confirming his dates of attendance. Sighing, Lawrence rose and rested the letters against the carriage clock on the mantlepiece, ready for Annie to post tomorrow. Then he returned to his desk to confront the unavoidable. Any longer and the problem would assume elephantine proportions.

The cream-coloured envelope lurking on the desk was postmark free and unstamped. Written at the top in capital letters, was the word 'urgent' with the name and office address below. The rest of the envelope was unremarkable and contained no clues to the sender. Lawrence took a deep breath and removed the contents keeping the picture face down, then steeled himself and turned it over. There it was. A perfect line and ink drawing of Catherine's crest with Celtic crosses on a red stripe and blue dolphins on a silver background. He would recognise it anywhere. Penmanship was one of the quirks he'd loved about Catherine. She was proud of her heritage, and a talented artist, regularly combining both through sketches of her coat of arms. This drawing was so close to her style that it could almost belong to her. Lawrence took a closer look. The similarity was uncanny. Who had sent it and why?

Finding no other clues, Lawrence put his head in his hands and stared at the crest. He sat motionlessly for several minutes, then pushed his chair back and walked to the rear of the office. Unlatching the door, Lawrence approached the kitchen area shared with the milliner above and placed a pan on the gas stove. He watched the unlit hob for a few moments, his mind elsewhere. Then shaking his head, he rummaged in the drawer for a packet of matches and struck one. Wearing a look of grim determination, Lawrence returned to the office. He discarded the crest and collected the envelope in which it had arrived. Lawrence paced the floor of the narrow kitchen, waiting for the pan to boil. Before long, the water began to bubble, and when he judged it ready, he took the envelope and held it over the boiling water. After a few moments, Lawrence removed the envelope and placed it on a low wooden cabinet. He waited, considering the futility of his actions and a plan doomed to failure. The uncanny resemblance of the crest with Catherine's drawing style had provoked memories. Memories of their courtship and time spent apart when they wiled away the hours by writing to each other. It had started when Lawrence was on duty in the Isle of Man. After three weeks of boredom and countless letters, he'd decided to write a secret message on the envelope flap. Catherine had found it and responded in kind, and this continued whenever he went away. They'd kept it up until motherhood stripped away the romance and much of Catherine's time.

Lawrence picked at the envelope flap, not expecting to find anything. Catherine was dead, and nobody else knew about their little game, yet he felt compelled to check. The steam had softened the envelope, and the flap pulled apart with ease. There, beneath the fold, written in dark blue ink, was the word 'Deceiver'. Lawrence dropped the envelope, recoiling in horror. He stumbled into his office, sat down heavily at his desk and pulled the bottom drawer open. Grasping the bottle inside, Lawrence fumbled for a glass, slamming it carelessly onto the table. It split in half, and he hurled it to the floor, splintering shards across the office. His eyes darted from the crest to the envelope. Deceiver, deceiver, DECEIVER. Never, never NEVER. The walls felt like they were closing in on him, and the silence in the office was deafening. He took a slug of whisky straight from the bottle and kept on drinking until darkness fell around him.

CHAPTER SEVENTEEN

Distress

Wednesday, April 1, 1895 – 7.30 am
To: Miss Violet Smith, Crown Hotel, Diss
From: Miss Hutchinson, Butter Market, Bury Saint Edmunds

Come home quickly. Mr Lawrence unwell. Recovering at the residence of Mr Farrow. Please do not delay.

CHAPTER EIGHTEEN

Netherwood House

Wednesday, May 1, 1895

Francis Farrow's residence in Westgate Street was an imposing three-storey building with an array of sash windows and a doorway set below a triglyph frieze. The Doric pilasters adorning the sides provided further grandeur, enhanced by a sizeable driveway leading to garaging for his carriage and a small formal garden. Farrow's three decades as a high ranking Suffolk detective had not generated quite enough income to buy such a magnificent property. As the eldest son, he had inherited the lion's share of his father's fortune, and this windfall allowed him to take early retirement and sole occupation of Netherwood House. Like his father before him, Francis lived alone except for the servants. His father had been a widower for over a decade, and Francis had never married. If his brother Michael had not chosen to follow his faith, he might have stayed in Bury with Francis. But Michael did not seem to envy his older brother's fortune and had never expressed a wish to live at their ancestral home. Anne Huntingdon, their older sister, was the only other living member of the Farrow family, and she had joined her husband in India many years before. Anne only visited England occasionally, and Francis was left to enjoy the quiet luxury of his home alone.

Violet had been to Netherwood on several previous occasions, and all were jolly affairs. She was therefore unaccustomed to the butterfly nerves that had settled inside her since catching the earlier train. It was almost three thirty by the time she arrived, accompanied by Michael who had insisted on joining her despite her protestations. She had already taken up too much of his time and was fearful that his superior would think he was neglecting his duties. But Michael had explained the situation and The Reverend John had been sympathetic. As long as Michael was back in Frenze before the weekend, he would manage.

Michael rang the doorbell of his childhood home more out of politeness than necessity. Their old retainer, Albert Floss, answered it with a welcoming smile before asking after Michael's health. Once he was satisfied with the reply, he guided them into the drawing room where Francis was sitting on a chaise longue. Beside him was a moustached man wearing a stethoscope around his neck. They stood as Violet entered the room.

"Ah, good to see you both," said Francis. "You know Doctor Mallory, don't you?"

Michael approached the doctor and shook his hand while Violet smiled uncertainly. Their paths had not crossed during her four years in Bury, and she was unaccountably nervous in his presence.

"Where is Lawrence?" asked Michael.

"Upstairs, in the blue room," said Francis.

"What happened?" Violet picked anxiously at the brocade on her jacket as she spoke.

"I'll let the doctor explain."

"Sit down." Doctor Mallory beckoned them towards the sofa. "Mr Harpham is suffering from nervous exhaustion. He has experienced a breakdown, not helped by the consumption of an excessive amount of alcohol. His spirits are low."

"Poor Lawrence." Violet's eyes filled with tears. "His health has improved so much over the last few years that I thought he was over the worst of it. Why has he relapsed?"

"It could be anything," said the doctor. "Sadly, it is all too common among the long term injured. Mr Farrow and I were discussing the possibility of moving Mr Harpham to a sanatorium."

"No." The word exploded from Violet's mouth. "He would hate that. He must recover in his own home."

"I understand your feelings," said the doctor, kindly, "but it is not always the case that home is best. Still, it is his choice, and if he refuses to go, I cannot make him unless he deteriorates further. But I have sedated him, and I strongly suggest that he is not left alone."

"Then, I will look after him. There is a spare room in my cottage. He can stay with me."

"Or here," said Francis. "You can stay too if you like."

"No," said Violet. "He will be better off with me."

"How will it look?" asked Francis. "Your reputation will suffer."

"I don't care. I will explain and if people want to imply something that isn't true, then let them. Lawrence is my friend, and I know I can help."

"Let her try," said Michael. "Violet has nursed him back to health once already."

"His father will decide, in the end," said Francis. "I contacted Lionel earlier, and he is already en route."

"I am sure he will agree," said Violet confidently. "Thank you for taking care of Lawrence, but my background as a companion is perfect for looking after him. Caring for people is what I do best."

PART TWO

CHAPTER NINETEEN

The Crown Hotel

Violet had cared for Lawrence well. Very well. So well, that he was sitting in The Crown Hotel, in Diss only two weeks later, waiting for her to join him. The first week after his breakdown had passed in a blur. Violet had fed him, cared for him and tended to his every need while dutifully keeping the office running. When Violet was working, she sent Annie to her cottage to watch over him and later in the evening, she cheerfully cooked dinner and chatted about the day's events. Her presence was a balm to his wounded soul, and he felt, as before, immeasurable gratitude towards her. By the start of the second week, Lawrence was beginning to improve. He stopped taking the sedative prescribed by the doctor and started taking an interest in Violet's current case. Two days later, she'd arrived home to find him sitting at the kitchen table surrounded by bits of paper and utensils. He had spread half the contents of her kitchen cupboard across the table at strategic intervals.

"What are you doing?" she'd asked.

"It makes no sense," said Lawrence, rearranging the crockery. "See. This is Moyse." He pointed to a pepper pot and moved it to the left of the table. "Needham is down here." He dragged a saucer towards him and pushed a china cup to his right. "And this is Miller," he said, pointing to the teacup. Finally, he grabbed a thimble and placed it above the pepper pot and saucer. "This thimble is the attic space. Now, they say that Miller attacked Moyse for money and no other reason. They were friends, and Moyse was kind to Miller. A purse of money was under Moyse's mattress, and Miller must have known that there was money in the house, even if he didn't know the location. Regardless, the mattress is the first place you would look for money."

"I agree," said Violet. "It is a pity that elderly people won't use banks. They often doubt that their money will be safe."

"Precisely," said Lawrence. "And that's why they hide their most valuable items close to their person. It is inconceivable that Miller would have gone to look for money and not checked the mattress. Especially as he had already killed the occupant of the bed."

"What did Miller say to you?" asked Violet gently. She had avoided mentioning anything about Liverpool while Lawrence was recovering, but things had rapidly changed. The man before her was the usual version of Lawrence and not the sick and broken creature from the previous week.

"Nothing," said Lawrence. "He neither confirmed nor denied it. But it's a question of logic. There was clear evidence that Miller was searching the attic. When I challenged him, he almost keeled over in shock. Now, Miller might have killed Moyse to prevent the old man from stopping his search. But if that was the case, then why attack Needham? He had already been into the loft before he hit the boy."

"Perhaps he was angry because he couldn't find what he was looking for."

"I agree," said Lawrence, returning the cup to the saucer. "Whatever he was looking for and couldn't find was crucially important to him. The frustration of being unable to find it enraged him to the point of murder."

"Do you think he was looking for money?"

"No, I do not. Miller was searching for something connected to the Scole Confession.

Violet frowned. "Are you sure?"

"Of course not. But instinctively it fits. Tell me everything you discovered while I was in Liverpool."

Violet chewed her lip, contemplating whether he was up to a long conversation. But Lawrence was adamant. He needed to know everything she did. They talked into the night. Violet recounted her experiences with

Mr and Mrs Jackson over and over again until Lawrence was satisfied and he finally decided that he had the measure of Moyse clear in his mind.

"We'll go to Diss tomorrow," he had said, but Violet refused. And because she had been so good to him, he didn't press it. But as the days passed by and he fought to keep Catherine from his thoughts, he knew he must carry on with the case. Finding out more about Fanny Nunn and the Scole Confession became his one focus. At the end of the second week, he returned to his apartment, and after a lot of persuading, Violet agreed to return to Diss. Lawrence made arrangements with Annie Hutchinson to mind the office, and Violet left a day earlier.

Friday, May 17, 1895

Safely back in Diss, Lawrence had unpacked and was waiting for Violet who had gone into the town for reasons best known to herself.

"Another coffee, sir?" Minnie Panks had returned to the lounge with a vase of flowers and two newspapers.

"Thank you," said Lawrence.

"Help yourself if you like." She nodded towards the papers as she collected his empty cup.

He picked up a paper and almost put it back when he realised it was local. *The Diss Express* was not likely to be a hotbed of exciting news. Lawrence half-heartedly read it not expecting much in the way of national coverage, but he was wrong. Between an article on the Rickinghall flower show and a report about the Bishop of Norwich's views on education, was an article headed 'The Liverpool Murder.'

Lawrence grasped the paper with both hands and read greedily. 'The trial of William Miller for the murder of Edward Moyse formerly of Scole, concluded at the Liverpool Assizes on Wednesday when the jury returned a verdict of guilty and the prisoner was sentenced to death.'

So that was the outcome. Miller would hang. Lawrence read on. All the details that he hadn't got from Tom Strettell or his uncle were in the newspaper report. Miller was poor and of bad character. He was an adulterer who had left his wife and children to run away to America with another woman, who he subsequently robbed. His wife had forgiven him only to find him back home and covered in blood from the murder. She had burned his clothes and done her best to help him. Lawrence shook his head. Miller was guilty. Of that, there could be no doubt. The only unknown was what he was trying to find. 'I don't suppose I will ever be sure,' he muttered aloud.

"What was that?"

Lawrence had failed to notice the arrival of three men, who had squeezed past him on their way to a window seat.

"Sorry," said Lawrence. "I was talking to myself."

"I do it all the time," said one of the men. "I find I get a much more civilised response."

One of the other men raised his eyes heavenwards and shook his head.

"Here you are," said Minnie Panks, bustling into the lounge and placing a cup of coffee on the table.

"Any sign of Violet yet?" asked Lawrence, hopefully.

Minnie shook her head. "Not yet."

"Are you looking for Violet Smith?" asked the slimmer man.

"Why, yes. Do you know her?"

"We had the pleasure of meeting Violet a few weeks ago," he continued, walking towards Lawrence. He offered his hand. "Harry Aldrich," he said, "and this is Joseph Pope and Robert Moore. We ran into Violet half an hour ago. She was on her way to the church."

"Thank you. I'm Lawrence Harpham. Violet and I will be staying here for a few days."

"Do you mind if we join you?" asked Joseph Pope, already moving towards him with a cup in his hand.

"Not at all. Please sit down," said Lawrence with more enthusiasm than he felt. Conversing with strangers this early in the morning had not been part of his plan. He folded the paper and put it to one side.

"How do you know Violet?" he asked.

"We met at the last lodge meeting." Harry Aldrich reached into his pocket for a pair of spectacles, picked up the paper and scrutinised the page. "Catching up with the cricket results, I see," he continued.

"Yes, it sounds like a good match," said Lawrence vaguely. He had no idea who had been playing or the outcome of the game, but it was easier than admitting to reading a report of the Liverpool slaying.

"They're a good team over at Thelnetham," said Moore, looking at the paper over Harry's shoulder.

"I beg to differ," said Joseph. "We won by more than an innings last time we met." He reeled off a long list of local cricketing statistics.

"How the devil do you remember all that information?" asked Aldrich.

"He's probably making it up." Robert Moore rested his chin on his hands and stared across the table.

Joseph Pope raised an eyebrow. His round face bore a quizzical expression.

"Check them, if you like," said Harry Aldrich. "I guarantee he will be right. He can't remember how to tie a shoelace, but remembers all the non-essential details."

"You enjoy cricket, then?" asked Lawrence.

"Not really," Pope replied. "It's a dull game. I don't play myself, but collecting scores – well, that's a different matter."

"That's what happens when you work in a bank." Robert Moore looked apologetically towards Lawrence. "He spends too much time adding numbers together. It has addled his brain."

"You work in Diss?" Lawrence was struggling for small talk in a group of three men who were evidently well acquainted. He was very much the outsider.

"The National Provincial Bank on Mere Street," said Joseph, looking at his pocket watch. "Which is where I should be now." He rose and tipped his forelock before leaving the room.

"Don't mind him," said Harry Aldrich. "He's one of the more eccentric members of our lodge."

"Are you Freemasons?" asked Lawrence, feeling on more solid territory at the mention of lodges.

"Oddfellows," said Aldrich. "We met your friend at the last lodge meeting."

"You did," said Robert Moore. "I was elsewhere at the Faith and Fidelity lodge trying to boost their spirits. I play the accordion," he continued, by way of explanation.

"And he plays it jolly well," said Harry.

"Was there a problem at the lodge?" asked Lawrence, wondering why spirits were low.

Aldrich flashed Moore a look, but he ignored it.

"The treasurer ran off with the bulk of their funds," he said frankly. "It's gone to court, and they secured a conviction, but it's too late. Their savings are gone. All that money, fraudulently used."

"Shocking," said Lawrence. "What a shame."

"They've appointed another treasurer," Moore continued. "But there's little money left to look after."

The irony of a fraud case in the Faith and Fidelity lodge was not lost on Lawrence, but he kept his counsel and made no comment.

"We are arranging a series of events to raise funds for our brothers," said Harry Aldrich. "A spring fair on Sunday week. You are welcome to come along."

"I expect we will be back in Bury by then," said Lawrence. "We're only here for a day or two."

"Work or pleasure?" asked Robert Moore.

Lawrence opened his mouth to answer just as Violet walked past the doorway.

"Violet," Lawrence called to her, but she sailed by. "Excuse me." He put down his coffee cup and followed her into the hall.

"I say, Violet."

She turned to face him. "Lawrence." She smiled at the sight of his face. "Where have you been?"

"To the church and the chemist. I am feeling a little under the weather this morning."

"Go back to bed then. I can carry on alone."

"It is nothing serious," she said. "Where shall we start?"

"I've been chatting to your new friends," said Lawrence. "We ought to say goodbye before we leave."

He returned to the lounge with Violet in tow.

Harry Aldrich rose and greeted her. "Did you find the vicar?" he asked.

"Yes, I did, thank you. He was very accommodating even though I unintentionally interrupted his meeting with Mr Garrod."

"Henry Garrod?" Robert lowered the newspaper and scratched his nose.

"Yes, I believe so."

"Solicitor and county coroner," said Harry helpfully.

"I wonder what he was doing there?"

"Any reason why he shouldn't be?" Harry peered over his glasses.

"The last time I saw the two of them together, they had words," said Robert.

"About what?"

"I couldn't hear what they were saying despite the raised voices."

"Unusual," said Harry, "they are both mild-mannered men."

Lawrence coughed and nodded imperceptibly towards Violet.

"We must go now," she said. "It was good to meet you again." She offered her hand, first to Harry Aldrich and then to Robert Moore before leaving the room ahead of Lawrence.

"Let's walk," said Lawrence following Violet into the hallway. "We won't get any privacy in here."

They proceeded down St Nicholas Street towards St Mary's Church. "How did you get on?" he asked.

"The Reverend Manning is charming," said Violet. "We got on rather well, once I'd apologised for interrupting him."

"Could he help?"

"Yes and no," said Violet. "He showed me the burial register, and there was just enough time to copy down a few names of women who were the right age and recently deceased. He has allowed me free access to the register whenever I like."

"Good." Lawrence nodded approvingly.

"I told him that I was looking into the death of someone who lived in Diss but did not give any further detail. I thought it would be unwise to say too much, even to a man of the cloth."

"Always best," murmured Lawrence.

"But then he asked if she died in Diss, and of course, we don't know."

"No, we don't." Lawrence squinted and shielded his eyes as the bright sun penetrated the market place. "The Bible came from Diss, and the address book directed us to Jackson in Scole. She could have died in either place."

"Or somewhere else altogether."

"Agreed. The burial records won't get us anywhere. We need to try another way."

They turned into Mere Street and walked past the National Provincial Bank on the right.

"I wonder if Mr Pope was late?"

"He doesn't strike me as the type to care one way or another," said Violet. "He is quite an unusual man."

"I didn't meet him long enough to form a judgement. Anyway, that only leaves us with Fanny Nunn," said Lawrence. "Did you ask about her?"

Violet nodded. "The Reverend confirmed that she drowned, but I couldn't get him to tell me any more than that."

"Nobody wants to talk about it. Odd when it happened such a long time ago."

"A wasted visit then?"

"No. Fanny's mother still lives in Diss. She is the proprietor of the Two Brewers Inn."

"Capital. She will know everything of note."

"If she will speak to us."

"Perhaps you could go and ask her? She is more likely to talk to you than me."

"And if she doesn't, her daughter might. Her daughter's name is Carrie Algar. She's a little younger than Fanny and resides with her mother at the inn."

"Good. And you will speak to them?"

"I'll try. Are you sure you won't come?"

"No," said Lawrence. "This Henry Garrod fellow that you met earlier. The county coroner, you say?"

"I didn't say that. I barely know him."

"It doesn't matter," said Lawrence. "I'm going to visit, regardless. Any coroner worth his salt will have full records about a local drowning. He might be able to assist with the recent female deaths too."

"As you wish." Violet smiled at Lawrence. Though not fully recovered, he had regained that glint in his eye with which she was all too familiar. She had her doubts about their investigation. There was little basis for it and no hope of a financial reward. But if anything could keep his mind off Catherine, it was an unusual case, and for once she was happy to indulge him.

CHAPTER TWENTY

The Two Brewers Inn

Not one to waste time in contemplation, Violet elected to visit the Two Brewers Inn in St Nicholas Street without delay. She waited outside while Lawrence called into the National Provincial Bank to ask for directions to Henry Garrod's offices. He returned five minutes later, and they parted in the Market Place. Violet went north, and Lawrence made his way past St Mary's Church and into Mount Street. It was a short walk to the Two Brewers Inn which allowed Violet the opportunity to call into the Corn Hall. She crossed through the covered portico and through the foyer where she stopped in front of a printed poster. It advertised a second showing of the Diss Choral Society's rendition of Handel's operetta, *Acis and Galatea*. She smiled, pleased at her excellent recollection. She had glimpsed an advertisement in the paper earlier that day but hadn't been sure of the date of the performance. It was as she'd hoped. If they were still in Diss tomorrow, the operetta would be an excellent way to spend their leisure time, if she could persuade Lawrence to come. If not, she would go alone.

The Two Brewers Inn stood next door to the Corn Hall. It was a two-storey, timber-framed building with a coach way and more modest than its ostentatious neighbour. It was early afternoon by the time Violet peered through the front window. The inn was full, and for a moment, she baulked at entering alone, but steadied her nerves and walked through the front door. As she passed through the crowd, she tried to think of a reason to bring up the sensitive subject of the publican's daughter's death.

On the way to the counter, Violet noticed a discarded newspaper on a wooden chair. It provoked immediate inspiration for a ruse that might be effective if handled well. Gaining confidence, she approached the young woman behind the counter who was busy serving drinks, and waited for her to finish. The girl poured two tankards of ale from a large jug which she placed on the bar before holding her hand out for money. An elderly man paid at a snail's pace then grasped the tankards with shaking hands and walked an unsteady path to a table by the window. The air in the public house was musty with the smell of hops and none too clean. Violet leaned on the sticky counter and immediately pulled her hand away, wiping it discreetly on her skirts. Her heart sank as she looked at the floor. A combination of dust and spilt ale had already leached over the bottom of her dress.

"Yes?" The girl's accent carried a familiar North Norfolk burr.

"Is Mrs Nunn available?" asked Violet.

"Who wants to know?"

"Miss Violet Smith."

"Is she expecting you?"

"No," said Violet.

"Then she's busy. She has asked me not to disturb her unless the coal merchant calls".

Violet bit her lip. "Well, can you give her a message?" she asked, crossing her fingers behind her back. "Tell her that I am a journalist. I am currently engaged in writing an article on selected East Anglian public houses and would be grateful if she would grant me an interview. Please say that she is free to decline, but to keep my visit secret. The Two Brewers is our first choice, but other inns in the town are under consideration. If she would rather not feature in the magazine, we will select another establishment instead.

The girl raised her eyebrows in surprise. "I'll be back in a moment," she said and left Violet alone in the busy bar.

Violet stood near the counter, trying to look unobtrusive and thanking her lucky stars that she'd recently read an article by journalist Eliza Lynn Linton. Although Violet disagreed with Mrs Linton's views on feminism, she admired her forthright opinions. Though Violet always regretted lying, she'd seen no other way to proceed without doing so. There had been a reluctance to discuss Fanny Nunn's death so far, and a direct approach would not work. Pretending to be a journalist might. She stared towards the window and waited for the barmaid to return, knowing that the first thing she would need to do is pour another pint. The poor old man had managed to carry the beers as far as the table, but within moments of arriving, had knocked one onto the floor. His companion stared dolefully at the growing puddle, but neither man made any attempt to clean the mess.

"This way." The girl had returned and was beckoning Violet to follow her towards the rear of the inn. "Up there, turn left at the top," she said, curtly. Violet wondered at the wisdom of employing a girl of so few words in a public house where exchanging pleasantries was key. But it was not her problem. Obtaining information was her only concern. She made her way up the creaking stairs, trying not to touch the grey film on the white wooden railing. At the top of the stairs, she opened the door to a room which served as a parlour. A plump woman with auburn coloured hair tinged with a smattering of grey was sitting in front of an unlit fire. She lounged in a reclining chair with her feet on top of an upturned basket, and she'd pulled up her black dress to expose unstockinged feet. Her ankles were red and swollen.

She looked over her shoulder. "Come in, Miss Smith," she said. "Excuse my state of dress. Doctor's orders. Now, take a seat over there." She gestured towards a padded armchair covered with an old shawl. "And tell me all about it."

Violet reached into her bag and pulled out the notebook and pencil she habitually carried. "I am a journalist," she said. "As I explained to your barmaid, I have been commissioned to produce an article on selected public houses in Norfolk and Suffolk."

"So I understand," said Mrs Nunn, scratching her calf. White tracks scored her legs and did not fade. Violet averted her eyes, feeling slightly uncomfortable.

"How did you select the Two Brewers Inn?" asked Mary.

Violet had already considered the question while she was waiting at the bar. "I didn't select it," she said. "Neither did my editor. One of your customers put it forward."

"Well, I'll be," said Mary Nunn. A smile spread across her face, and her blue eyes twinkled. She tucked a lock of hair into her lace cap before

107

continuing. "I am not altogether surprised," she said. "There are no airs and graces in my establishment. Not like others, I could mention. People are free to say what they will and come and go as they please. What publication do you represent?"

"The Wymondham Courant," Violet replied, hoping she sounded convincing. "Now, tell me. What hours do you keep?" she continued.

Mary Nunn responded, counting on her fingers as she spoke and Violet scribbled a series of unreadable notes across her book.

"Who works with you?"

"My daughter Carrie, and my servant Maria both live and work here," Mary Nunn replied. "The barmaid Susan who showed you upstairs and another girl, Beatrice live out with family but come in daily to work behind the bar. Thomas Clark is the barrel man and helps with any heavy work. I am a widow, you see."

"I am sorry," said Violet sympathetically.

"Yes, two times over," continued Mary Nunn staring into the distance with misty eyes. "Henry Murton and Henry Nunn. I outlived both of them."

"How sad." Violet leaned over and touched Mary's hand. The older woman's eyes filled with tears at the small gesture of kindness.

"And my poor children," she continued. "Ellen and Fanny. Both girls died young."

Violet stopped writing and looked up with interest. "It's one thing losing your husband, but losing a child – that is a tragedy for a parent to endure."

"It was," Mary agreed. "Ellen died naturally, but poor Fanny. I still do not know to this day whether she did away with herself or whether somebody killed her."

Violet gasped and put her hand to her chest, surprised at the sudden offering of information. "You poor thing."

Mary hoisted herself upright and leaned forwards looking directly into Violet's eyes. "I fear I was too hard on her," she said. "I drove her to it, one way or another."

"What do you mean?"

"She drowned in the mere," said Mary. "They called it murder at the trial, but I am not so sure. I wanted her to go to Norwich to take a situation. You see, I still had younger children at home to care for, and I thought it would be good for Fanny to make her way in life. But she didn't

want to leave. Her sweetheart lived here in Diss. Young Alfred Wylie."
Mary's eyes filled with tears again. "If I had not sent her away, she might
still be alive."

"I am sure that is not the case." Violet felt a surge of empathy for the
ageing woman who had buried two daughters.

"She was unhappy about leaving," said Mary, "and she told me that she
would not trouble me long."

"What do you think she meant by that?"

"I would not have thought anything of it if she had said it only once.
But she mentioned it several times. 'I won't trouble anyone long.' That is
what she uttered."

"But that is not the same as threatening suicide," said Violet.

Mary Nunn shuddered at Violet's words.

"I know it is not germane to my article," said Violet, taking a chance.
"But I would be glad to hear what happened that day. You might feel
better talking about it."

Mary nodded. "It has been a long time since I have spoken of Fanny.
Carrie does not like to remember her sister's death. Nobody talks about
Fanny any more. The trial divided the town."

"How?"

"Half the people thought she had made away with herself and the other
half agreed with the jury. In the end, most people came around to thinking
that she was responsible for her death."

"I can see why they might," said Violet. "After all, the alternative
would mean a murderer in their midst. What do you believe?"

"I don't know, but I fear it was a suicide, and that means I must bear
some responsibility. But worse still is the possibility that somebody killed
my poor girl."

"Did she have any enemies?"

"No." Mary shook her head. "She helped me in the inn and was always
chatty, always interested in people. She enjoyed a drink, loved to talk and
naturally became a great favourite among our customers."

"What happened on the day that she died?" asked Violet gently.

Mary let out a deep sigh and sank back into her chair. "I last saw her
alive on the twenty-ninth of November 1877. It was a Thursday and a
little after eleven o'clock at night."

CHAPTER TWENTY ONE

The Mere

"It's a day I will never forget," said Mary Nunn, sadly. "My last ever sighting of Fanny was in the passageway at the rear of the inn. The dailies had left, and we were all set to turn in. It had been a long night, and the inn had been full due to a celebration. One of the young men had secured a position in London and prepared himself to leave the next day, just like Fanny. His friends were drunk and quite rowdy. But they left at eleven o'clock, and we closed the doors."

"Was Fanny alone?"

"She was then, but her sweetheart, Alfred, had been with her for most of the evening."

"What was she doing in the passageway?"

"Nothing. She seemed to be waiting. I said to her, 'Fanny, dear, take the light. It is time to go to bed,' and I handed her the oil lamp. She took it without a word, and I suppose she went upstairs. I did not follow as I had to check the doors and windows downstairs."

"Did you always secure the inn?"

"Not always," said Mary. "But some money had gone missing the previous week. Not a lot, but I did not know how or when it disappeared, so I was more careful than usual."

"Did she bid you goodnight later on?"

"She may have, but if she did, I never noticed as I was still locking up."

"And she had been out of sorts, you said?"

"She had been low-spirited all week. I could not make out what the matter was. I knew that she was unhappy about leaving and would not have gone by choice, but it was more than that. She had left home before, you see. I'd secured her an unpaid position in North Walsham as a favour for a friend to get her used to the idea of working away. She had not been unhappy there. Quite the contrary."

Violet turned a page in her notebook, having covered two sides with her small, compact writing. She glanced at Mary Nunn, wondering how she felt about seeing her take notes. If she had an objection, she did not voice it.

"Was Fanny ready to leave for her new position?"

"Not really. She was due to journey to Norwich and should have gone on Wednesday, but she didn't start making preparations to pack until Thursday, the day she died. I'd put the trunk in her bedroom and said, 'Why don't you get on packing your box?' Fanny seemed worried and said that she was in no hurry and that she didn't want to pack more than was necessary. I told her that she could take as much or as little as she needed because she could come home on Sunday morning and spend the day here. Then she could take away extra clothes if she wanted."

"Did she intend to live with her new employer?"

"No." Mary rubbed her hands together as if trying to improve her circulation. "She was going to stay in Bedford Street with my married daughter Ellen Hammond, her stepsister."

"So, you went to bed once you had locked up?"

"Not straight away. I sat up for a while."

"But you didn't hear her come downstairs."

"No. I had no idea that Fanny was out."

Violet lowered her notebook and leaned forward. "I know this will be difficult, but can you tell me how you came to find out that your daughter was dead."

Mary sighed deeply. For a moment, she seemed reluctant to continue, and Violet wondered if she had pushed her too far. She sat quietly, hardly breathing and hoped that Mary would speak.

"It was about seven o'clock on Friday morning. I had been awake since dawn and was tidying and preparing for the day. The busman came in to collect Fanny and take her to Norwich, and I went up to her room."

"Was she usually late up?"

"Yes, often. Fanny was in the habit of taking a little too much drink at times and was not an early riser."

"Did she sleep alone?"

"Yes. Fanny had a room of her own. I went upstairs to wake her as soon as the busman arrived, but she had not slept in her bed. The bedclothes were undisturbed, and her trunk was lying open on the floor."

"Had she packed anything?"

Mary's brow knitted in concentration. "Yes," she said. "Now I come to think of it her trunk was fully packed. Not just the bits I had put in, but most of her clothes and all of her shoes."

"So she intended to leave?"

"I have never been sure," said Mary. "In recent years, I have veered more towards the suggestion that she did away with herself. But today is the first time that I have thought about the trunk. Would she have bothered with it, if she had intended to throw herself into the mere?"

"What did you do when you saw that her room was empty?"

"I went back down to tell the busman, John Rudd. When I said that Fanny was not in her room, he asked me if I had seen Mr Wood that morning. I said that I had not been outside yet and had not spoken to anyone. 'Then you won't have heard the news,' he said."

"News about Fanny?"

"News about a young woman jumping into the mere. I knew at once, as soon as he said it, that it must be Fanny. She was not in her room, and a girl was lying dead in the water. Of course, it must be my daughter. My servant at the time was Elizabeth Peake. I sent her over to Inspector Amis to ask for his help. He came straight back to the inn, but it wasn't until midday that they retrieved her poor body."

"How dreadful." The account almost moved Violet to tears. "Why did they think that she might have met her end by foul play?" she asked. "Though it grieves me to say so, your story suggests that Fanny either jumped or fell into the mere."

"There were many witnesses who thought otherwise," said Mary Nunn. "Upstanding, professional people. John Aldrich, his son Henry and daughters Louisa and Alice, and John and Sarah Wood of the Sun Inn. There is no reason for them to lie."

"No, none at all," agreed Violet. "It must have been a dreadful time for you."

"I was in bed for several days," said Mary. "I could not move or function with the pain of it. I sent my son Christopher to Norwich to fetch Ellen, my eldest daughter. She kept the inn until I was well enough to work again and took care of the funeral with the burial club money. But a week later, I was ordered to give evidence at the inquest."

"And you were not yet recovered?"

"My body was weak and my mind, weaker still. The coroner asked many questions of me as if I was a prisoner on the stand."

"You should have had more time to mend," said Violet.

Mary nodded. "You should write about that," she said. "There was no sympathy for me, yet I had done nothing wrong."

"Did you say that the jury found Fanny's death felonious?"

"Yes. They said she'd been killed. The verdict was murder by person or persons unknown?"

"But they never found her killer?"

"They never looked. It was only the jury that believed in a murder – and the Aldriches who said they heard her cries for help. Within a few months, they'd forgotten Fanny as if she had never existed. As I told you, most people thought she had taken her own life, and like them, I did not see any purpose in an investigation for its own sake."

"And now?"

"And now, I wonder whether I should have done more to find out. Could a killer have lived among us these last twenty years?"

CHAPTER TWENTY TWO

A Revelation

Henry Garrod's office formed part of a large terraced house in Mount Street a short distance away from the National and Provincial Bank. Lawrence had asked the clerk for directions and was in luck. Mr Garrod had conducted his banking earlier that day and had mentioned his intent to return to his office. Sure enough, Lawrence pushed the door open to find a young clerk writing in a ledger with studious concentration. The young man looked up as Lawrence entered and placed his pen in the inkstand. "May I help?" he asked in a faltering voice that sounded as if it hadn't quite broken.

"Is Mr Garrod available?" asked Lawrence.

"I'll check," said the clerk, rising to his feet. He was short; a full head shorter than Lawrence with fine, wispy, blond hairs covering the lower half of his face. "who will I say is calling?" he asked.

"Lawrence Harpham."

He hesitated as if about to ask a further question, then changed his mind. Lawrence watched as the boy walked timidly towards a wooden door at the end of the room and knocked twice.

"Yes?" A gruff voice came from the room beyond.

"A Mr Harpham to see you, sir," said the young clerk.

"What does he want?"

"I don't know," said the clerk, biting his lip.

The sigh from the other room was loud enough for Lawrence to hear. There was a short silence, then the door swung open to reveal a stout, grey-haired man of between sixty and seventy years. He was sporting a handlebar moustache.

"Pleased to meet you, Mr Harpham," he said, extending his hand. "This way," he gestured to the door through which he had come. "Take a seat, and I will be with you shortly."

Lawrence made himself comfortable in one of a pair of chairs at the front of a sturdy oak desk. A bookcase stacked with law books filled the right-hand side of the back wall while a tall bureau stood to the left of the fireplace. The side window overlooked a pretty cottage garden with tall, yellow foxgloves swaying against the glass in the light May breeze. Lawrence tried not to listen to the raised voice coming from the other room. The young clerk was getting a dressing down for some failing in his service.

Mr Garrod returned and pushed the door a little too firmly. It slammed against the frame, making Lawrence jump.

"Sorry about that," he said, as he sat behind the desk. He leaned forward on his elbows and steepled his hands. "He's only been with me a month," he continued. "Good at his numbers and letters but short on common sense. I'm not at all sure that he will cut the mustard."

"Good men are hard to find," muttered Lawrence, vaguely.

"Indeed, they are. Anyway, Mr Harpham. We've met before, haven't we?"

"Not as far as I know," said Lawrence.

"Are you sure? There's something familiar about you."

Lawrence shook his head. "I think I would have remembered."

"Never mind, must be imagining it. Perhaps I should retire, after all. Ellen is always saying that I should step back and leave things to my business partner, but I cannot agree. When a man stops working, he stops thinking. My friends all seem to die when they give up their occupation. Now, what can I do for you?"

"I hoped for some information. Am I correct in thinking that you are a coroner?"

"I am coroner for the liberties of the Duke of Norfolk."

"And you carry out inquests?"

"I do."

"Would you have conducted an inquest in Diss in 1877?"

"No. That would have been Mr Culley."

"Ah. How may I contact him?"

"That won't be possible without a medium. Culley died a long time ago. What is it you would like to know?"

"A young woman, Fanny Nunn, died in 1877. I wondered if you could tell me a little more about the inquest."

"It was nothing to do with me. A different jurisdiction, you see. Culley was deputy coroner for Norfolk."

"That's a shame."

"Not necessarily. I take it upon myself to collect copies of all inquests and autopsies relevant to Diss and the surrounding areas. It makes my work much easier."

"Then you have records for all suspicious deaths?"

"Yes, in theory. But whether a death is suspicious is a subjective matter."

"Meaning?"

"Well, a coroner is only notified if the policeman in attendance deems it necessary. Suspicion must exist in the first place."

"Are you saying the opinion of one man alone precipitates a coroner's investigation.?"

"Yes. That is often the case."

"So any flaw in logic, or laziness on the part of the policeman concerned, could prevent the reporting of a questionable death?"

"In principle, but there is no reason for a man of the law to disregard such a crime."

"And it did not happen in the case of Fanny Nunn. There was an inquest."

"From what you say, there would have been. I have an hour before my next appointment. I can check my records if it helps?"

"Thank you." Lawrence nodded appreciatively and waited while the solicitor opened the glass doors of the bookcase. He extracted a sizeable hard-backed register which he placed on the desk and within moments had located the relevant record. He turned the register to face Lawrence and pointed to an entry.

"That's it," he said. "You can read it while I take this document to young Mr Jones."

Henry Garrod left the room while Lawrence read the report. Mr Culley had presided over the well-attended inquest, and Mr John Aldrich was

foreman of the jury. A dozen or so witnesses gave statements, all
reputable members of Diss society. Two surgeons conducted the post-
mortem, and neither found any marks of violence. Fanny Nunn was not
pregnant at the time of her death, and the cause of death was suffocation
by drowning. The coroner directed the jury to establish why the deceased
was in the water. Was she there by her own hands or due to the actions of
another? Evidence indicated that the deceased might have been of
unsound mind at the time of her death, and there were discrepancies
between the testimony of Alfred Wylie and that of Inspector Amis. The
coroner allowed the jury to return a verdict of 'found drowned' if they had
any doubt, but the jury was not so minded. After about an hour's
deliberation, the public returned to hear a verdict of wilful murder by
person or persons unknown. Lawrence closed the register and pondered.
The conclusion was a surprise. The coroner had given a clear steer
towards suicide or an open verdict, which had not swayed the jury. Either
they were mistaken or had heard something that concerned them. Henry
Garrod interrupted his thoughts as he returned to his office.

"How did you get on?" he asked.

"I'm not sure," said Lawrence. "This account has raised as many
questions as it has answered."

"I am sorry that I could not have been more helpful. You're not local to
Diss, are you?"

"No," said Lawrence." I'm here on business. I'll be returning to Bury in
a few days. Thank you for your help anyway." He stood and held his hand
out to the solicitor.

Henry Garrod clicked his fingers. "That's how I know you," he
exclaimed. "Oh," his face clouded as a further thought crossed his mind.
"It's a delicate matter."

"What is? How do we know each other?"

Garrod sighed, seemingly regretting his recollection. He gestured to
Lawrence to sit down.

"We have never met," he said. "I don't know you, but I know your
name. I am sorry that you lost your wife in such tragic circumstances."

Lawrence slumped in the chair, dazed at the unexpected reference to
Catherine. "You conducted her inquest?"

Henry Garrod nodded his head." I would not typically have done so,
but from time to time, we cover other jurisdictions. It just so happens that
I was available that night."

"I have never seen a report of Catherine's autopsy," said Lawrence. "I was unwell and in no mood to attend the inquest."

"That's probably for the best. Facts cannot undo the tragedy or lessen the sorrow."

"Yet I owe her a responsibility. I should have gone."

"You know how she met her end. Isn't that enough?"

"She died in a fire. She must have suffered terribly."

Henry Garrod turned to the cabinet once again. This time he selected a different volume with red binding and gold letters down the spine. He licked his fingers and turned the pages.

"Mr Harpham. On that fact, at least, I can reassure you. Your wife died of smoke inhalation. It is most unlikely that she suffered at all."

Lawrence expelled a deep breath. "Thank God," he said. "The thought of her last moments have haunted me for years. And my daughter, Lily?"

"The same. Lily was in her bed, and there was no evidence that she ever woke."

Lawrence's eyes filled with tears. "Thank you," he said. "I cannot tell you how much that helps." He managed a weak smile. "At least it must have been a quick inquest," he continued.

Henry Garrod nodded. "Yes. Once they discounted the arson theory, proceedings were straightforward. As you know, the verdict was an accidental death."

"Arson theory?" Lawrence pushed the chair away and walked to the window with his hands over his mouth. "Arson? Nobody has ever mentioned the possibility that the fire was deliberate."

Henry Garrod scanned the report. "As I said, the theory was raised and disregarded. Arson was mentioned only in passing at the inquest."

"I never knew."

"It is a hard thing for a man who has lost his family to hear. And unnecessary, it would appear."

"But I was in the police force. They had an obligation to tell me."

Henry Garrod raised his eyebrows. "I expect your colleagues were trying to spare your feelings," he said.

"Even so..." the words trailed away as Lawrence fought to regain his composure. "Mr Garrod. Thank you for your help. Forgive my reaction. I am truly grateful."

He reached out for Garrod's hand and returned to The Crown, so deep in thought that he remembered nothing of the journey.

Lawrence located Violet in the sitting room of The Crown Hotel. She was occupying a seat by the window and frowning in deep concentration as she studied the contents of her notebook.

He slid into the opposite seat, and she looked up.

"At last. I expected you back hours ago."

"I went for a walk around the mere."

"You should have come with me. Mary Nunn was very helpful. I feel as if I know Fanny much better now."

"Good," Lawrence murmured noncommittally.

"Only the jury believed it was murder. Everyone else thought the poor girl killed herself. It's only now that Mary Nunn is beginning to wonder."

"I know. I read the inquest report," said Lawrence. "The coroner directed the jury to return an open verdict or one of drowning while of unsound mind."

"Yet they didn't. There must be a reason. Are you listening?"

"Sorry." Lawrence was staring into the distance, lost in thought. "Well?"

Lawrence regarded Violet impatiently. "The foreman was a Mr John Aldrich," he said. "And the main witnesses all carried the Aldrich surname. Assuming they were members of the same family, it is hardly surprising that their similar stories influenced the jury. Be that as it may, I do not think there is anything sinister in it."

"That's a sudden change of opinion on your part."

Lawrence sighed. "The whole case is ridiculous. I've created a mystery where there is none. We are wasting our time. I am surprised you have gone along with it."

Violet closed her notebook. "I thought it was what you wanted," she said, studying his face.

"You're my equal partner," said Lawrence, coldly. "If you think a case is not worth pursuing, you should say so."

"What's wrong, Lawrence?"

"Nothing."

"Yes, there is."

"Why must something always be wrong if we don't agree?"

"I know you better than that. Something has happened, and I don't think it has anything to do with the Aldriches."

Lawrence put his head in his hands. "I don't want to talk about it."

"But you will," said Violet. "And when you do, come and find me. I will be in my room." She gathered her notebook and papers and stood up.

"Violet." Lawrence looked at her helplessly.

She sat down again and reached for his hand. "What is it?"

"Catherine," he said. "Henry Garrod told me that he performed her autopsy. I never knew. And there's something else. The police considered the possibility of arson for a while."

Violet sat quietly, listening without interruption. "Poor Lawrence," she said when he had finished. "What are you going to do?"

"I don't know," he said, shaking his head. "I cannot seem to free myself from the past. Every time I accept Catherine's death, something comes along and knocks me off track."

"The best way to carry on is to embrace the present," said Violet.

"How?"

"By dealing with the task at hand. Our positions on the Scole case have altered," she said. "You have come to think of it as a waste of our time, but I do not. It is only a small thing, but Fanny packed her trunk to go. Why would she have bothered if she intended to do away with herself? And we have met Harry Aldrich. He is a reasonable man, a successful auctioneer and well regarded around the town. Let us give full attention to this matter. Forget the past for a while."

"I cannot."

Violet squeezed his hand. "Yes, you can. You must."

"What do you suggest?"

"Let's move forward with our investigation. I will speak to Alfred Wylie. He was Fanny Nunn's sweetheart. I have already checked with Minnie Panks, and Wylie still lives in Diss. While I'm doing that, you can visit Inspector Amis. He was in charge of the investigation but is now retired. He left Diss, but I have it on good authority that he resides in Attleborough. As you were both in the police force at the same time, he is bound to speak to you."

"I have met him once or twice," said Lawrence. "I do not know him well, but you are right. He is a decent chap and will no doubt cooperate."

"So that is settled?"

"No. Forgive me, Violet, but I must go back to Bury first."

"Why?"

"To see William Clarke."

"Who?"

"Superintendent William Clarke."

"Can he help?"

"Not with this. I used to work for Clarke. If they considered arson, he would have known. And it would have been his decision to keep it from me."

Violet was still holding his hand. "Is that wise?" she asked, with a gentle squeeze.

"Probably not, but I need to know."

"You are picking at a scab that will never heal."

"I cannot let things lie as they are, Violet. I have known for years that something was amiss. I have felt it and deliberately ignored it. If I am ever going to be free, then I must confront what happened. Do you understand what I mean?"

Violet nodded without speaking.

"I will go to Bury, and then I will go to Attleborough, I promise. Will you come with me?"

"No. You must go alone. I will track down Alfred Wylie."

"Get Michael to help."

"He is too busy, Lawrence. Michael has responsibilities of his own. I will manage it alone."

"Again," said Lawrence. "I am sorry."

"Don't say it." Violet left The Crown and walked to the church. By the time she returned, Lawrence had gone.

CHAPTER TWENTY THREE

In Pursuit of William Clarke

Saturday, May 18, 1895 – 05.30 am

"Have you any idea what time it is?" Francis Farrow thundered down the stairs, clad in a dressing gown. His butler, Albert Floss, followed meekly behind.

"Yes, thank you," said Lawrence advancing towards him. "My pocket watch is functioning perfectly well today. Did you know that it could have been arson?"

"What are you talking about?"

"Catherine, of course. How many other people do you know who died in a house fire?"

"Ah. No need to be rude, Lawrence. Come and sit down. Albert, fetch some coffee please." He guided Lawrence into the breakfast room. "Now sit down and tell me all about it."

"No, you tell me. You must have known."

"Well, I didn't. Don't forget – I was stationed in Ipswich when Catherine died."

"You must have heard something."

Francis sighed. "There was the merest suggestion that her death might not be accidental. I don't know why. They quashed the idea almost immediately, and nothing further came of it."

"And you didn't think to mention it to me?"

"Of course not. You were in no condition."

"Then I'll go and see what Superintendent Clarke has to say."

"No, you won't. Not today at any rate."

"Why? Has he been posted away?"

"No, he's still in Bury. But it's Saturday, and we're hosting the Quatuor Coronati lodge for luncheon."

"Then take me as your guest."

"Certainly not."

"Why?"

"Because I hold a senior position in the lodge, and you will cause a scene."

"I only want to speak to Clarke."

"It's neither the time nor the place."

"Take me, and I'll be discreet. Otherwise, I'll meet him outside when it finishes."

"Don't do this, Lawrence." Francis tried to appeal to his better nature.

"I have to. As you would if you were in my position."

"Then don't involve me and don't involve the lodge."

"I don't know where he lives, and I cannot wait until Monday."

Francis stood and walked to the window. He stared across the garden, watching the rosy hues of the rising sun as he tried to think of the least worse option. "Are you determined to push the boundaries of our friendship to this degree?" he asked.

Lawrence bowed his head and shielded his eyes as he mulled over the dilemma. His behaviour was unreasonable, and he knew it. But it had taken eight years to confront the details of Catherine's death, and now that he'd started, he could not stop. "I am determined to do whatever it takes," he said finally. "I hope that as my friend, you will understand. I would not put you in this position for any other reason, but I must speak to Superintendent Clarke. I give you my word that I will not embarrass you, and I will not confront him. I will only ask him what he knew in a calm and orderly manner."

Francis nodded. "Very well. Go home and get dressed into something suitable. I will sign you in, and you will tell anyone who asks that you have a current membership with another lodge. I will vouch for you, but please do not damage my reputation."

"Thank you, Francis," said Lawrence, rising and touching him on the arm. "You are a good friend."

Francis nodded. "Meet me outside the lodge at a quarter past twelve. Don't be late."

Lawrence arrived in Chequer Square a fraction before midday. He had already searched through his old trunk in the eaves of his apartment in the hope that he still had some Masonic regalia left. Lawrence had lost many of his possessions in the house fire, but the trunk and its contents had survived. He found the Masonic clothing squashed inside a canvas bag below some educational books. After a quick shake and a half-hearted press with an unheated iron, they were more or less wearable. He was now standing by the obelisk in Chequer Square dressed in a crumpled lambswool Masonic apron. A couple of jewels were pinned to his breast pocket, both of which had seen better days.

Lawrence had never progressed beyond the first degree of Masonry, much to the chagrin of his father. He had been willing to dedicate time to charitable activities but found the ceremony and tradition of the Masonic rituals tedious. He didn't see the point. But as a police inspector, Masonry was almost mandatory, and it wasn't easy to progress without membership. Lawrence deplored the practice of secret handshakes, but it was an inevitable part of his world. Handshakes were regularly delivered, and conveyed the rank of the person concerned. Even to someone as unambitious as Lawrence, it was disconcerting to learn someone's status without a single word being uttered. He always dreaded being the recipient of a handshake from a senior lodge member with influence and connections, while on police duty.

Lawrence loitered around the obelisk for twenty minutes waiting for Francis to arrive. Finally, he saw him in the distance walking down Angel Hill and set off to greet him.

Francis sported a colourful pale blue and burgundy collar with matching apron and an impressive array of lodge jewels. He looked Lawrence up and down and sighed. "That's not what I had in mind, Lawrence. You could have made more of an effort."

"It's the best I can do," muttered Lawrence, flushing. He dressed smartly by inclination and was not proud of the condition of his regalia despite his apathy towards Masonry. Now he could add self-consciousness to his growing list of problems.

"Come on then," said Francis, striding towards the Royal Saint Edmund lodge.

Inside, the manorial room had barely changed since Lawrence had last seen it weeks before the grand opening almost five years earlier. The only significant difference was the temporary addition of two long rows of tables and chairs in the inner temple. A further table bridged the gap at the top of the room. Near it, a smartly dressed man with slicked-back hair leaned over while he rearranged the cutlery. His suit was plain, with no indicators of Freemasonry.

"Good afternoon, Baxter," said Francis. "Is everything ready?"

"Almost, sir," he replied. "Colonel Dade is unwell and will not be attending. I was changing the place settings to give you more room."

"Good," said Francis. "Mr Harpham is unexpectedly joining us. Please change them back again, and sit him next to me. Where have you put Brother Clarke?"

"Over there, sir." Baxter pointed to a position at the far end of the table.

Francis nodded. Clarke would be too distant for Lawrence to disturb him over dinner. The meal might not turn into the disaster he feared, after all. "Stay here," he said to Lawrence. "The other lodge members will be arriving shortly, and I must greet them."

Lawrence strolled around the outside of the room while Francis made his way to the entrance hall. After five minutes, he heard the low murmur of voices as guests arrived. He almost lost his composure when he saw the first entrant through the doorway. It was the familiar face of Superintendent Clarke who recognised Lawrence immediately. "Harpham, Good Lord. How are you? It's been a long time."

Lawrence held out his hand, unsure of what to say. He had expected to be angry at the sight of his former superintendent, but Clarke's greeting was cordial, and there was no reason for it to be otherwise.

"Good to see you, sir," he said, from force of habit.

"No need for that here," said William Clarke. "It's good to see you back among us. I know you are working in town as a private investigator now, but we never see you any more."

"I left the Masons," said Lawrence, then, following Francis's earlier instructions, corrected himself. "But I rejoined again when I was working in London."

"Capital," said Clarke as the room began to fill with men in full Masonic dress. The number of men that he recognised came as a surprise to Lawrence. He seemed to be the only one who had moved on, leaving the Masons behind. Francis spotted him talking to Clarke across the room and weaved his way over. "Almost time to sit down," he said, guiding William Clarke away. Lawrence grimaced. He was desperate to speak to Clarke privately, but it had been an inopportune time. There were too many people milling around. Reluctantly, he took his place at the table almost as far away from Clarke as it was possible to get.

Luncheon was a cold buffet brought straight to the table with no money spared in the preparation. Generous portions of raised game pie and plates of ham and tongue adorned the table with baskets of pastries and pots of strawberries in jelly to finish. The delicious spread was small consolation for the series of boring speeches that followed. Lawrence had forgotten what a self-congratulatory bunch the Masons could be. Though he appreciated their charitable endeavours, the constant referencing of individual achievements left him wondering how much altruism existed outside of their egos. He fidgeted as he listened, each word preventing swift completion of his task. Finally, the members stood for a toast, and the formalities were over. Lawrence watched as William Clarke shook hands with one of the blue-collared Master Freemasons beside him before making his way to the door. It was now or never. Lawrence bolted from behind the table and negotiated his way through the crowd. Clarke was not in the hallway or the opposite room, so he darted outside to see him striding up Crown Street. "Wait," he yelled. William Clarke stopped in his tracks and turned around.

"Hello again, Lawrence," Clarke said, politely. "Are you walking this way?"

"Yes, I am," said Lawrence. "Do you mind if I join you?"

"Not at all," said Clarke, "although you'll have to shake a leg. I have another appointment. Bad planning on my part."

"In that case, I will come straight to the point. I have a question concerning the events of May Day '87 when Catherine and Lily died."

William Clarke stopped walking. "Ask me anything, and I will do my utmost to answer. I will never forget that dark day."

Lawrence cleared his throat. "It has recently come to my notice that somebody raised the possibility of arson at the time of their deaths."

"I see." Superintendent Clarke nodded and began walking again. His pace was slow, and he bowed his head in concentration. "Who gave you this information?"

"Does it matter?"

"No, I suppose not, but whoever mentioned it did you a disservice. The matter of arson was briefly speculated upon but did not amount to anything substantial in the end."

"Why?

"Why was it considered, or why was it discounted?"

"Both."

"I will tell you, Lawrence. But don't read too much into it. You probably remember that the fire began at night. The fire brigade arrived and extinguished it after several hours. It was all over by daylight. Now, do you remember Police Constable Brame?"

"Yes. Wasn't Brame's beat in Livermere?"

"Eventually. But at the time Brame worked in Bury. Anyway, he was the constable sent to secure your property and keep your surviving possessions safe while you were in the hospital."

"I didn't know," said Lawrence. "I owe him my thanks and yours for sending him. I remember very little about the events of that awful night."

"Naturally." William Clarke smiled sympathetically.

"But how is this relevant?"

"PC Brame spent several hours waiting outside your property while the workmen cleared as many of your effects as they could salvage. I don't know if you returned before they pulled the building down, but the rooms overlooking your garden were largely unscathed."

"I never returned. I could not bear the thought of it."

"I'm sure I would have done the same under similar circumstances. But, as I said, Brame was there for some time. On his return, he gave a statement. And in that statement, he noted the presence of several matches beside your boot scraper, some burnt out and some intact. Not Lucifer's either, but red phosphorus safety matches."

Lawrence frowned. "I cannot think of any reason for struck matches to be near my front door."

"Did you not have a lantern on your wall?"

"No. It was not necessary. The street lamp was directly outside my house, and there was no reason for more light. Did you investigate why they were there?"

"We did. Brame's report arrived on my desk the very next day. I searched him out, and we both returned to your home, but the matches had gone. Not one remained, nor any evidence that they had ever been there."

"Good God, man. Isn't that evidence in itself?"

Clarke pursed his lips. "No, it is not. There was no other indication that the fire could have been deliberate. None whatsoever. That is why I took the decision not to tell you to avoid any further distress."

"But what about the matches?"

"Only Brame ever saw them. He could have been mistaken, or perhaps they belonged to somebody else. If there had been any other sign of arson, we would have made a thorough investigation. I deeply regret that someone has seen fit to tell you of this matter. Trust me when I say that there was nothing in it."

CHAPTER TWENTY FOUR

Another Letter

Lawrence turned without another word and walked back in the direction of Chequer Square, his mind ablaze with questions. Every instinct in his body was alive, tortured by the significance of the matches. He had known PC Brame for a long time, and they had worked together once or twice. Brame was a good man and experienced. If he said that he saw matches, then he did, and if he thought they were worthy of mention in his statement, then it should have been taken seriously. There were only two possible explanations. Either Brame had been wrong which Lawrence doubted, or someone else removed the matches. A passer-by could have picked them up to use. But if that had happened, what became of the burnt ones? Perhaps the wind blew them away. But would bad weather dislodge them all? Lawrence shut his eyes and tried to remember what the weather had been like that week. Nothing came to mind. He had been in so much pain that he could hardly remember his name, much less whether there was a high wind or not.

Lawrence found himself outside his office in Butter Market, having walked there without thinking. He looked through the window and saw the familiar shape of Annie Hutchinson leaning over his desk. Lawrence wondered what she was doing there so late on a Saturday afternoon. He considered walking past rather than disturb her, but loitered for a moment, then thought better of it and went inside.

"Good Lord," Annie exclaimed, clutching her hand to her chest. She picked up a sheet of paper and fanned her face. "You frightened me to death," she continued. "There I was, singing to myself like a proper Charlie."

"I didn't hear you," said Lawrence smiling. "It's not your usual day," he continued.

"No, sir. I didn't come in yesterday. My sister, Mary, was visiting from London and I spent the day with her. I thought you wouldn't mind as long as I cleaned up today."

"I don't mind at all," said Lawrence. "Have you much left to do?"

"No. I'm almost finished. I'll make you a drink, and then I'll leave you in peace. Your post is on the mantlepiece."

"Thank you." Lawrence collected the small pile of letters stacked against the clock, then returned to his desk. He discarded three brown envelopes and stared at the remaining two. One was a plain white envelope with no stamp, and the other bore a Liverpool postmark. Lawrence stared at the white envelope for a long time. It was disturbingly familiar. He waited until Annie deposited a cup of coffee on his desk, then made his way to the kitchen while she tidied her cleaning materials away. It took no time to steam the envelope open. Inside, exactly as he anticipated, was another copy of Catherine's crest. The word hidden beneath the gummed down envelope flap was different. It read 'betrayed'. Lawrence gritted his teeth. The first crest had released an unbearable sadness. This time, it made him angry. Lawrence strode into his office and waved the envelope in front of Annie. "Did you see who delivered this?" he asked.

"No, sir. It was on the doormat when I arrived. Is it important?"

"No," said Lawrence curtly. "I'm sorry," he continued. "I don't mean to be rude."

Annie blinked in surprise. She had witnessed him losing his temper often but had never heard him apologise.

Lawrence examined the crest one more time, expecting an overwhelming sense of loss again with the weighty blow of regret. But fury boiled inside him instead. Somebody was deliberately trying to make him suffer. It had worked the first time, but they had gone too far, and it had nullified the effect. Devastation had turned to irritation and weakness to strength. He felt buoyed in the certain knowledge that the perpetrator was a living, breathing person and not a ghost from the past.

He slit open the second envelope with a brass letter opener and removed the single sheet of paper inside. It contained a warrant to visit William Miller in Walton gaol. Miller must have something to tell him, or why would he bother?

It was a sign. He should go to Liverpool and continue with the Moyse investigation. The identity of the anonymous letter sender and the matter of the arson suspicion could wait a while longer. Lawrence scribbled a few words onto a sheet of paper and passed it to Annie. "Drop this at the post office on your way out," he said.

CHAPTER TWENTY FIVE

Alone Again

Saturday, May 18, 1895 – 4.30 pm
To: Miss Violet Smith, Crown Hotel, Diss
From: Miss Hutchinson, Butter Market, Bury Saint Edmunds

Good afternoon Miss Violet. Mr Harpham has finished in Bury and is proceeding directly to Liverpool. He will arrive back in Diss on Tuesday.

CHAPTER TWENTY SIX

Alfred Wylie

Sunday, May 19, 1895

There were rough times and smooth in every occupation, but Violet felt fortunate as she sauntered along Saint Nicholas Street on her way to Market Hill. She had woken to a sunny day having attended the Corn Hall alone the previous evening where she had delighted in the operetta. While Violet would have enjoyed Lawrence's company, she had become too independent to be reliant upon it. Violet had arrived alone, but it was not long before she was engaged in small talk both before and after the performance. It had been a splendid evening, and today had started well too. Unsure how to locate Alfred Wylie, she had asked Minnie Panks. Minnie rewarded her with enough information to find him and the bonus of a potted history of his background. Minnie was a tremendous asset. She had a sound knowledge of many of the townsfolk, whether high ranking or ordinary. And the guileless way she gave information without requiring an explanation in return, was both useful and endearing.

So now, Violet was on her way to Rose Cottage in Mount Street expecting to find Alfred tending to the extensive, formal gardens at the rear. The property was only a short distance from Market Hill, and she found it with ease. An elaborate ironwork gate led into a pretty courtyard with an arbour covered in sweet-smelling climbing roses in shades of red.

She passed through, hoping that she would encounter Alfred before bumping into the owner of the property. It was hard enough to know what to say to Alfred without also having to explain it to his employer. The day continued well when Violet spotted a man digging a trench at the side of the garden who appeared to be the right age for Alfred. She walked towards him and announced herself, and he confirmed his identity.

Violet chewed her lip. "Minnie sent me," she said. "She thought you might be able to help."

"With what?"

Violet debated whether to continue with her new persona as a journalist. But the scruffy man in front regarded her with a dour expression, and she didn't think it would impress him.

"Do you know Fanny Nunn?" she blurted out.

His mouth set into a thin line until his lips almost vanished. "What business is it of yours?" he asked, thrusting the spade into the ground.

"It isn't exactly," she said in a faltering voice.

"Then leave me alone."

"But I need your help."

"You need to go before I set the dogs on you."

Violet scanned the garden. There wasn't a dog in sight. Wylie was blustering, and it gave her the confidence to continue.

"I'm not going to try and deceive you," she said.

"That's good of you." He scowled at her with undisguised contempt.

"I am sorry. I appear to have upset you, and it's quite understandable given the circumstances of your loss. But I'm not being nosy. I could make up a reason for my questions, but the truth of the matter is that Fanny's name has appeared in a diary in unusual circumstances. I don't know why and I would like to understand what happened to your sweetheart. Everyone I meet is reluctant to speak about her, apart from Mrs Nunn, that is."

Alfred grunted, turned his back on Violet, and picked up the spade before resuming his task. Violet sighed. She had never encountered a circumstance where her natural empathy failed to gain trust, and by now, the conversation was usually flowing. She considered leaving, then noticed that her shoe buckle was hanging by a thread. Violet pulled the buckle off and dropped it into her bag, then stood with her arms crossed and a sullen expression on her face. She waited and watched Alfred Wylie dig. After a few moments, he stopped. "Are you still here?" he growled.

"Obviously."

"I should throw you off the property."

"If you were going to, you would have done it already."

He moved towards her and lowered the spade. "You're sparky, like Fanny," he said.

"That's the first time anybody has described her character," said Violet. "Sparky. It makes her sound like a real person."

"She was a real person and full of life," said Wylie. "Until that last week. I could tell you a lot about Fanny Nunn."

"Then why don't you? Fanny deserves better than to be forgotten."

He stared into the distance as if conjuring up a memory. "Walk with me," he said.

"Where?"

"I'll show you," he continued, striding through the rose arbour. Violet walked behind him, frowning in trepidation. Moments before he had threatened to evict her from the garden. Now she was obediently following him to goodness knows where.

"This way," he said, turning left. Violet struggled to keep up as he marched down Mount Street. She was panting with exertion by the time they arrived in Heywood Road some ten minutes later.

"Here," he said, pointing to a long pathway. It led to a flint-covered church with a large archway to the cemetery beyond. They walked through and towards a small plot under a low boughed tree. "This is where she lies."

Violet lowered her head respectfully, wondering why he had brought her to this lonely cemetery. But two elderly ladies were paying their respects by a tall gravestone only a few yards beyond which gave her a sense of security.

"I shouldn't do this," said Alfred, perching on the edge of a weathered marble tomb. "It's not right using a man's grave for a seat, but I often sit here and talk to Fanny. I tell her about my day. I never married, you know. We were only young and foolish, but she was the right girl for me."

"I'm sorry for your loss," said Violet, feeling empathy towards him for the first time.

"You sit here," said Alfred. "I'll stand. It's not right to sit in the presence of a lady. Sorry that it's not more suitable."

"It will do well enough," said Violet. Sitting on a tomb might be disrespectful, but he had set off so fast that she'd almost run to keep up. Now she needed to take the weight off her hot and swollen feet.

"I'll tell you about Fanny," he said. "Good and bad alike. She was not perfect. Not by a long way. But she did not deserve to die. Where do you want me to start?"

"Tell me what happened on the night she died."

Alfred took a deep breath. "I was in the market room at The Crown all night. It's one of the drinking areas, but it's quieter than the other public room. Fanny and I were having a beer with my friends. She liked a drink."

"Was she in good spirits?"

"Not really. The old bitch was sending her away, and she didn't want to go."

"Did she have to leave?"

He nodded. "Fanny had no choice. No money of her own, you see. And with younger children in the house, her mother didn't want her."

"Too many mouths to feed?"

"So the mother said, but she didn't want for money of her own. She took all the profits from the inn and had recently received a legacy. Fanny expected to get some money, but her mother would not part with so much as a farthing."

"Did she help Mrs Nunn to keep the inn?"

"Sometimes, though her mother did not always pay for her services. As I said, Fanny liked a drink, and on occasion, she would have too many and get up late the next day. Her mother said she was fat and lazy and true enough, she was a well-built girl, but a comely lass all the same."

"Was she unhappy that evening."

"You could say that, but she was not devastated. She did not want to leave me, but she knew that I would not stray and that she could return at the weekend."

"And you don't know of any other reason why she might have been unhappy."

"As I said, she was still mithering about the money in the will that she believed was intended for her. And she'd been quieter than usual for a few days, as if something was on her mind."

Violet licked her lips before choosing her words carefully. "Do you think Fanny might have taken her own life?"

"I don't know. I did not think so at the time."

"Even though she was quieter than usual?"

"She wasn't especially unhappy – more pensive than anything. As if something was playing on her mind."

"And she didn't tell you what it was?"

"No. And I wouldn't have listened if she had," he admitted. "We were all too jolly. The ale was flowing, and the conversation was light-hearted. Fanny laughed with us too, when she wasn't fidgeting and staring out of the window."

"When did you last see her?"

"A few minutes past eleven, it was. I left the Two Brewers with a couple of the other lads. Fanny grabbed me by the arm as I walked towards the door and said, "Alf, I want to speak to you.""

"Even though you had been together all night?"

"Yes. I suppose Fanny wanted to say something privately."

"And did she?"

"Eventually. Fanny pulled me back into the market room, which was empty by then and burst into tears. I asked her what was wrong, and she did not reply. Instead, she reached into her pocket and pulled out a small parcel wrapped in brown paper. She shook it, and I heard a few coins jingle. 'There are thirty pounds in here,' she said."

"I thought she had no money?"

"She didn't. That parcel couldn't possibly have contained thirty pounds. At most, it was a pound or two."

"Did she show you?"

"No. But Fanny told me that if the thirty pounds weren't in there now, they would be by the time I saw it next."

"How strange. Was Fanny expecting some money?"

"I don't think so, but she was behaving oddly. She said that if I saw her at the weekend, we would treat ourselves. And if I did not, I would find the packet in her Ulster coat pocket the following morning. It would be twenty yards from Mr Muskett's staithe in the mere under the weeping willow."

"And was it?"

"No. I searched for it when I knew Fanny had drowned and I scoured the area more than once. There was no sign of the package, and I had heard it said that she was wearing her Ulster coat when they pulled her from the mere."

"Did she say anything else before you parted?"

"She gave me a note, as I left," said Alfred. "It was dark outside, so I made no attempt to read it, but put it in my greatcoat pocket. I told her I would see her when she returned from Norwich, waved her goodbye and went home, thinking no more about it."

"Was that the last time you saw her?"

Alfred nodded. "Yes. It was. Then, Inspector Amis called me up just after seven the next morning. I opened the window and asked what he wanted, and he replied that Fanny was missing from her mother's house and there was a body in the mere."

"How dreadful."

"It was. I knew it must be Fanny and I remembered the envelope she had given me the previous night. I opened it and showed it to the inspector."

"What did it say?"

"Nothing. It contained a likeness of Fanny. She wanted me to remember her." He reached into his breast pocket and removed a battered leather wallet held together with a cord. He untied it and removed a piece of paper. "Here."

The tomb upon which Violet was sitting lay in shadow from the trees above. She stood and moved towards the pathway and into the sunlight before looking at the paper. It contained a pencil sketch of a well-built, homely looking girl with dark eyes and hair. She turned it over, but there was nothing on the reverse.

"Thank you," she said, handing it back to Alfred. He tucked it into the wallet and carefully folded the cord around. "What do you think happened to Fanny?" she asked.

"I suppose she was more unhappy than I realised," he said sighing. "I did not notice at the time, but I was younger then and selfish in my ways."

"You think she took her own life?"

He nodded. "I suppose it is the only explanation. Why else would Fanny leave me her likeness?"

"It is a good question," said Violet. "But it doesn't explain why she told you where to find her money. Did it ever turn up?"

"There was no money," said Alfred. "And there was nowhere for her to get it. She made it up. She wasn't in her right mind that night and must have known what she was going to do. It was a long time ago, now. Let the poor girl lie." He nodded towards Fanny's grave and touched his cap. "I must go now, or Mr Brookes will notice my absence."

"Thank you," said Violet. "I do appreciate you talking to me." She watched as Alfred Wylie walked briskly away and thought about how lonely he must have been. He appeared to be in his forties, and there was time enough to find love again if he wanted to. Then, snapping out of her reverie, Violet spotted a clump of bluebells beside a tree. She picked a bunch and placed them on Fanny's grave before leaving the cemetery; head bowed in contemplation. Alfred Wylie's explanation was convincing, and he had known Fanny very well. But the mention of thirty pounds troubled her. Fanny was either a fantasist or was expecting money. But from whom? By the time Violet returned to The Crown, she had talked herself out of believing Alfred's theory. Fanny's death was far from solved and Violet was as baffled as ever.

CHAPTER TWENTY SEVEN

A Bad Year for the Young

Violet was still pondering the meaning of love as she walked back to the town. Romance had largely evaded her which was hardly surprising. She had spent the better part of her forty years in domestic servitude to others, first as a governess and later as a companion to several elderly ladies. There had been a young man once; a fleeting romance which had fizzled out almost as quickly as it began. She had not been particularly upset and had soon realised that their attachment was not as strong as she'd initially thought. Employment as a ladies' companion had been rewarding and never strenuous, but it was solitary, and Violet rarely found the opportunity to mix with suitable young men. She had not been unduly concerned to begin with, but as she left her twenties and thirties behind, the passing of time became more apparent. By the time she reached her forties, she had reconciled herself to the solitude of spinsterhood and was, for the most, content. But it was an uneasy peace. Loneliness could strike at any moment.

She shrugged off her thoughts and entered The Crown Hotel, hanging her hat and coat on the stand before entering the dining room for a light lunch. A jam tart followed bread, cheese and a slice of brawn. She patted her bodice after eating, convinced that her waist was thickening. Violet had never been slight, but neither was she plump. She was fortunate in having an hourglass figure and was still wearing dresses that fit her twenty years ago. Violet examined the backs of her hands as she pondered, clenching them to hide the ugly veins that were becoming more prominent. She couldn't quite straighten her fingers anymore. Not the ring and little finger anyway. She was starting to look matronly but was sensible enough not to be unduly concerned. Violet stood and made her way into the sitting room, hoping that it would be quiet. She wanted to read her book, but not alone in her room. One or two companions in the lounge would be ideal, but when Violet opened the door, a buzz of noise indicated it was full. She turned away, and then a friendly voice shouted her over.

"Miss Smith. Do come and join us." It was Arthur Thompson. He waved at her from the other side of the room. Harry Aldrich and Joseph Pope were sitting beside him. Their faces were solemn, and they appeared less animated than usual. "How are you?" she asked, pleased to see their familiar faces.

"Not so good," said Harry. "But better now you are here to take our minds off it."

Violet smiled. She wanted to ask what was wrong, but it was evident that Harry did not want to discuss it. "Are you here on business or pleasure?" she asked.

"It's the Lord's day, so we must be here for pleasure," said Joseph Pope with none of his usual jocularity.

"And a little business," said Arthur. "We are having an informal meeting of the Oddfellows."

Harry Aldrich flashed him a glance, but Arthur ignored it.

"On a Sunday?" Violet teased.

"As long as we've been to church, the Lord will forgive us. And we did," said Harry.

The men fell silent again, and Violet began to feel uncomfortable and wished she had retired to her room.

"What have you been doing today?" asked Arthur. "Have you enjoyed the fine weather?"

Violet smiled. "I took a stroll along Heywood Road," she said, "and I found myself in the cemetery. It is a beautiful resting place."

"It's getting rather full," said Joseph glumly.

Violet cocked her head. "What do you mean?"

"I think he is referring to the children's graves," said Harry. "It's not been a good year for the youngsters."

"In what way?"

"There was an outbreak of smallpox earlier in the year," said Harry. "It took a few adults but many more children. Then last week little Doris Edwards died, and today we found out that young Samuel Grainger drowned in the well."

"Poor little chap." Violet's hands flew to her mouth. "What a terrible thing to happen."

Harry nodded. "It looks like he fell in and couldn't get out again. His mother is distraught. And she's a widow too."

"What will she do?"

"We will look after her," said Joseph. "Her husband was one of us, and she still pays her dues. There will be enough to bury the little fellow and a bit more besides."

"Does she have other children?"

"Plenty," Joseph replied. "Not as many as George Fairweather, but she's lost three and still has five."

"A hard life," Violet murmured, thinking about her childhood. She was one of three and her mother one of two. They were a small family and had been fortunate enough never to have suffered the loss of a child. Violet could only imagine the pain.

"Let us speak of happier things," said Harry Aldrich, banging his hand down on the table. "It's the spring fair on Wednesday afternoon. Are you coming?"

"I would love to. Where is it?"

"By the mere, near Lait's Coach Builder's."

"I know it," said Violet. "I will be there."

"And bring Reverend Michael too."

Violet nodded. She would be meeting Michael later and was looking forward to it. Alfred Wylie's loneliness had made her wistful for the family life that had passed her by. After tales of smallpox and a little boy's drowning, she was more than ready to indulge in something pleasurable.

CHAPTER TWENTY EIGHT

Miller Talks

Lawrence dropped his overnight bag in the upstairs room of the boarding house. He had opted to stay there on the spur of the moment after leaving the railway station. It was a last-minute decision, over which Lawrence had agonised, having intended initially to lodge with his uncle. As the journey progressed and the train drew closer to Liverpool, he'd begun to dread the prospect of making small talk. Staying with his uncle was a sensible option, but as he started walking towards Lord Street, he realised he couldn't go through with it. There would be too many questions. The minute he arrived, his uncle would ask why he was back in Liverpool so soon. An explanation would be unavoidable, and he was still pre-occupied with Catherine. He wasn't in a fit state of mind to insert himself into the domestic bliss in which his uncle and Connie now dwelled.

So he had changed direction and applied to a lodging house near to the prison. Now, as he drew the curtains and gazed out of the dirty window onto Rawcliffe Road, he wondered whether he had made the right decision. The room smelled damp, the bed squeaked when he placed his bag on it, and the wallpaper was peeling. Still, it would only be for one night. Lawrence reached into his jacket pocket and rechecked the visiting warrant. He was due to see Miller at two thirty in the afternoon. If he left now, he would arrive too early, but anything was better than being stuck in this room longer than necessary. Besides, it was sunny outside, and the walk would be pleasant.

He returned down the staircase, taking care not to touch the bannister which was thick with grime. As he reached the bottom stair, the door to the sitting room opened, and the landlady appeared wearing a dark dress, her hair concealed beneath a lace cap. Her thin face was set in a scowl.

"I'll be locking the door at ten thirty," she said. "Don't be late, or you'll spend the night on the doorstep."

"I'll be back by ten," said Lawrence, putting his hat on and feeling aggrieved. He was in his forties, and the landlady had treated him like a child. If he hadn't already paid, he would have packed his bags and left. Instead, he politely requested directions. "Where is Hornby Road?" he asked.

"Hornby Road is very long," said the landlady. "Where do you want to go?"

"The gaol," he said without thinking, then sighed knowing what she would assume.

She looked him up and down and pursed her lips before opening the front door. "Go left until you reach the bottom of the road, cross over and through the cemetery. You can't miss it," she said, crossing her arms under her chest. She stared at him, accusingly. "Is it a relative?"

"Who?"

"The man you are visiting."

Lawrence restrained himself from telling her to mind her own business. "It's a professional matter," he said.

Her thin lips relaxed, and she uncrossed her arms. "I see. Don't be late." She returned through the door without a backward glance, and Lawrence walked down the street, glad to be away from the dingy house.

Lawrence entered the gaol, relieved to be there with official authority for once. Though he had achieved his objective on the previous visit, it had not been without risks and had created a different problem. An eagle-eyed guard might spot the similarity between his photographer guise and his real identity. But Lawrence had thought ahead. The possibility of being recognised had occurred to him en route to Mrs Bramwell's lodging establishment. He had located a public convenience and applied the moustache he habitually carried and was wearing it when he entered. The landlady had been none the wiser, and he expected it to pass without scrutiny from the gaol staff. But for all the years Lawrence had worn the moustache, it remained tickly and uncomfortable. He would have preferred to leave it behind.

Lawrence approached the building confidently, walked to the entrance and presented the warrant. The guard grunted and directed him through the courtyard to a room at the front of the inner building. After ten minutes, another guard appeared handcuffed to Miller. He nodded to Lawrence, unfastened the cuff and sat in the corner watching them. Miller took a seat opposite Lawrence and nodded his head.

William Miller had lost a considerable amount of weight since they'd last met. His bloodshot eyes stared from a thin, gaunt face, the right eye twitching uncontrollably. The haunted look of a condemned man had replaced the calm demeanour he had presented before.

"How are you keeping?" asked Lawrence.

"How do you think?" Miller's Liverpool accent was strong and his voice gruff. "I'm going to swing. How would you feel?"

Lawrence ignored the question. "Did you do it?"

Miller glanced towards the guard. "Don't I get any privacy?"

The guard crossed his legs and unfurled a newspaper without speaking. Miller shook his head. "I don't want to talk in front of the guard."

"You don't have much choice. And it's too late to matter."

"Thank you for the reminder," said Miller bitterly. He stared at the floor without speaking. Lawrence began to worry that his visit might be fruitless.

"Why have you asked me here? Do you need my help?"

"Not exactly."

"Then, why?"

"I'll be dead in two weeks. I want to put my affairs in order."

"Go on."

Miller swallowed. His mouth and eye were twitching in tandem. "I did it," he said. "I'm guilty as sin, and I will die like the dog that I am."

Lawrence regarded him with a furrowed brow. He had expected a declaration of innocence, not a bold confession. "Then I'm not sure how I can help," he said.

"You can listen," said Miller. "I will tell you exactly what I did and why I did it. I am resigned to my fate and deserve nothing less. There is a reason why I killed Moyse and attacked the boy. I wasn't going to confess while there was a chance that I might get away with it. But since the trial, I've tried to tell my story, and now nobody believes me."

"Start from the beginning," said Lawrence. "Why did you go to the Moyse house?"

"It was like this," said Miller. "Last year, I left Sissy, my wife. I have always liked women, and for some reason, they like me. I cannot resist the thrill of it, you see. I started seeing a married woman last year. Her name was Mrs Goss, and she had money. Lots of it. I stayed with her until the money ran out, then I took her last few coins and came home."

"You abandoned her?"

Miller bowed his head. "You could say that. Anyway, I came back to Sissy, but she would not have me. She was angry and refused to let me back into the home."

"Understandably," said Lawrence thinking about Catherine. Some men didn't deserve their loyal, faithful wives.

"So I spent a few nights in a coffee house in Great Charlotte Street. I often went there when Sissy got angry. But my money was running out, and I needed some more."

"You could have earned it," said Lawrence, feeling little sympathy with Miller and his lack of morals.

"That's what I was doing," said Miller. "I was on my way to see the gangers on George's Dock when I saw a man hanging around the bookstall."

"Moyse's bookstall?"

"Yes, but Moyse wasn't there. Just one of his half-witted boys."

"What do you mean when you say the man was hanging around?"

"I mean that he was watching the bookstall from a distance as if he was waiting for someone."

"What did you do?"

"I walked past him and over to the gangers. There were no jobs left that day. It was too late, so I came back again, and he was still there. Moyse was back at the stall, but the man was still watching, and I knew there was something odd about him."

"What did he look like?"

"Like Moyse. The same height, with a full beard, but not thin like Moyse who always looked like he needed a good meal. I couldn't see much of his face under the beard, and a cloth cap covered his head. He looked like a working man but didn't speak like one, and he wasn't from around here."

"You talked to him?"

Miller nodded. "I was curious, so I asked him what he was doing. He went to walk away, but turned back instead and asked if I wanted to earn some money. I questioned him further, and he nodded towards the bookstall and asked whether Moyse and I were acquainted."

"Were you?"

"Yes. I lodged with Moyse once when Sissy threw me out and had known him for several years. I passed his bookstall every day when I was working, and we often spoke."

"What happened next?"

"The man said that Moyse had something belonging to him. I asked what it was, and he said it was a Bible containing a letter. Well, I laughed at him. Moyse is a Bible seller. He has hundreds, but the man said that it wasn't the Bible that was important. It was the letter inside. It was unlikely that Moyse would part with it so it must be in his house. He asked me if I could retrieve it and offered to pay me well."

"And you agreed?"

"Of course, I agreed. The price was good, and it was an easy task. Moyse wouldn't miss the letter, and I knew he would let me into his home. There didn't seem any harm in it."

"So you went to Redcross Street?"

"I called in that very evening at about six o'clock. Moyse wasn't there, but one of his boys let me in, and we talked for a while. He said that his master wasn't due to return until much later, so I left. But on my way back to Great Catherine Street, a further thought occurred to me. The boy might know where Moyse kept his valuables which could save a great deal of time. So I returned an hour before Moyse was due and spoke with the boy again. He was useless and said he knew nothing of Moyse's personal affairs."

"That's why you sat at the table with him?"

"Yes. How did you know?"

"I talked to Needham."

Miller spoke without meeting Lawrence's eyes. "Has he recovered?"

"Physically," said Lawrence. "But he will never be the same."

Miller flushed and lowered his head further still. "I don't know what came over me."

"I cannot begin to understand it," said Lawrence. "You enter the house to retrieve a letter and come out a murderer. Nearly a double murderer, as a point of fact."

"And I will pay with my life," muttered Miller.

"What happened to make you risk everything?"

"I panicked. That is all."

"Why?"

"When Moyse returned, he welcomed me and said I could spend the night on the sofa. His bedroom was on the same floor, and Needham slept in the room above. The boy turned in first and then Moyse. I waited until he blew out his lamp then gave it another half hour. When I was sure that he was asleep, I searched every part of the house. There were Bibles everywhere, but no letters that fitted the description. It was worth a lot of money to me, and I had to find it, so I thought long and hard. The only places I hadn't checked were the bedrooms. It wasn't likely to be in Needham's room, so it ought to be in with Moyse. And it made sense for it to be there. Old people like to keep their valuables close."

"Agreed," said Lawrence. "I suppose he saw you. Was that why you killed him?"

Miller exhaled loudly. His face contorted in an expression somewhere between anger and shame. "Don't ever mention this to anyone else," he growled.

Lawrence raised an eyebrow. "What?"

"Yes, he found me in his room. I carried a candle because it was pitch black, and I needed to see to search for the Bible. I thought he would not notice the faint illumination. Moyse was snoring and in a deep sleep. It felt safe to continue, but it wasn't. The floor was a mess with boxes of books stacked on every available space. I nearly tripped over a poker by the fire then noticed a chest at the end of the room with papers strewn across the top. Not those I was looking for, as it turned out. I crept past his bed and opened a drawer. It creaked. My God, it screeched like the scream of a banshee. I stopped dead and extinguished the candle and waited, barely breathing. Moyse started snoring again, so I made for the door, planning to find a way to divert his attention on the morrow. Then I could search his bedroom in daylight. But he was only half asleep. He saw me tiptoe past the bed and sat up."

"And you hit him to stop him crying out?"

"He didn't cry out."

"Then, what did he say?"

Miller turned his head away. "He made a suggestion so revolting, so utterly unexpected and repugnant that I could hardly believe what I was hearing." Miller's words trailed away as he stared out the window with a glazed look across his face.

"What suggestion?"

"I will not say." Miller spat the words out staccato.

"It made you angry?"

"So angry that I could not think straight. I grabbed the poker and slammed it on Moyse's head. His skull split open, and blood poured from the wound. He stared at me whimpering, so I hit him again and kept hitting him until he stopped moving. Then I searched through the chest and the boxes and found nothing. Nothing. Without that letter, there would be no money, and I would have killed a man for no reason."

Lawrence exhaled and put his hand on his forehead, wondering how he had once assumed Miller's innocence.

"You might well look disgusted," said Miller. "I am. I could stomach it while I was still angry, but not now. His face haunts me. What I did to that man, who had been my friend." He shook his head.

"Then you attacked the boy."

"It was not my intention," said Miller. "I went to his room to get him out of bed and asked him to go downstairs and cut up some wood for the fire. I searched his room just in case, but couldn't find anything, so I returned downstairs. I passed the loft hatch on the way to the kitchen and realised that I hadn't looked there. Needham wasn't in sight, so I took a chair and my candle and peered inside. I could barely see and felt around the hatch with my bare hand, but there was nothing but dust. Then I heard Needham snigger, and I looked down to see him staring up at me, with a stupid grin on his face. Then, his jaw dropped in horror. I jumped from the chair and blew out the candle, but it was too late. Needham had already seen my bloody hands. He dropped the hatchet and ran towards his bedroom. I picked it up and followed him up the stairs striking a blow that hit him, but did not bring him down. He struggled past me and headed back to the kitchen. I couldn't let him go, couldn't let him live. His head wound had slowed him down, and I caught up with ease. He screamed and begged me not to kill him. There was another poker by the kitchen fire. I hit him over the head with it, and he fell. He cowered in the corner, staring at me and trembling in fear. Then the anger left me as quickly as it had come. The boy did not know me well and was so badly injured that had he survived; he still might not recognise me. I told him to go to Moyse and that I would not kill him if he did not tell. Then I left."

"Thankfully, the boy survived," said Lawrence, grimly. "And you were not discovered immediately. What did you do in the meantime?"

"I waited at the docks until midday. I had arranged to meet the stranger there to hand over the goods. He was standing in the same place that I had first encountered him. He saw me and held out his hand for the letter, and I told him that I did not have it. There was no document in any Bible in Moyse's home. The man stared at my bloody hands with an expression of disgust and made as if to walk away. I said,' what about my money?' and he said,' you shall not have it'. I told him that I had killed Moyse and he smiled and said that it was as good an outcome as finding the letter and remedied his problem. I asked for my money again, offering to relinquish half if that was all he was willing to give me. He raised an eyebrow and regarded me with cold eyes, then walked briskly to the other side of the road and boarded a bus before I could regain my composure. I wandered the streets, trying to create an alibi, and you know the rest."

"What a waste of a life," said Lawrence. "Can you tell me anything more about this man."

"Nothing at all."

"You said he resembled Moyse. Could he have been related?"

"No. The resemblance was contrived and most likely a disguise."

Lawrence nodded. "Quite possibly. Anything else?"

"Nothing. I would tell you if I knew more. I have lived a sinful life and made bad choices, but that man has blood on his hands too. My life is over, and he walks free. Find him and bring him to justice, Mr Harpham. Let my soul rest in peace."

CHAPTER TWENTY NINE

The Language of Flowers

Lawrence emerged from Walton Gaol into glorious sunshine. The skies were blue and cloudless, and the temperature was warm without being humid. He had only been inside for a bare hour, but it felt like days had passed. Miller was guilty and would justifiably die. Lawrence felt no sympathy for him. He had killed a man in cold blood out of greed. And it was only by God's grace that John Needham had survived. Miller deserved his fate, but he had not acted alone. The bearded man who had sought the letter had blood on his hands by association and should lose his freedom too. But who was he and where did he go? Miller had not recognised him, and the description he'd given could have applied to half the men in the country. Lawrence did not know where to start. But of one thing, he was certain. He could not face spending the rest of the day in Mrs Bramwell's lodging house.

He crossed over Hornby Road and made his way back towards the city when a yellow tram, the colour of mustard, pulled up. Lawrence removed his jacket, boarded the tram, and climbed the metal staircase to the top seats with no thought to its destination. After a pleasant journey, the tram came to a halt in the centre of the city only ten minutes away from his uncle's house. He briefly considered visiting, but although he felt better, he was still more inclined towards solitude and decided to go for a walk instead. Wandering east along Ranelagh Street, he was admiring the

151

exterior of the grand hotel in front of him when he heard a familiar voice. "Lawrence Harpham. Well, I never."

He turned to see a slender young woman wearing a burgundy ribbed silk dress overlaid with white lace and braid trimming. She carried a brown paper parcel and a lace parasol.

"Do I know you?" Lawrence said, then recognition dawned. "Loveday," he exclaimed.

"You are looking well, Lawrence," she said, smiling.

"Allow me," he said, taking the parcel from her.

"That is very kind, but I am only going to the Adelphi." She pointed to the building that he had been watching.

"Aren't you lucky. But what are you doing here, Loveday? I thought you were in India."

"I was. It's the first time I have been back from Calcutta in four years."

"Are you visiting family?"

"No. My family live mostly abroad now. I'm staying with friends in Cheltenham."

"Why are you in Liverpool?"

"Because that is where my ship docked. You are nosy, Lawrence."

"I'm only making conversation," he said tersely.

"And I am only teasing," she replied. "I am not expected in Cheltenham for another two days. Meanwhile, I am all alone and friendless in this big city."

"Well, we can't have that, can we?"

She smiled as they reached the hotel entrance. "Here we are, then. I am going inside to freshen up. The Adelphi serves a splendid dinner. You should join me."

"Should I?"

"You know you want to. It will be fun."

Lawrence considered it. Loveday was over twenty years his junior, but breathtakingly assured and masterfully manipulative. He remembered their time together in Fressingfield. She had flirted disgracefully, dropping him the moment she met Doctor Taylor. Not that the young doctor had fared any better in her long term affections. She'd left him without a backward glance too. Under any other circumstance, Lawrence would wish her well and walk away. But spending the evening with Loveday was a hundred times better than watching paper peel off the damp lodging house walls.

"Why not," he said.

"Meet me at six," she commanded, holding her hand out for a kiss. Lawrence obliged.

"Haven't you forgotten something?" she asked.

"Ah, yes. Your parcel."

"It's a silk shawl," she said.

"Only the best for you." He could not help but flatter her. She was, if anything, more beautiful than when he last saw her at the vicarage all those years ago. But flirting with Loveday was like teasing a cobra with a stick. He was living dangerously, yet he continued to wave at her as she walked past the doorman and into the hotel lobby.

Lawrence whistled as he walked away from the Adelphi. He waited until Loveday was out of sight, then checked his pocket watch. Two hours to kill until their meal. There wasn't enough time to go back to Rawcliffe Road, even if he had wanted to. Instead, he opted to wander around the city centre, calling into a flower shop where he enquired about purchasing a bouquet. The flower girl was alarmingly direct.

"For a young lady, is it, sir?"

"Yes," he said cautiously.

"Your intended?"

"No. The lady is a friend."

"A particular friend?"

"Just a friend. Nothing more."

The girl smiled knowingly. "If you say so, sir. Might I recommend a tussie-mussie?"

"What kind of flower is that?"

"It's a nosegay, sir. A posy. Flowers arranged together with aromatic herbs – like this." She thrust a small arrangement towards him, and the sweet scent of lavender drifted through the air.

"That will do," he said.

"But I haven't told you what it means?"

"I beg your pardon?"

"The language of flowers."

Lawrence sighed, wondering whether to leave. The simple purchase was becoming unnecessarily complicated. "What does it mean?"

"True love," she said, holding her hand over her heart.

"Not that one, then," he said quickly. "Do all women know this floral code?"

"Many of them."

"Then it makes buying flowers a dangerous thing. How is a man supposed to know what sentiment he is portraying?"

The girl laughed. "That is why you need an experienced florist."

"Tell me what to choose."

"Do you like this girl?"

"Of course I like her. Why would I buy flowers if I didn't?"

"I mean, really like her."

"I've told you. The young lady is a friend. A friend that I haven't seen in a long time."

The flower girl watched as a red flush settled across Lawrence's cheeks. "Here," she said, selecting a spray of yellow   flowers from a water-filled trough. She teased them expertly into a small posy and passed them to Lawrence. "Primrose and rue," she said.

"What does that mean?"

"Friendship," said the girl, crossing her fingers behind her back.

"Ideal," said Lawrence. He paid her and left the shop.

She smiled as she watched him walk away, hoping that she had done the right thing. Despite her youth, Verity Naylor had been working with flowers and lovesick men for a long time. She understood them better than they understood themselves. She hoped the young lady concerned would appreciate the pretty yellow nosegay and its underlying message – eternal love with a trace of regret.

Lawrence had always adhered to an exacting standard of dress. He was smart by nature, whether working or socialising. So, although he had visited the gaol that day, his attire was still acceptable for dining in a high-class hotel. He arrived at the Adelphi, handed his coat to the doorman, and found a nearby gentlemen's convenience. There, he straightened his bow tie and checked his jacket for dust and hairs. He nodded at his reflection, satisfied that nothing was out of place and proceeded to the reception hall. Three smartly-dressed hotel staff were sitting behind a long counter. As he approached, two of them stood and offered to help, almost competing to be the most useful. Lawrence asked for Loveday, and the shorter of the two men directed him to a small seating area with comfortable sofas in which to recline. But he was in no mood for sitting and paced the small room. Now and then he examined his reflection in a mirror conveniently set above an empty fireplace.

He had only been waiting a short time, though it felt a lot longer, when Loveday appeared. She was a vision of beauty clad in a blue satin dress with a scooped neck and a shaped waist that accentuated her graceful figure. She beckoned him from the doorway, and as he walked towards her, she turned away. He followed her across the reception hall and into an opulent sitting room with a long bar down the side. She sat on a leather sofa and patted the seat beside her. "Sit down," she said.

A waiter appeared in front of them before Lawrence had a chance to reply. "What drinks can I get for sir and madam?" he asked.

Loveday grinned. "What would you recommend?"

"A cocktail, perhaps?" said the waiter.

"Oh, yes. Choose one for me."

"As you wish. What would you like to drink, sir?"

"I would like a brandy," said Lawrence. "Don't put anything in it."

The waiter nodded and proceeded in the direction of the bar.

"Are they for me?" asked Loveday.

Lawrence looked at the posy in his hand. "Of course," he said. "Sorry. The waiter distracted me."

He presented the flowers to Loveday. "They smell beautiful," she said, placing them on the table in front. "I like it here," she continued. "It's a pity I have to get on a rotten old train on Wednesday."

"It won't take long."

"But I have to change at Crewe," she said, her mouth set in a downward turn. "Still, it could be worse. At least I'm travelling first class."

Lawrence thought about his rail journey between Bury and Liverpool. He had been perfectly comfortable in second class, and it had not occurred to him to travel otherwise.

"I suppose someone will meet you at the other end?" he asked.

"Naturally," said Loveday. "I am staying in Pittville Circus Road with my schoolfriend and her family. They will send a carriage."

"Then I am sure your journey will not be too arduous," he assured her. "You may even enjoy it."

The waiter returned with two drinks on a silver salver. "A white lady for you, madam," he said, placing the glass on the table in front. "And your brandy, sir."

Loveday raised her glass and clinked it against Lawrence's. "Your very good health," she said, sipping the delicate cocktail. "Delicious."

Another drink followed before they made their way into the dining room. They sat at a table for two and shared a bottle of wine over a three-course dinner – a sumptuous and no doubt expensive dinner, the cost of which Lawrence had already considered. The next stop after the flower shop had been the bank where he had withdrawn a sizeable sum. Though Lawrence had known the meal wouldn't be cheap, nothing had prepared him for the size of the bill when it arrived. He swallowed, and carefully peeled several high denomination notes from his wallet, hoping that there would be enough to cover the cost. He already regretted not drawing a more substantial sum earlier and had just enough money to save him from embarrassment. But the thought of explaining the extravagance to Violet left him cold. He would have to replace it with cash from his resources rather than count it as a business expense. Loveday was blissfully unaware of all these concerns as Lawrence smiled at the waiter and paid with the confidence of a man of means.

"What now?" asked Loveday as they rose from the dinner table.

"Would you like to take a walk?" asked Lawrence.

Loveday snorted. "It's only nine o'clock, and we have the whole night ahead of us. I would like to do something more exciting than that."

"The whole night?" Lawrence echoed, taken aback. His plans had gone no further than the end of the meal, and the idea of the redoubtable Mrs Bramwell and his ten thirty curfew did not appeal.

"Well, I have nothing better to do," said Loveday. "Have you?"

Lawrence shook his head and held out his arm. Loveday took it, and they left the Adelphi hotel, strolling in a northerly direction.

"Look," said Loveday, pointing towards a grand neoclassical building ahead in the distance. "I think that's a concert hall. Shall we take a look?"

They drew nearer and joined the crowd of people making their way up the stone steps and through the columns beneath the portico. "There is a concert," said Loveday. "Let's go inside."

"I must get back," said Lawrence.

"Don't be silly. You have all night."

"I don't..." he began to say before realising that any further protestation would mean that he had to disclose the reason why. Lawrence could not bring himself to tell Loveday that he was spending the night in a low lodging establishment with a curfew. He swallowed and decided to go inside and take whatever fate decided to throw at him.

The concert turned out to be an organ recital given by a talented young musician. Even so, Lawrence was ambivalent to the performance and preoccupied with his watch. Loveday seemed equally distracted, chatting to Lawrence at inappropriate moments. She earned a series of pointed glances from ladies nearby to whom she appeared oblivious. It was eleven o'clock by the time they returned to the Adelphi.

"Are you coming inside?" asked Loveday.

"No," said Lawrence. "I must return to Bury tomorrow. I am only here on business."

"I know. You said. Your work sounds thrilling. I will visit your office one day."

Lawrence smiled. He had told Loveday about some of his more interesting cases over dinner, and it was fair to say that he'd exaggerated a little. "It's not as exciting as you might think," he said. "My cases are rather dull and routine most of the time."

"Don't go back, then," said Loveday. "Spend tomorrow with me. Then you can come to the railway station and see me off on Wednesday morning."

"Absolutely not," said Lawrence.

"At least come and see me tomorrow," she said plaintively.

"I can't."

"Why not? Who are you rushing back for?"

Lawrence opened his mouth to explain, then realised he hadn't told her about Violet. Not a word. Loveday had no idea that Violet was his business partner. He had not revealed that they were still acquainted nor that they had recently returned from a holiday together. Lawrence idly wondered why he hadn't thought to mention it, then dismissed the idea. His friendship with Violet wasn't relevant, and he could tell Loveday another time. Tomorrow perhaps.

"I will come for you at midday," said Lawrence eventually. "Think of somewhere you would like to visit, and I will take you there."

Loveday beamed. He took her hand and kissed it gently, then she waved goodbye and disappeared through the door of the Adelphi Hotel. Lawrence tightened his bow tie, then proceeded down Ranelagh Street, wondering where he was going to find a bed for the night.

CHAPTER THIRTY

The Spring Fair

Wednesday, May 22, 1895

"Cheer up," Michael patted Violet's hand, encouragingly. "It's a beautiful day. See the children enjoying themselves."

Violet raised a weak smile. The maypole was still standing from earlier May Day celebrations, and three little girls weaved coloured ribbons around the pole as they danced. The spring fair was busy with many of the town's inhabitants outside enjoying the festivities. There were chairs and blankets spread across the grass. Trestle tables groaned under the weight of cakes and sandwiches, all provided by the town's tradesmen. The spring fair was free, and all from the wealthy to the most impoverished families were made welcome. Michael and Violet had chosen chairs overlooking the mere. The sun was out, and there was no trace of a breeze. The mere was peaceful and serene, which was more than could be said of Violet.

"Where is he, Michael?" she asked for the third time that day. "He has vanished off the face of the earth."

"You know where he is," said Michael reassuringly. "He sent a telegram."

"That was days ago, and I have sent another since," said Violet. "To Annie and she hasn't heard from him either, so I sent a telegram to Frederick Harpham and what do you think?"

"I can't imagine," said Michael, as if she hadn't already told him.

"He hasn't seen him. Not once, since his first visit. So where is he and more importantly, is he safe and well?"

"Lawrence has nine lives," said Michael. "You know that."

Violet glowered. "He nearly died last time."

"I know." Michael patted her hand. "But he isn't doing anything dangerous."

"He's visiting a gaol."

"Where there are guards to keep an eye on him. You don't need to worry."

Violet sighed, then smiled as she saw Joseph Pope and Arthur Thompson in the distance. She waved, and both men doffed their hats before disappearing into a canvas tent trimmed with yellow and red bunting. "They are running the tea tent," said Violet. "Would you like a cup?"

"Yes. Let's go inside," said Michael, glad of the opportunity to distract Violet from her worries.

The front and sides of the large tent were open to take full advantage of the evening sun. Rows of benches were half full of people enjoying a fine array of cakes. Violet sat down while Michael collected the teas. He returned carrying a plate of scones.

Violet pulled one apart and buttered it moodily.

"Jam?" asked Michael, pushing a small dish of preserve towards her.

She accepted and spooned a little onto her scone, smiling again at the men by the tea urn. Half a dozen Oddfellows, dressed in full regalia, were standing with Joseph and Arthur. She recognised one as George Fairweather who she'd met on her first visit to Diss.

"Their altruism is commendable," she said. "Very kind men."

"All lodges encourage charity," said Michael, "Masonic or otherwise."

"I didn't know that until I met Francis," said Violet. "I thought these organisations were men's clubs – more for socialising than anything else."

"Hmmm." The conversation ground to a halt as Michael finished his scone and Violet watched the mere in front of them through faraway eyes.

"How are you getting on with your investigation?" he asked, snapping her out of her reverie.

"I've ground to a halt," she confessed. "Lawrence asked me to get a list of all women old enough to be the writer of the Scole confession."

"I didn't think you knew much about her?"

"We don't."

"Then how do you know what age she is?"

"Oh, I see. Well, we made certain assumptions. The writer referred to Fanny Nunn who died almost twenty years ago, and she would have been well into her maturity then, but probably older still. So I've drawn up a list of females aged fifty or over who died between 1887 and 1892."

"Why those years?"

"Because William Jackson said that Moyse went to Liverpool in 1892 and we know he left the Antipodes in 1887. It's quite a tidy timeframe."

"Yes. That makes sense," said Michael. "Then you have made progress."

"Not really." Violet looked glumly at the list that she had retrieved from her bag. "I've only noted entries from Saint Mary's. We realised soon after, that the writer could have died in one of the other villages or she could have been a Catholic, Methodist or Baptist – any denomination really. We realised we were chasing our tails and gave up."

"That's a shame. I can help if you like. It's not such a big task when you consider that you only need records for five years."

"I suppose so. It couldn't do any harm."

"Show me what you have written."

Violet passed her notebook to Michael and finished off the last of her scone while he read. After a few moments, he looked up at her with a frown.

"Have you looked closely at this?"

"Not since I wrote it."

"There are an awful lot of deaths from drowning."

"Yes, I noticed that. But Lawrence and I have dealt with coastal cases, and there are always more drownings in villages by the sea. I suppose it's the same for any large body of water?"

"No. The sea is tidal and dangerous. Ships are not always seaworthy, or men get washed overboard. There are many reasons why drownings are more prevalent by the coast. The mere is still and quiet. There shouldn't be the same number of deaths associated with it at all."

Violet pulled the book towards her and looked again. "I see what you mean," she said. "Yes. I will look further into it. I'll go to Saint Mary's again tomorrow and recheck the register. Perhaps I'll collect records back to the year of Fanny's death."

She was about to elaborate when Harry Aldrich walked up to their table and clapped Michael on the back.

"Good to see you again, Vicar," he said.

Michael stood and shook his hand. "Splendid weather for the fair," he replied. "It seems to be going very well, indeed."

"Yes. We couldn't have asked for a finer day. Now, my little boy William is outside and about to race his young playmates on their hobby horses. I must go outside and cheer him on."

"I can't miss that," said Michael, rising to join him. "Are you coming, Violet?"

Violet shook her head and continued reading through the list of names. Michael was right about the drownings. The number was unnaturally high, and she had been dimly aware, but not enough to react. Michael's comment had solidified her concerns. She would ask Lawrence's opinion, as soon as she managed to track him down.

CHAPTER THIRTY ONE

Trapped

Thursday, May 23, 1895

Lawrence Harpham was the first thing on Violet's mind when she woke the next morning. The second was the unexplained presence of a note by the door of her bedroom. She peered at it with unfocused eyes, then sat up to see if it became more explicable when viewed from a different angle. Finally, she got out of bed, padded over to the door and picked it up.

The handwriting on the envelope was unfamiliar, with Violet's name scrawled on the front in block capitals. Inside, was a single sheet of paper covered in green ink. It read "Meet me at the disused house by the Baptist Church in Denmark Street. I have some information that may help you in your quest. Come at two o'clock Tell no one."

Violet bit her lip as she scrutinised the paper. If the writer of the note thought that she would go wandering into an empty house without mentioning it to anyone else, he didn't know her at all. She was far too intelligent to do anything that foolish. But clearly, somebody had gone to a lot of trouble to make contact, and there must be a reason. She decided to follow the lead in the safest possible way. She would tell Michael and make sure that he was nearby and in a position to watch over her in case of trouble.

She dressed quickly and decided not to bother with breakfast. Her appetite had vanished over the last few days, and she preferred to make an early start at Saint Mary's instead. She located the vicar and sat quietly copying death dates for the women of the parish from the years 1875 until 1887. These, together with the records she already possessed, gave her almost twenty years' worth of information. Then, glad that she'd had the foresight to wear flat-heeled boots, she embarked on the long walk to Michael's parish church in Frenze. She arrived at Saint Andrew's a little after eleven thirty, out of breath and very warm. The tiny church, surrounded by stone pillars and wrought iron railings, stood at the end of a long footpath. The sun was high, and the grass was beginning to dry out after several days without rain. She walked inside and found Michael sitting in the vestry, writing in a large register.

"Violet. I wasn't expecting you."

"No. Sorry. I need your help."

Michael closed the heavy book. "I was planning to spend today on church matters," he said ruefully.

"I know. I am sorry to have kept you away from your work so often. You will be glad when I have gone."

"No, I won't," he sighed. "But I am busy today. Can it wait?"

Violet shook her head. "No, it can't. Look."

She thrust the note towards him.

"You're not going, are you?"

She nodded.

"It's a terrible idea, Violet. It is either a hoax or dangerous. Either way, you shouldn't be doing it."

"I must. Don't you see? Something is going on around here. Some days I can't be sure if there is a problem, and other days, it is staring me in the face. Today is one of them. If I don't go and find out what this man has to say, I will regret it."

"Man?"

"I assume a man wrote it."

"Doesn't it say?"

"No. Perhaps it's from a woman, then. That would be safer."

"None of it is safe, Violet. Please don't go."

"I hoped you would come with me."

"I will if you insist on this ill-advised meeting. But I doubt whoever it is will make an appearance if I'm with you."

163

"No. I must go alone. But you could hide within sight of the house. Then, I will meet them, and if I don't return within a quarter of an hour, you can come and find me."

Michael sighed. "And if I say no?"

"Whoever wrote that note will be there at two o'clock   . It's my only chance to find out what they want and whether it connects to this case."

"So you will go with or without me?"

Violet nodded. "I must."

Michael sighed and looked at the clock on the vestry wall. "We had better be on our way," he said, getting to his feet. "And when Lawrence does reappear from wherever he has gone, he will be getting a bill for my time."

The disused house in Denmark Road was an unprepossessing property which had lain unloved for a long time. The door was intact, but grime caked the window panes, masking the view inside. Violet knocked on the peeling door, and it creaked open. She stepped cautiously inside, treading on rotten squeaky floorboards peppered with wormholes. The smell of rising damp hung heavy in the hallway and paint was peeling from the walls. Though warm outside, the house was unnaturally cold. Violet called out in an uncertain voice. "Hello. Is anyone there?"

She stood silently, listening for a reply but none came. Then she ventured further inside and through the door at the end of the hallway, taking care to leave the front door open.

The inner door hung uselessly from one hinge allowing a partial view into the kitchen beyond. Violet squeezed past the door, hoping not to dislodge it from its precarious position and called out again. Silence descended until she heard a rustling – a scrabbling sound which seemed to be coming from the floorboards. Violet surveyed the dingy kitchen. The only illumination came from a hole in the broken glass window by the rear door. She peered through the gloom and examined the floor again, but there was nothing untoward. Violet waited, hardly breathing, then the noise began once more, and this time, it came from under the sink. Biting her lip, she tiptoed towards a filthy linen curtain slung between two nails. She lifted the corner. A half-starved rat with a torn ear stared at her through dead eyes. Her gasp disturbed its scavenging, and it slunk furtively away while she stopped and clutched her heart, hoping to calm her breathing. Violet's fingers shook as she counted aloud trying to distract her fears and steady her nerves and pulse. After a few moments, she felt able to carry on, frightened, but secure in the knowledge that Michael was only a short distance away and would hear if she screamed.

Taking a deep breath, she turned towards the inner doorway by the stairs. She was about to ascend when the front door slammed shut with a force so shocking that it took her a few moments to comprehend what had happened. She ran towards the hallway, nudging the inner door which spun off its hinge and crashed to the floor, hitting her shoulder as it fell. The force of the impact propelled Violet forwards onto her knees. And as she knelt there, with dust and debris coating her long skirt, something bright dropped through the letterbox and fell onto a damp patch by the door that she hadn't noticed earlier. It hit the floor, and the area ignited with a roar, as flames blazed along the hallway and straight towards Violet. She gathered her skirts and ran ahead of the fire into the kitchen and towards the rear door. She tugged the brass doorknob with both hands, rattling the glass with her efforts, and the doorknob came away in her hands. She looked over her shoulder to see the hallway aflame, and thick smoke billowing into the kitchen. Violet could hear Michael shouting outside the front door. He must have seen what happened, but was unable to gain access. She scanned the kitchen.

The window with the broken pane was tiny, and she would never fit through, but there was another oddly shaped window set higher up the wall. She might be able to squeeze through if she could reach it before the smoke overwhelmed her. For the second time that day, she thanked her lucky stars for sensible boots. She headed for the chipped and stained fireclay sink set beneath the window with its solitary brass tap listing drunkenly to one side. She pushed down on it, testing her weight as pieces of plaster crumbled around her. The fire had not yet entered the kitchen, but the smoke was acrid. Violet coughed uncontrollably before ripping a piece of decorative satin from her bodice to cover her mouth.

The unsteady sink was the only thing standing between escape and imminent death from smoke inhalation. She would have to take a chance and hope it stayed fixed to the wall. She gulped a deep breath through her satin mask, before plunging the material into her pocket and hauled herself onto the wobbling sink. It tilted to the side as she grabbed the narrow window ledge and fought to balance. Holding tight with one trembling hand, she edged the other towards her pocket, retrieved the satin and wrapped it around her knuckles. Then she slammed her hand into the window punching blindly above. The brittle glass exploded, scattering shards into her hair. Violet grimaced as she cleared loose pieces of glass from the window frame with her barely protected hand as blood poured from deep gouges. Then she lunged for the opening, kicking against the sink which fell from the wall with an almighty crash. With her head hanging from the window, Violet hauled herself free of the kitchen and tumbled to the garden below. She was still lying in a heap, winded and bloody, lungs screaming for air when Michael hurtled into the garden and fell on his knees beside her.

"Stand up," he said urgently. "Violet. Stand up now."

She coughed as her muscles began to relax and gulped the air.

"Come on. Stand up. You're too close to the house."

She lifted her head and gazed at the building. Flames licked at the edges of the window sill from where she had fallen. Michael reached out his hand. "Come on."

He grabbed her and pulled her off the ground. She winced as glass shards pressed further into her wounds, but said nothing and limped towards the open yard behind the house.

"Quickly." Michael pulled her behind him, and they were a bare twenty yards away when the house exploded, and flaming tiles tumbled from the roof.

The door of the adjoining house opened, and a couple ran towards the safety of the road. By the time they reached Denmark Street, the town's men were already forming a line towards the mere, while women fetched pails from their homes. Violet slumped on the roadside, unwrapped the satin from her hand and examined her wounds. "Stay here," said Michael. "I'm fetching the doctor."

Violet was too tired and shocked to argue. She lay there panting as a kindly woman placed a cup of warm milk into her hand. She sipped it and waited for Michael to return. In five minutes, he reappeared and waited while the doctor took her to the nearest house to clean her hand and make a private examination of her wounds.

"How is she?" Michael asked as soon as the doctor returned.

"I have dressed and cleaned her hands," he said.

"Any broken bones?"

"I don't know. She wouldn't let me check."

"Let him help," pleaded Michael.

"There's no need," Violet insisted. "I'm only a little nauseous, and I've felt like that for days. It's got nothing to do with the fire."

"You're not a doctor. You could have a concussion."

"I fell on my back," she said. "And I did not hit my head. Please don't make a fuss."

"Talking of making a fuss," said Michael as a uniformed man came into view.

The man approached Violet. "Are you responsible for this?" he asked, nodding towards the fire. She opened her mouth, but he did not give her time to respond. "You're coming to the police house with me, and you're going to tell me exactly what happened."

CHAPTER THIRTY TWO

Murder in the Mere

Friday, May 24, 1895

Violet reached her hat from the top of the wardrobe, wincing as a muscle in her back spasmed. The hat dropped to the floor, and she lowered herself onto the edge of the bed, staring at her bandaged hands dejectedly. She ached all over, mostly from tiredness and the shock of winding herself when she'd fallen. Her injuries were confined mainly to cuts and grazes, though she still felt nauseous. But worse than her physical condition was the feeling of utter abandonment. Lawrence had been away for a whole week and should have returned to Diss on Tuesday. Here she was three days later, suffering the after-effects of an attack and he hadn't bothered to contact her to explain himself. She was both angry and worried.

Violet reached forward for the fallen hat and placed it on top of her case, then opened the wardrobe door and re-checked for any forgotten garments. She was leaving Diss today at Michael's insistence. He had accompanied her to the police house, listening while she gave the constable a sketchy account of her actions. When asked why Violet had been in the abandoned property, she'd prevaricated as much as possible. The constable was not amused but would have been even less impressed had Violet elaborated on her reasons for being in Diss. If Lawrence had been with her, she might have stayed. There was safety in numbers, and more importantly, it brought confidence. She felt tired and out of her depth. Michael had been an enormous support, but she knew she was taking up too much of his time and was fast becoming a nuisance. Whatever mysteries remained in Diss, were not worth the way she felt today. Violet dabbed her eyes with a lace handkerchief monogrammed with a lilac V. Then, remembering that her old and much-loved former employer had given it to her one birthday, she let out an involuntary sob. A tear trickled down her cheek and more followed, streaming down her face and plopping into her lap. She put her hand to her forehead and shook her head. "What's wrong with me today?" she whispered. "Enough." She stood and shoved her damp handkerchief into her case and closed it with a snap. Then looked in the mirror and re-pinned an unruly curl. "Control yourself," she said under her breath, then standing tall, she exhaled before striding towards the bedroom door, bag in hand.

Minnie Panks was emerging from the dining room as Violet lugged the case down the stairs.

"You needn't have done that, miss," she said.

"I wanted to," Violet replied. She wasn't an invalid and was getting fed up of the constant attention since the attack.

"You'll be wanting a good breakfast after all your troubles yesterday," said Minnie.

Violet sighed. She wasn't hungry for the third day running, but it was easier to dine than engage in a debate with the good-natured and well-intentioned serving girl.

"Go and sit down and I'll bring you a nice pot of tea."

Violet obeyed, hoping that Minnie would ask her what she wanted for breakfast. A few days ago, Minnie had plonked a large plate of cooked food in front of her without asking. Violet might manage a small bowl of porridge, but anything else was beyond her. She waited quietly, too tired to read her book, then involuntarily jumped when she heard shouting from outside the building. Violet cocked her head and listened. Multiple voices were speaking excitedly, too distant for her to hear what they were saying. She considered walking into the passageway to find out what was going on, but was too tired to move and remained where she was. Her solitude did not last long. Minnie rushed into the room, slamming a tray onto the dining table and sloshing the contents of the teapot over the lace mat on which it stood. "Cor blarst me," she exclaimed, slipping into a stronger version of her usual Norfolk accent. "Oh dear. Oh dear." She waved her hand across her face as if to cool herself.

"Whatever is it?" asked Violet, temporarily distracted from her problems.

"It's a body, miss. Another body in the mere."

Violet gasped. "Who is it?"

"I don't know. They didn't say."

"I must go."

"But you haven't had your tea."

"Sorry, Minnie. You drink it."

Violet left the dining room and rushed out of The Crown, heading down Saint Nicholas Street towards Market Hill. She was not alone. A large group of people surged towards the mere. She turned into Mere Street, where she saw two men walking against the direction of the crowd. They were Harry Aldrich and Joseph Pope. Harry's face glowed red, and he clenched his jaw, doffing his hat without smiling. "Have you seen Henry Garrod?" he asked.

"Sorry, no," said Violet.

"Damn the man." Harry scowled, his usual mild manner replaced with an impatient snarl.

"Steady," said Joseph, patting him on the arm.

"What's happened?" asked Violet, wondering at the change in the two men. Harry was furious, and Joseph looked as if he was about to cry.

"He's dead," said Joseph.

"Who?"

"Robert Moore. They dragged his body from the mere earlier. The surgeon's there now, and he's asked for the coroner."

"The coroner?"

Joseph took a deep breath before continuing. "Yes. He's checked the body. It wasn't an accident. Robert was murdered."

Violet was nursing a mug of tea in the market room of The Crown Hotel when she felt a hand on her shoulder. She spun around, nerves still frayed from the events of the last few days.

"You're looking well," said a familiar voice.

She glanced up to see the tall figure of Lawrence Harpham smiling down at her.

"You think I look well!" she exclaimed, raising her bandaged hands.

The smile fell from his face.

"Good Lord, Violet. What happened?"

"Never mind what happened. Where on earth have you been?"

Lawrence sighed and pulled a wooden chair from the table opposite. He turned it towards her, sat down and reached for her hand.

"No." Violet snatched her arm away and glared at him.

"Don't be angry, Violet."

"Well, I am. You could have been dead in a ditch for all I knew."

"I wasn't."

"Then where did you go and why did you take so long? I couldn't even reach you by telegram."

"It was wrong of me. I should have made contact."

"Then, why didn't you?"

Lawrence shifted uncomfortably in his seat. There were two reasons why he hadn't been in touch with Violet. One was Catherine and the other, Loveday. He could explain the former, but even he did not understand his compulsion to keep Loveday company for the best part of a week. And now that he was back in Norfolk, she did not occupy his thoughts at all. He felt ashamed of his treatment of Violet and relieved that Loveday would be going back to India when she left Cheltenham. He decided there was no need to mention her to Violet and cleared his throat.

"I found out a little more about Catherine," he said.

Violet's face softened. "What did you learn?"

"That there was clear evidence of arson, but it disappeared. And without the proof, there was no case to answer. That is the reason William Clarke kept it from me."

"Poor Lawrence. What evidence?"

"Spent matches. They were there one day and not the next."

"Were there many?"

"Enough to be sure."

"What will you do?"

"Nothing. What can I do?"

Violet shook her head. "So, you went to Liverpool?"

"Yes. I saw Miller. He told me what he did to Moyse."

Violet leaned forward and put her bandaged hands on her knees. "What did he say?"

"What on earth happened to you?" Lawrence leaned forward and picked up her hand. This time, she let it rest in his.

171

"There was a fire."

Lawrence stared at her, eyes wide. The colour drained from his face.

"Don't worry," she said sympathetically. She had always understood Lawrence's fear of fire and the depth of loss he had suffered from it. "I was never in any real danger."

"I should have been here," he said. "Tell me about it."

She gave him a sanitised version – one where she was unafraid, and escape had been easy. He gazed at her with soft blue eyes, brows knitted in concern. He did not look convinced.

"I've let you down," he said, raising her hand to his lips and kissing her fingertips.

She shook her head. "You weren't to know. How could you?"

"Do you know who set the fire?"

"No, but there's one person it couldn't have been?"

Lawrence tilted his head and looked at her quizzically.

"Haven't you heard?"

"I came straight from the station and haven't spoken to anyone."

"They pulled Robert Moore from the mere this morning."

Lawrence whistled. "An accident?"

"Apparently not."

"Do I know him."

Violet glared. "You spent half an hour with him in this hotel on the first day you arrived."

"Ah, yes. With Aldrich and Pope. He seemed like a nice fellow."

"He was. And now he's dead. Violet shuddered. "Death by drowning – a horrible way to go."

"It must be an accident, though?"

"Not according to the coroner, and he should know with all the other recent drownings."

"Other drownings?" Lawrence raised an eyebrow.

"Yes," said Violet, rummaging for her notebook. "I copied down the burial records for St Mary's and noted any unnatural deaths. There have been eight drownings since 1874."

"That's not a particularly high number over two decades," said Lawrence.

"It is when you consider that it's only relative to women of a certain age who died in St Mary's parish."

"I see. In that case, we ought to check every death record. It's an important detail. Well done, Violet."

"We still don't know what is going on, though. There is no evidence to prove a crime ever happened."

"We do know. I will go into detail another time, but Edward Moyse died because of the Scole confession."

"That's only our assumption."

"No. Miller confirmed it. A stranger paid him to locate the letter, no doubt to conceal the identity of the writer. Had he succeeded, Moyse would still be alive and we would be none the wiser."

"Where is the letter now?"

"It could be anywhere. It's not at Moyse's house in Redcross Street. I checked."

"But what can we do?"

Lawrence shrugged. "We can get more records, but the detail is important. A drowning alone is not evidence of foul play. And we need to find out who wrote the confession. Is it linked to these deaths? We still have much to learn."

Violet nodded. "If you hadn't arrived today, you would have missed me altogether," she said. "Staying seemed pointless and I'm glad you are here." Violet smiled and released her hand. "We must see this through, or someone will get away with murder."

CHAPTER THIRTY THREE

The Printworks

Saturday, May 25, 1895

Lawrence knocked on the door of the coroner's office for the third time, then slammed his palm against a wooden panel.

"He isn't in, no matter how many times you try," said Violet, reasonably.

"It's frustrating," said Lawrence.

"It's Saturday," Violet retorted. "You will have to wait until Monday now."

Lawrence opened his mouth to snap a reply when he saw a familiar figure ahead. His frown changed to a smile, and he waved. "It's Michael."

Michael strode out towards them, and Lawrence thrust his hand out. Michael faltered, and for an awful moment, Violet thought he might refuse the handshake. But good manners and his position in the church got the better of him.

"Good to see you at last," he said. "Where have you been?"

"In Liverpool."

"For a whole week?"

"Yes."

"It's none of my business," said Michael, abruptly. "I suppose Violet has told you what happened to her?"

"She did, and it sounds like she handled herself magnificently."

"She nearly died, Lawrence, trapped like a rat in a cage."

Violet glared at Michael, and he stopped, surprised at her demeanour.

"I didn't realise it was that serious," said Lawrence.

"Well, it was." Michael was in no mood to spare his feelings. "What brings you here?" he continued.

"We were hoping to see Mr Garrod," said Violet. "About the list of unnatural deaths."

"Why?"

"For further clarity," said Lawrence, speaking before Violet could answer. "We need to know the exact circumstance of the deaths to know if they are suspicious."

"You'll have to wait until Monday," said Michael.

"We know," said Lawrence, uncertainly. In all the years he had known Michael, the younger man had always been friendly. His attitude today was curt and his anger, barely concealed. Lawrence already regretted his behaviour well enough without criticism from his friends.

"Or, if you can't wait until then, go and see Edward Abbott."

"Who?"

"Abbott. The owner of the local printworks." Michael pointed to a large building further up Mere Street. "I've just walked past the print shop, and it's open."

"How will that help?" asked Lawrence.

"An excellent idea," said Violet clapping her hands together. "At least some of the deaths will have made it into the newspapers."

"Oh, that type of printworks," said Lawrence, enlightened.

"Edward Abbot has produced the *Diss Express* since the 1860s," Michael explained. "I expect he keeps back copies."

"Thank you," said Lawrence, holding out his hand again. "We will speak soon."

Michael nodded in full comprehension of his meaning. "Until then," he said.

Lawrence opened the door to the printworks to find an entrance hall with a long counter running almost the entire width of the room. An open doorway behind the worktop allowed a glimpse of the heavy printing press which creaked and groaned beyond. A young man dressed in work clothes and a leather apron was standing behind the counter squinting at a sheet of writing. He lifted his glasses and looked again before shaking his head in frustration.

Lawrence coughed, and the man looked up.

"Can I help you?" he asked, placing the paper into an overflowing wooden tray.

"Do you keep old copies of your newspapers?" asked Lawrence.

"Of course. We hold copies of every paper that ever went to press."

"Can I view them?"

"Not today. It's far too busy. We are only open because of the extra print run. No time for anything else."

Violet flashed a smile. "That's a lot to get through," she said, gesturing to the tray. "Must you finish it today?"

"Most of it, if I want to keep my job," said the young man. "This is the most important one of all," he continued, brandishing a sheet of heavy cream paper covered in tiny handwriting. "I would stand half a chance of completing it if I could only read Henry's scrawl."

"Can I see?" asked Violet. He hesitated, then passed it to her, and she peered at the page.

"Pass me that pencil," Violet commanded, pointing to a pot on the desk. "And a piece of paper."

He handed her the items, and she marked the document with neat, precise strokes and passed it back again.

"Are you sure that's what it says?" he asked, scrutinising the page.

She nodded. "Once you know shorthand, any writing style becomes easier to read."

"I didn't know you'd learned shorthand," said Lawrence.

"There's a lot you don't know about me." Violet smiled towards the young man again. "Is Mr Abbott available?"

"Not yet. He might come by later."

"And what's your name?"

"Charles. I am Mr Abbott's apprentice compositor."

"I see," said Violet. "So it's your job to set the lettering for the press."

He nodded. "Yes. I must produce two hundred characters an hour, which isn't difficult as long as I can read the original document. Most of them are readable, but anything from Henry – well, I don't know why he can't make his writing bigger. It's my first time alone, and I don't want to let Mr Abbott down."

"Perhaps, we can help each other," said Violet. "Why don't you let us see the back copies of the newspapers, and we'll sit quietly out of your way. You won't even know we're there. Then if you have any problems with Henry's writing, you can ask me for help. How does that sound?"

Charles pondered the offer. "I don't see that it can do any harm," he said. "Come through."

They followed him into the printworks which smelled of paper and chemicals. Heavy wooden presses and compositors' cabinets filled the room. A desk had been set directly below the large window, and a composing stick full of letters was lying next to a handwritten design for a sales pamphlet.

"I'll be working here," said Charles pointing to the desk. "And the door to the paper room is through here."

He opened another door to a well-lit room which was sparsely furnished apart from a desk, two chairs and a gaslight. A large window dominated one end of the room and chunky wooden shelves, stacked with binders, covered the adjoining wall.

"Don't come outside if you hear any voices," said Charles. "I'm not sure what Mr Abbott would have to say about this."

"We won't," promised Violet as she sat at the desk. The door closed, and Lawrence moved the second chair opposite her.

"Where should we start?" he asked.

Violet retrieved her list and pushed it across the table. "I have written an asterisk by the suspicious deaths," she said. "You locate the binders, and I'll make a start."

Lawrence nodded and reached for the first weighty tome, then manoeuvred it on the desk in front of Violet. She blew a layer of dust away, then located her handkerchief and wiped the residue.

"It's been a while since anyone's read that," said Lawrence, unnecessarily, pulling down another binder. Silence fell upon the reading room save for the rustle of pages as they both examined the newspapers. Ten minutes later, they had found nothing of note. Deep sighs from Lawrence punctuated the rustling pages. Patience was not one of his virtues. After another ten minutes, he considered leaving the printworks and forgetting all about it when an article caught his eye. He was halfway through reading it when Violet spoke.

"There," she said, pointing to a dog-eared newspaper dated April 1885.

"What have you found?" he asked.

"A suspicious death. It wasn't from drowning," said Violet, "but I marked it with an asterisk and having read the report, it's certainly questionable."

"Who died?"

"Susan Reynolds," she replied. "Her husband found her dead in the wash house. She was laying by the mangle and had fallen and injured her head."

"It doesn't sound very suspicious to me."

"But she was in perfectly good health. There was nothing wrong with her at all. The coroner ruled it natural causes because he could find no evidence of disease."

"She could have lost her balance."

"I suppose so. But the paper describes the wound on Susan's head as severe."

"Mark it as possible if you like," said Lawrence. "But I'm not convinced. This one is worth checking further though," he continued poring over the page. "It doesn't sound right at all, and I bet it isn't on your list."

"Why not?"

"Because it concerned a young child," he said. "It was a real tragedy. The poor little chap drowned in a barrel."

"Oh, no." Violet closed her eyes. "How awful. The poor parents."

"According to the account, he went missing. When the searchers had exhausted all other avenues, one of the constables opened the lid of a barrel, and there he was."

"He must have fallen in."

"And lowered the lid at the same time? He couldn't have."

"Did they treat it as murder?"

"No. The coroner assumed that he had fallen in and that later on, when the light was failing, someone must have inadvertently placed the lid on the barrel."

"That sounds silly."

"I agree. But that is what the report says."

"Then I'll make a note, and we had better keep looking."

Two hours later, Lawrence pushed his binder into the middle of the desk. "That's it," he said. "I can't see straight, and I've got the devil of a headache. Have we got enough to be going on with?"

Violet scanned her journal. "More than enough. We've found reports for about half the names I listed. Those, together with the other records, gives well over twenty inexplicable deaths."

Lawrence took the list from her. "They're not in order," he said. "Wait a moment." He opened his notebook and re-listed them, putting a tick against each of Violet's entries as he wrote it down. "Right. The first name on the list is Solomon Derby who fell in front of a cart in March 1876. Next, is Mary Green who drowned in December of that year and Mary Clarke who fell down the stairs in January of '77. Charlie Green was found dead in his bed in May '77..."

"Any relation to Mary?"

"Her eight-year-old son. The verdict on his death was unknown. The boy was perfectly healthy when he retired to bed. The father went to get him up in the morning, and he was cold and stiff. A drop of blood in the right nostril was the only unusual sign."

"There are too many children on this list. I don't like it."

"Next is Althea Carter and then Fanny Nunn. Ah, strange."

"What?"

"The next inexplicable death after Fanny is Charlie Adams in 1880. Nearly a three-year gap. But since then, there have been at least one and often two deaths a year. Extraordinary."

"My goodness." Violet's hand flew to her mouth. "How dreadful. Don't you see what this means?"

Lawrence nodded. "Oh, yes. There's a definite pattern. The murders started before the death of Fanny Nunn, and they have continued unabated ever since."

CHAPTER THIRTY FOUR

The Ironmongers

"I can't believe it," said Violet for the third time, as she worried at her bandages with pale fingers.

"Stop that," said Lawrence, placing his hand over hers. "They will unravel, and you'll need to see the doctor again."

"It's just so horrible," she continued. "Could we have made a mistake?"

"Nothing is certain," said Lawrence. "Our evidence is largely circumstantial, but we know that somebody killed Moyse and his murderer is probably still living in Diss. Even if only one of the deaths is unnatural, it is one too many."

"And we don't know who did it or why. Do you think anyone suspects that we are investigating?"

"They must do. Someone lured you into that empty house with the sole purpose of causing you harm."

"But how could they know?"

"Have you told anyone why you are here?"

"Only Michael. Mary Nunn thinks I am a journalist, at least that's the story I gave her, and I think she believed me. But anyone could have heard you and me talking. Or perhaps listened to one of my conversations with Michael."

"We can't trust anyone," said Lawrence, lowering his voice.

"What do we do?"

Lawrence walked towards the window and stared at the whitewashed wall beyond. "We need to know why Fanny Nunn was so important. She was the only person named in the confession."

"Why don't we look at the newspaper report of her death while we are here. Her mother gave me lots of useful information but there may be something more in the papers."

Lawrence scanned the bookshelves and removed the volume covering December 1877. He drew his chair to the other side of the desk and sat next to Violet. Fanny's death had been the subject of several reports, and he located them quickly. They read the articles, side by side, their heads bent close together.

"I'm not sure this helps," said Lawrence, when they had finished.

"There's a dearth of available witnesses."

"Yes. Both the surgeons are dead," said Violet. "I found that out several days ago. Fanny's brother Christopher lives in London, and we can't speak to him. John Aldrich died last year according to Minnie, and Harry Aldrich won't talk to anybody about Fanny."

"What about his sisters?" asked Lawrence. "Both of them were witnesses. And the newspaper report suggests that the coroner took their evidence seriously."

Violet scanned the paper again. "I agree. They both heard Fanny drown. Do you think we should go and see them?"

"If they haven't gone to meet their maker. Everyone else involved seems to have passed away."

Violet smiled. "But they were well past their prime. There's nothing sinister about their deaths, and yes, the Aldrich girls are very much alive. They've been running the ironmongers in Market Hill since their father died. We could go there now."

"Good. I think we should. And let's hope they are a little more forthcoming than their brother."

The Misses Aldrich were a long way past their prime which momentarily confused Violet who still had the 1877 newspaper reports fresh in her mind. She'd overlooked the fact that almost two decades had passed and they were no longer young women. From the moment Lawrence opened the door to the ironmongers and ushered her through, Violet was ill at ease. She reached the counter first and asked the middle-aged woman behind it, where she might find Miss Louisa Aldrich. When the woman replied that she was Louisa, Violet could not conceal her surprise.

Louisa Aldrich wore a smart, black brocade dress. Though the modest dress looked simple, it was finely tailored and of excellent quality. Louisa was taller than Violet and looked older. It was difficult to estimate her age, but fine crow's feet and raised veins on the back of her hands gave clues to the passage of time. Slim, with pale, unblemished skin, Louisa wore her hair in a tight bun exposing a long, slender neck. Her deportment was elegant, and she carried herself with the confident poise of a woman who knows her place in the world.

The well-organised ironmongers in which Louisa kept shop smelled like the blacksmiths in Violet's childhood village. Items of metalwork hung from hooks on the ceiling with smaller pieces arranged in drawers or tidy stacks. Violet felt a wave of nostalgia, half expecting a horse to push its head through the stable door at the rear.

"How may I help?" asked Louisa.

"A pair of hinges and nails to fit," said Lawrence pointing to a half-open drawer containing a small and hopefully cheap set of brass fittings.

Louisa retrieved them and deftly wrapped the items in a piece of newspaper which Lawrence recognised as last week's copy of the *Diss Express*.

"Will that be all?"

"And some information, please," Violet added.

"Certainly. What would you like to know? I'll fetch Mr Baxter if you need something forged."

"It's not that sort of information," said Violet. "Nothing to do with the shop."

"Oh?" Louisa's brow knitted momentarily.

"I hoped you would answer some questions about Fanny Nunn."

"Why? The poor girl died a long time ago."

Violet caught Lawrence's eye and hoped he would follow her lead. Her persona as a reporter had worked well with Mary Nunn, and she thought it worth repeating.

"I'm working for a magazine," she said.

"I don't believe you," said Louisa, directly.

Violet opened her mouth to protest, but the words would not come. Something close to a smile played across Lawrence's lips. Violet scowled at him, furious at his enjoyment of her discomfort.

"I saw Mary Nunn yesterday," said Louisa. "She has told half the town that she will be receiving an award from your magazine."

"That's not what I said," Violet protested.

"It's the way she has interpreted your words," said Louisa. "Take whatever you said and multiply it by a large dose of wishful thinking. The result will be Mary Nunn's version of events."

"Isn't she reliable?" asked Violet.

"To a certain degree," said Louisa, "She does not lie, so much as exaggerate the truth."

"Then what she feels about her daughter's death is not necessarily what happened?"

"It might be. But equally, Mary could have embellished things. She is a good woman, but prone to overstating the situation."

"And she is singularly indiscreet," said Lawrence.

"Yes. I asked Mary not to say anything about the award." Violet was intentionally curt, hoping that her faux outrage would distract Louisa from further questions. She did not want her to guess their real purpose. In the event, it did not matter.

"Well, now we've got that out of the way, what do you want to know? I won't ask why you are enquiring. Be as nosy as you like. My brother has already spoken about you, Miss Smith and a friend of his is a friend of mine."

"Thank you." Violet smiled weakly. She had feared a hostile reception from Louisa. "You already know that I've spoken to Fanny's mother. She mentioned you briefly, but I didn't realise your close involvement until I read it in the newspaper."

"Yes. It was an unsettling experience," said Louisa. "And one that I shared with my sister. We were home together that night, but Alice heard the cries first. Perhaps it's best if I fetch her."

Louisa unlatched the stable door and disappeared out of sight.

"Well recovered," said Lawrence grinning.

Violet shook her head. "You enjoyed that, didn't you?"

"I don't think I have ever seen you lost for words."

"I have some choice words for you," she hissed as the door re-opened.

"This is Alice," said Louisa Aldrich presenting an identically clad and similar-looking woman, also in her late forties. It was only Alice's slighter stature and a large silver cross that she wore on a chain, that differentiated one sister from another. "Alice has agreed to tell you everything she heard. Please, take a seat."

Violet murmured her thanks and moved towards a small table tucked away in the back corner of the store. The three women sat down on the only three seats available, and Lawrence loitered by the counter feeling awkward. Louisa was about to speak when the door opened, and an elderly man, hunched painfully over a walking stick, hobbled into the shop.

He approached Lawrence and looked him up and down. "New boy, are you?" he asked.

Lawrence forced a smile as Louisa Aldrich glided towards the counter. "Mr Seeley, how are you today?"

"Middling," he said. "My poor old bones are playing up."

"I'm sorry to hear that. What can I do for you?"

"You sent this," he said accusingly, producing a crumpled piece of paper. "It says I owe fifteen pounds."

"That is correct."

"I don't have fifteen pounds."

"You do surprise me," said Louisa, with the air of a woman facing a regular problem.

"So I can't pay you." The man propped his stick against the counter and crossed his arms.

"Can you pay any of it?"

"I might manage five pounds, at a push," he said, pursing his lips.

"Then give me five pounds today and another five pounds for the next two months."

"That's more like it," he said, reaching into his pocket. "Fancy sending me a bill for the whole amount. I don't know what your father would say."

"I've written it in the book," said Louisa, ignoring the slight. "Look. Five pounds paid, ten pounds due. I'll see you again next month."

The old man grunted and retreated towards the doorway.

"Let's try again," said Louisa, taking a seat.

"My sister says you have been asking about Fanny Nunn," said Alice. Her voice was quiet with a distinctive lisp.

"Yes," said Violet. "It would be helpful if you could tell us everything you remember about Fanny."

Alice gazed into her lap. She seemed less confident than her sister and struggled to make eye contact. "I remember a great deal," she said. "It is not the sort of night easily forgotten. It was late, getting on for midnight, I think, when Harry called me to the window and asked if I could hear noises. I opened the latch and listened." She paused and transferred her glance from her lap to the window pane.

"Go on," said Violet.

Alice blinked and continued, still staring into the distance. "I distinctly heard a cry," she said. "A female voice was wailing in distress."

"What did she say?"

"She said, 'Don't' and she said it several times. The words were unmistakable."

"What did you do?" Violet leaned forward and looked into Alice's eyes. She did not return her gaze.

"I went to Louisa's room to seek her opinion."

"Yes," said Louisa. "So I opened my window and heard the same shrill cries. 'Oh, don't, save me, help me,' the voice moaned, and then there was a dreadful silence followed by a long shriek."

Violet shuddered. "How awful."

"It was," said Alice, turning to her sister.

Louisa reached for her hand and squeezed it. "It affected us all in different ways. Harry will not speak of it at all and Alice still has nightmares, even after all these years."

"Did you hear anything else?"

"Yes. Gurgling sounds which were coming from the direction of the mere near Park Fields. I heard this immediately after the cries."

"Many believe that Fanny took her own life," said Violet.

Alice shook her head, vigorously. "She did not."

"Are you certain?"

"Positive. The cries were quite distinctive. Fanny was screaming for her life."

"Did you hear anyone else?"

"No. Only Fanny's voice."

"What happened next?" Lawrence spoke from his vantage point midway along the counter. Both sisters jumped at the sound of his voice.

"My father and brother went to look for her," said Louisa. They thought she must be in the area of the mere near Mr Muskett's garden. They met a police constable in the street, and he joined them in their search. They followed the sounds until, by the light of their lanterns, they saw a young girl struggling in the water . She was about twenty feet from the bank. By then, she was no longer crying, and all they could hear were a series of groans. They called out to her, but she did not reply."

"Did they try to save her?"

"Of course." Louisa's voice rose in indignation. "There were two boats moored nearby. My father and brother attempted to push off, trying first one boat, then the other. But both boats were in a state of disrepair and utterly useless. My father called to a passer-by to fetch a length of rope. By the time it arrived, it was already too late, and the poor girl had disappeared into the water. There was no moon that night. It was pitch black and too cold to make any further progress, so they abandoned the search until dawn."

"Poor Fanny." Violet sighed as she imagined the terror of the drowning girl.

"Next day," Louisa continued," they dragged the mere and recovered Fanny's body. You know the rest."

The sisters fell silent. Violet tried to find something comforting to say, but nothing came to mind.

"Thank you for your help," she said finally. "We understand better now."

"Do you?" said Alice. She met Violet's eyes for the first time.

"I think so," said Violet, slowly.

"There's something I haven't told you yet. I don't believe I mentioned it to you, Louisa. It didn't seem important at the time. Fanny was in the shop on the day she died. I happened to be there with my father when she came in looking for straps for her suitcase. She was in good spirits and told me that she was going away to Norwich, but would be back the following week."

"Curious," said Violet. "I have heard that she was in low spirits and upset."

Alice cocked her head. "Not upset. Nervous would be a better description. She didn't express any concern or upset about the journey she was about to undertake. Her only reservation was a meeting later that day."

"Meeting?" Louisa appeared surprised by her sister's statement.

"Yes. Fanny had arranged to meet someone before leaving for Norwich and anticipated a difficult conversation."

"You didn't mention this at the inquest?"

"Didn't I? I haven't thought about it for nearly twenty years. I can't remember if I said anything at the time or not. I don't suppose it's of any importance."

Lawrence and Violet exchanged glances. "It could be, if Fanny was murdered," he said.

"But the meeting could have been with a friend," protested Alice. "The comment about the meeting didn't sound sinister, and the fact that she purchased the straps for her case has more relevance. It proves that she intended to leave Diss."

"Your recollections have been most interesting. Thank you again," said Violet rising from her chair. "I cannot tell you how much we appreciate your time."

They emerged from the ironmongery and into Market Hill. "That changes things," said Lawrence.

Violet nodded. "Possibly. But she could have been referring to a meeting with her sweetheart, Alfred."

"I thought you said she spent the evening with him."

"She did."

"Then it wasn't that. We need to find out who else Fanny met that night. And why she was so nervous."

CHAPTER THIRTY FIVE

The Cupboard

"Didn't you like it?" asked Lawrence as Violet pushed her dinner plate away, almost untouched.

"I liked it well enough," said Violet. But I've lost my appetite recently. Hardly surprising with all the worry."

"Haven't I apologised enough?" Lawrence gave a half-smile as he leaned across the table and looked into Violet's eyes. "I shouldn't have left you on your own. I don't know what I would have done if your injuries had been any worse. It won't happen again."

"I wasn't asking for another apology," said Violet. "There is no need. Can we forget all about it and please stop monitoring how much I eat? It's annoying."

"Shall we retire to the lounge?"

"We may as well." Violet was still angry. Her relief at having Lawrence safely back was waning, and his insistence at clucking around her like an old hen was taking its toll.

They walked into the front room of The Crown. There was nobody around, and they took their choice of seating to the side of the fireplace. Violet sat by the window and Lawrence drew up a chair to face her.

"Where is everybody?" asked Lawrence.

"In the market room, I suppose," said Violet. "There's enough noise coming from it." She stared distractedly towards the fireplace and sighed. "I want to go home," she said suddenly.

Lawrence raised his head in surprise. "But we haven't finished," he exclaimed.

"We may never finish. This investigation lurches on and on. I want to sleep in my own bed, for once."

"We shouldn't be here much longer."

"How do you know? Do you think that a confession will magically materialise in front of you? It's not going to happen, Lawrence."

He opened his mouth, but she continued in full flow. "It's not been the same for you, swanning off to Liverpool for days on end. You've left me here alone, feeling ill much of the time and to what purpose?"

Violet looked as if she was about to cry. Lawrence took her hand. "Come on, old thing. It's not like you to complain."

She flashed him a withering look. "I want to go back to Bury. You stay here if you must."

"Very well. If that's what you want."

She nodded her head.

"Then I'll take you to the station tomorrow, but let's talk about what we have learned while we are still together. Give me the benefit of your wisdom so I can manage without you." Lawrence was downcast as he spoke.

"Where shall I start?"

"With your opinion on the whole affair."

She nodded. "There is some evidence of a crime," she said. "For once, it's worth investigating. Somebody pushed Fanny into the water, and her depressed behaviour leading up her death caused doubt over the guilty verdict. Some think she was suicidal, but the evidence suggests otherwise."

"I agree," said Lawrence.

"And Alice Aldrich thinks that she was meeting someone. I spoke to Alfred Wylie and he did not mention a meeting. Neither did Mary Nunn, but she told me that Fanny was loitering as if she was waiting for something."

"Interesting."

"And Alfred said that Fanny told him she would be leaving thirty pounds in the pocket of her Ulster under the willow."

"Which wasn't there."

The arrival of a large group of young men carrying tankards interrupted their musings. The men weaved towards the other window seat, too close for comfort.

Lawrence raised his eyes and grimaced. "Great," he said. "Just when we were making progress."

"Oy, Barney." One of the men stood and held up his half-empty tankard. He waved it in the direction of a man coming through the doorway. The other man waved a hand towards him and retreated.

"You were saying," continued Lawrence.

"I said, the money wasn't there." Violet lowered her voice as she moved closer to Lawrence.

"Do you think she intended to leave it?"

"She had nothing to give him. Unless..."

Violet put her hand to her mouth. "Oh."

She turned away, distracted, as a roar came from the group of men. They'd clinked glasses together and were starting to sing.

"We're leaving," said Lawrence. "Come on."

"Wait. I've had a thought. What if Fanny had a means of getting money, but it was risky."

"I don't understand." Lawrence moved from the table and sat next to Violet.

"She could have met someone with the expectation of procuring money."

"You mean blackmail?"

"Yes."

"That would explain why she was nervous."

The singing petered out as Minnie Panks bustled into the room. "Keep it down," she snapped. "Go in the market room if you want to behave like that". She glanced sympathetically towards Violet.

"Get me another one, Min," said a hang-toothed, wiry man.

"I'll serve you in the market room."

"Oh, go on."

"Don't do it," said another man. "Ratty has nothing left except his burial club money, and his missus will do for him if he spends that."

They all laughed.

"That's it," exclaimed Lawrence, grabbing Violet by the hand. He pulled her into the hallway and peered into the dining room. It was empty. "This way."

They sat down at a table in the corner. "What do you know about burial clubs?"

"Only that they are the salvation of the poor. Two young children died last week, and their parents were only able to give them a decent funeral because of The Oddfellows money."

"Edward Bowden paid burial dues," said Lawrence.

"And Mary Nunn. What are you suggesting?"

Lawrence thought for a moment. "Only that it is very convenient."

"But it's not a large amount of money. Only enough to cover funeral costs with a little over."

"The little over could mean a lot in a poor household. And even more, if there was an insurance policy."

"Really?" Violet seemed doubtful.

"Don't you remember the Liverpool scandal? Perhaps not. You were in the wrong part of the country. It was all my uncle spoke of for weeks. A chap called Higgins died. His mother-in-law poisoned him and collected something in the region of a hundred pounds in burial club payments."

"That's a lot of money."

"And worth a thirty-pound bribe if someone found out."

"You mean Fanny?"

Lawrence nodded.

"You don't think the Oddfellows are involved?"

"Not directly. But we might be able to find out who benefited from the payments by checking their records."

"They won't agree to that."

"I know, and I wouldn't ask them. Where do the Oddfellows keep their paraphernalia?"

"Here, of course. That's one of the reasons they meet at The Crown. They have no premises of their own. There's a large cupboard out the back where they store banners, regalia and the like. I suppose they might keep documents too."

"Good," said Lawrence, stroking his chin. "Well, there's only one way to find out."

There was a stark contrast between The Crown in the evening and during the early hours of the morning. The busy public house had quietened into a silent creaking menace ready to waken any of the occupants with the slightest misstep. Lawrence inwardly cursed for the third time as he tiptoed down the passageway to the groan of floorboards. He passed Violet's room, hoping that she had followed his request to get some sleep, ignoring the temptation to check. As he reached the top of the stairs, he glanced towards the landing windows. They were both open, and the curtains billowed in the light breeze. Lawrence covered the stump of his candle which he'd concealed in a tin top to protect it from draughts. He could ill-afford to lose his only source of illumination.

Every tread of the stairs produced another moan from the ancient wood until Lawrence finally reached the bottom. Holding his makeshift lamp aloft, he surveyed the area to the right by the reception area. Light glinted off the gun cabinet opposite the wooden counter housing the room keys. Lawrence edged through the small gap in the counter facing a wall containing several rows of hooks. Bunches of keys were hanging there, each affixed to rough-hewn wooden tags etched with room numbers. The end hooks held two chunky keys, probably for the external doors and the other, a bunch of varying sized keys of indeterminate purpose. Lawrence grabbed the latter and made for the rear of the building.

Moonlight illuminated the sizeable rear room revealing a double-doored recess with twin brass fingerplates and a lock set below. Lawrence crept past the room and almost tripped over the Panks' elderly cat which lay prone on the rug by the fireplace. It's yowl pierced the silence and Lawrence grimaced as it stared balefully towards him, hackles raised and spitting in fury. He waited with bated breath, for the proprietor to descend, but silence reigned, and he continued in his task. Lawrence tried one key after another from the enormous bunch and was beginning to lose hope when a tarnished brass key turned in the lock. He opened the double doors and entered a storage cupboard large enough to be a separate room, but for the lack of natural light. The commodious closet could easily have held a double bed and furniture. Instead, it contained shelving stacked with various items of Oddfellows equipment.

The cupboard hid a treasure trove of regalia. Large banners leaned against the side wall and items of apparel adorned the rear shelving. Lawrence set his paltry candle on a round table in the centre of the space. He advanced towards the shelves and picked up a black-trimmed apron from a shelf marked 'mourning' and examined it. The words 'memento finis' lay between a depiction of the sun and stars. He shivered as the candlelight picked out crossed keys above a skull and returned the item to its place next to a set of black sashes. Lawrence checked the shelving and noted a dozen sets of ceramic mugs beneath which were dusty tomes of records coated in a thick layer of dust. They looked as if they had lain unused for years.

Lawrence collected his light source and settled, cross-legged beside the books. He pulled one out and tilted it towards the candle, squinting at the untidy handwriting. Inside, was a register of Oddfellows members dated 1883 and of little use. He tried another and another until he opened the fourth register which turned out to be a ledger full of accounting records. Gritting his teeth, he turned the pages and peered at the entries. The writing was clear and easily readable. The Oddfellows treasurer must have been methodical. Each page recorded the month and year of the starting transaction and the book contained about twelve years' worth of records. The accounts were in two parts, the first being general expenses, and the second a history of fund payments for burials and sickness. Lawrence scanned the pages. On first glance, everything seemed in order. There were instances of multiple payments to the same family member. That might have been suspicious, but it was a sad fact of life that death was commonplace, especially when caused by disease. The amounts involved were not vast, though they could have been tempting if money was in short supply.

But all in all, there didn't seem anything untoward in the records. Lawrence sighed, and returned to the front of the cash book, this time focusing on the description. The ruled columns recorded information about the deceased. They included their relationship to the claimant and a witness who was usually a doctor.

Entries started in 1882 and the pages ran out in January 1894, at which point a new ledger began. Lawrence sighed. It was getting cold and he was sitting on a stone floor. He manoeuvred himself into a squatting position and took a final look at the register. As he considered the attraction of returning to his warm bed, a record caught his eye. The entry bore the witness signature of a woman, notable because the majority of the others were by men. The woman's name was Amy Sullivan. Lawrence flicked through the pages a second time searching for more records in her name. She featured on all the preceding pages, but entries petered out in 1891 with the last one early in 1892. Who was Amy Sullivan? And more importantly, where was she? Lawrence closed the book and returned it to the shelf, all the time wondering how old she was. The dates of her entries were significant, for no other reason than her disappearance from the records in the early 1890s. Could Amy Sullivan be the woman they were seeking?

As Lawrence stood, his numb legs buckled and he tripped into one of the banners. It fell to the floor with a clatter. The candle tipped over splattering wax over the floor and across the spines of the registers. "Not again," he sighed as the cupboard plunged into darkness. He waited alone in the unlit closet while his eyes grew accustomed to the dark. The outlines of the unfamiliar regalia took on monstrous proportions, and the metal jewels glinted like eyes. A headless mannikin wearing a Grand Master sash seemed to have moved ever so slightly from its original place. Lawrence gulped. His imagination was running wild. He would rather risk explaining himself than spend another moment where he was. He pushed open the cupboard and scanned the room. It was empty, and even the cat had disappeared. Encouraged, he tiptoed into the rear lobby and then into the entrance hall. With a sigh of relief, he alighted the stairs, before feeling ice-cold metal shoved against the nape of his neck. A low voice growled, "One move and I'll shoot."

CHAPTER THIRTY SIX

Seeking Amy

Sunday, May 26, 1895

Lawrence was rarely embarrassed and considered it a wasted emotion. Once a thing had happened, there was no reversing it and no point in worrying what people thought. But today was an exception. He had crept into the dining room behind Violet and sat in the furthest corner in a futile attempt to avoid bumping into George Panks.

"What's wrong?" Violet had asked, and Lawrence shrugged as if it was unimportant. "You seem like a cat on hot coals," she continued. "Anyway, how did you get on last night."

"I found out something interesting," he said, neglecting to mention his encounter with their host in the early hours of the morning. Lawrence could still feel the cold barrel of the shotgun in the nape of his neck. He squirmed at the thought of the awkward moment when he'd had to explain why he was prowling downstairs with a large bunch of keys in his hand. Unable to think of anything more convincing, he had told George Panks that he was hungry and looking for something to eat. Panks had lowered his gun and, in deeply sarcastic tones, had offered to fetch him some pie. Lawrence had no choice but to accept and suffered the further humiliation of George Panks serving him at a table in the dining room. His host sat opposite and watched silently across the table until he had finished every last crumb.

"I've found a candidate for the Scole confessor," he said, quickly.

"Have you?"

"I think so. Her name frequently appears as a witness to the funeral payments."

"Who is she, and what makes you think she might be the writer?"

"Amy Sullivan. I'm only speculating about her involvement, but the entries she witnessed stopped suddenly, and I wondered if she'd died."

"Or left the parish," said Violet.

"It's worth a look." Lawrence protested.

Violet agreed and returned to her room to collect the notebook in which she had written a list of burials at St Mary's.

"It's no good," she said, closing the notebook. "She isn't here. I didn't think she would be. I would have remembered a name like that."

"We can look elsewhere."

"Don't forget that I'm leaving today."

Lawrence sighed. "I hoped you'd have a change of heart."

"Well, I haven't."

"Why don't we try the Scole parish records?"

"If you insist," said Violet." But, it's like looking for a needle in a haystack. We don't even know that she's dead."

"I've got a strong feeling about this," said Lawrence as they left the hotel and took the Scole Road.

"You always say that when you want me to do something that's against my better judgement," Violet complained.

They arrived at Scole church to the peal of bells as the congregation departed from the Sunday morning service.

"Good timing," muttered Lawrence.

"We should have made an effort to get here earlier. I haven't been to church for weeks."

"You don't go every Sunday in Bury."

"And you only go on high days and holidays."

The arrival of the vicar interrupted their bickering, and he greeted them like old friends.

"Ah, there you are," he said. "Come in, come in."

They exchanged puzzled glances and followed him into the porch.

"Which one of you is Molly," said the Vicar, jovially. "Only joking," he continued, watching Lawrence's stern expression.

"Neither one of us," said Violet.

"Oh. You're not here to talk about marriage?"

"No. We're here see your burial records."

"I'm sorry. I thought you were Mrs Davenport's niece. Forgive me."

"There's nothing to forgive," said Violet, pleasantly. "But may we see your parish register?"

"Certainly," said the vicar. "Are you looking for anyone in particular?"

"Yes," said Lawrence. "Amy Sullivan."

"Oh, yes. Poor Amy. Death came quickly in the end."

"You knew her?"

"For many years. Amy's family came from Ireland and settled here while she was still a young child."

"She died young?"

"No. Amy must have been fifty or more. She lies in the churchyard now and has been there for at least three years."

"How did she die?" asked Violet.

"She died of cancer," said the vicar. "But she did not suffer for long."

"How sad for her family."

"You didn't know them then?"

"Not at all."

"Quite. Or you would have known that all of Amy's family predeceased her. Mother and father, as you would expect, but she was the last of her siblings. Even her niece died young, poor little mite."

"She must have been lonely," said Violet.

The vicar smiled. "Anything but," he said. "She was a nurse and before that, a midwife. There was a good turnout for her funeral, though I expect Polly was responsible for that."

"Polly?" Lawrence spoke for the first time, having been content up to then for Violet to take control.

"Polly Grundy. Her best friend. They were thick as thieves at school and stayed close all their lives. Speak to Polly if you want to know more about her."

"Where does she live?"

"Ivy cottage. Come." He beckoned them from the church and strode in the direction of the Norwich Road. "There," he said, pointing to a small cottage in the distance. "You should find her at home. She only left church half an hour ago."

Lawrence and Violet approached Ivy Cottage to see a stout woman clad in a brown dress with her face and hands hidden from view. One gloved arm held a woven skep, and the other grasped a smoker into which she was blowing assiduously. Bees buzzed lazily from an open hive as she peered inside. Lawrence leaned over the stone wall and coughed. She carried on, oblivious to his presence and he tried again, this time with more success. She walked towards him, lowering her veiled hat.

"Yes?" she asked, cocking her head in a gesture of mild curiosity.

"We've come about Amy Sullivan," said Violet.

"Amy Sullivan," Polly echoed. "I haven't heard her name in a few years. What's she to you?"

"A cousin of my mother's," said Violet without batting an eyelid. Her conscience had become less troublesome over the years, and she was fast becoming an accomplished liar.

"Who was your mother?"

"Bridie Smith." Another lie dripped from her lips without a moments delay.

"She never mentioned her," said Polly suspiciously.

"My mother's Irish," Violet replied.

"Of course," said Polly. "Amy went back to Cork a few times. I never heard her mention a Smith."

"That's my mother's married name."

"Well, that explains it," said Polly, evidently satisfied. "You know that she died, don't you?"

Violet shook her head sadly. "I know now," she said, "but not when I set off. My mother is frail, and when I told her I was visiting Diss, she asked me to call in and pay my respects on her behalf."

"You will be returning with sad news, then," said Polly. "I wish it wasn't so. She was a good friend, and I still miss her."

"Can you tell me anything about her? Mother hasn't seen her for over a decade. It will make the loss more bearable if she knows a little of how she fared."

"Of course, my dear," said Polly. "Why don't you come inside and I'll make a pot of tea."

They followed Polly up the path to the front door of her stone cottage, and Lawrence stooped as they entered the small porch. The cottage stood in stark contrast to the pretty, sunlit gardens. It was cold, dark and even smaller than it seemed on the outside. Polly opened the door into her tiny parlour and gestured to a pair of wooden chairs. "Sit there, my dears, and I'll fetch your drinks through."

They sat in silence and admired the bucolic view beyond the garden, wishing Polly had chosen to talk outside. The door creaked, and Polly appeared bearing a wooden tray with three chipped cups and a pair of saucers. She stirred the tea, set the cups out and waited for it to brew.

"What do you want to know?" she asked, a smile flickering across her weather-beaten face. Violet tried to guess her age. She'd likely be close in age to Amy and therefore in her early fifties. But if her appearance was anything to go by, she'd had a hard life. Her eyebrows were grey and sparse, and tiny hairs protruded from her chin. Deep grooves furrowed her brow, and the tendrils of hair beneath her white cap bore only a trace of chestnut brown. A patchwork of age spots covered her gnarled hands, and her knuckles looked red and painful.

"Tell me anything," said Violet. "Anything about her recent life."

"First and foremost, she was a nurse," said Polly. "Caring was in her nature and looking after people was all she wanted to do. She put their needs before her own and was kindness itself, especially at life's end. She had a particular horror of dying alone and would be there to hold a hand or provide comfort to those approaching their final hours."

"Did she ever marry?"

"Goodness, no. She might have, had she not been so cynical about men. An unrequited love early on, you see. It put her off for the rest of her life."

"Who was he?"

"I don't know," said Polly. "She would not say, and although I often asked, she refused to tell me. It was a source of shame to her because he did not love her back. Well, not enough to make an honest woman of her."

"Perhaps he couldn't marry," said Lawrence, incautiously. "If he already had a wife."

Polly raised an eyebrow. "I don't think that is likely," she said, lifting the lid of the teapot.

"How long did this infatuation last?"

"Decades for all I know." Polly picked up the teapot and poured. She pushed the cups with saucers towards her guests and took the one without. "He must have liked her somewhat," she continued. "She owned nice things that she could not have bought from a nurse's pay."

"Does Amy have any living relatives?" asked Violet.

Polly shook her head. "She was the last of the Sullivan line. There's nobody, except your mother and perhaps a few distant kin in Ireland."

"That's a pity. I would have liked to have met Amy's family and asked for a memento for my mother. A likeness or a letter would mean a lot to her."

"I can help with that," said Polly.

"You have a picture of Amy?"

"I might have. When Amy died, her furniture went to Aldrich's auction house, but she left me a box of personal items. Nothing expensive and only of sentimental value, but you are welcome to see them and choose something for your mother."

Violet felt a momentary pang of guilt at her kindness, but it was too good an opportunity to waste. "Yes, please," she said, "and thank you so much."

"Come this way."

Polly guided them up a narrow flight of stairs to an even darker landing with a door on the right and two uneven steps up to another door in front. "Mind your head," she said as they trod on the spongy floorboards. "I won't come in. It's more of a box room than a bedroom, and it won't fit us all. I'll be downstairs if you need me."

Lawrence squeezed into the room behind Violet and stood at the doorway with his head bowed. "Calling it a box room is a gross exaggeration," he complained. "I'll stay here otherwise I'll get in your way."

Violet reached for the wooden crate which was the only box-shaped item in the room and presumably the one to which Polly Grundy had been referring. She blew a thick layer of dust from the top and sent the choking particles into the damp air of the room. Lawrence sneezed and retrieved a handkerchief from his pocket.

Polly's description had been accurate. The box contained trinkets of no discernible value. Amy seemed to have a penchant for carved wooden animals. A small collection of elephants, a tapir and a rhinoceros were gathering dust in a chipped glass fruit bowl. Violet removed them together with a bevelled hand mirror and placed them on the floorboards. An ugly vase, a brass ring and a hair comb soon joined them. Violet continued removing objects until the box was almost empty. Then she noticed something underneath a leather-bound notebook. Violet pulled the shiny object out and held it aloft. At first glance, it looked like a medallion, but when she took a closer look, it was an Oddfellows jewel.

Lawrence whistled. "Where did she get that from?" He reached for the medallion and examined the back for identifying marks. There were none. Violet, in the meantime, had opened the notebook. She passed it to Lawrence without speaking.

He licked his fingers and turned the pages. "Accounts," he said unnecessarily. "Records of money collected with dates by all the entries."

"Her wages, perhaps?" asked Violet.

"Or something more sinister? Hello, what's this?" He extracted a piece of folded paper from the back of the notebook. "A letter from an admirer," he said. "Listen to this."

'My dearest Amy, you are the cleverest girl. Brains and beauty personified. I will act at once upon your suggestion. The mere again, or is it too soon? Either way, there will be a bit for you and a bit for me, as always."

"No, doubting it now," said Lawrence. "Amy was right in the thick of this business. The only question remaining is who was there with her?"

CHAPTER THIRTY SEVEN

Cat Among the Pigeons

Lawrence and Violet walked towards Diss, both preoccupied with the exact nature of the crimes involving Amy Sullivan. She'd been colluding with somebody, probably male, and they'd conspired to obtain burial money for profit. "But," said Lawrence, stopping to emphasise his point, "it's not a great deal of money. The largest amount in the book was a hundred pounds. If Amy and the other party had shared the proceeds, after factoring in a funeral payment there would be barely any money left. A lot of risk for little benefit."

"I know," said Violet. "I am not happy with the logic behind our theory. There must be something else that we are missing."

"And someone else," said Lawrence.

Violet shuddered. "It makes my skin crawl," she said, "to think that it could be somebody we know."

"And we still have to determine what we are dealing with. We don't know how many deaths were natural and how many were criminal."

"Or whether they were opportunistic or planned."

"And if the latter, then it's cold-blooded murder for sure. Anyway, Violet, we must hurry along now. You have a train to catch."

"I thought you didn't want me to go."

"I will be a lot happier when you have left."

Violet fell quiet, and they walked in silence as Lawrence considered his previous remark.

"That is to say, I won't have to worry about your safety when you are away from this snake pit," he said hurriedly.

"I know what you meant," she said. "My feelings weren't hurt – I was just thinking."

"About what?"

"About what we ought to do next. There isn't enough evidence to bring the matter to the attention of the police force. I expect they would laugh at us."

"My thoughts exactly," said Lawrence. "The time for subtlety is over. I'm going to set the cat among the pigeons."

"How?"

"By making our suspicions public."

"And where are you going to do that?"

"I'm not sure yet," he admitted. "But it's one of the reasons why I would like you well out of the way."

They had walked briskly and taken a more direct route leading past the railway station.

"It's a pity we didn't think to send your bag on, " said Lawrence over the rattle of a passing train. He watched the brightly painted engine chug into the distance, steam billowing from its funnel. His heart sank at the thought of Violet leaving, but he knew it was for the best.

"We should talk about suspects," said Violet. "Have you any thoughts?"

"Not really," said Lawrence. "It's reasonable to suppose the involvement of the Oddfellows, but it may not be direct. I'm not suggesting it was one of them, but at the least, they must know the perpetrator. This person is probably a male, but not a young man. He would have to be in his forties."

"But more likely in his fifties, if he was an admirer of Amy Sullivan."

"We should have hung onto that note," said Lawrence. "Someone may have recognised the handwriting."

"Not after almost twenty years," said Violet. "And the writing was terrible. But the fact that it exists at all rules out the illiterate."

"And the crime itself involves a low cunning, more likely found in someone with a good education," said Lawrence.

"Let's assume that it was an Oddfellow," said Violet. "There was a jewel in Amy's possessions which could connect to the note. Now, the Oddfellows meet at The Crown every Sunday."

"This evening?"

"Yes, every Sunday evening. So why not make a public declaration there? Even if the Oddfellows are not involved, there will be enough of them to hear and repeat what you have to say. It will be around the whole town by tomorrow."

"Good. Yes, that could work well. In that case, let's go back to The Crown and pack your bag," Lawrence said, looking at his pocket watch. "You can be in Bury by five o'clock."

"Or Overstrand," said Violet.

"Why on earth would you go back to Overstrand?"

"Because I've had a fascinating thought."

"Go on."

"You didn't find the Scole confession in Redhill Street, did you?"

"No."

"And neither did William Miller."

"You know he didn't. Where is this leading?"

"You didn't find it, because it wasn't there. It had already gone by then."

"Gone where?"

"It could have gone anywhere, but I am hoping against hope that it went to Overstrand."

"You mean, that it was in Edward Bowden's Bible? I didn't see it."

"Did you open every page?"

"No, but it was in my possession for the best part of a day. I think I would have noticed."

"Not necessarily."

"And Bowden was fond of the Bible. If it had been there, he would have found it."

They had reached The Crown by now and Lawrence held the door open as Violet entered.

"That's all true," said Violet, walking past the empty lounge and towards the stairs. "But I still intend to check."

"I thought you wanted to go home."

"I do, desperately," she said, climbing the first stair. "But I can't sit idly by while you place yourself in danger." She clung to the newel post as she turned and spoke. Lawrence gazed up at her in admiration. She was plucky and spirited, and he had mistreated her. Never again.

"It's not worth it," he said. "Go home, and I will return as soon as I have announced the presence of a murderer in their midst."

"No." She shook her head. "I will find somewhere to stay overnight and send you a telegram tomorrow. I will be back in Bury in no time. By then, your plan may have come to fruition."

Lawrence smiled. "As you wish," he said, before following her upstairs to help with her packing. Neither one of them heard the rustle of a newspaper coming from the lounge, which had not been as empty as it first appeared. The sole occupant of the room glowered and lowered a copy of the *Diss Express*. Once again, their luck had held. Once again, there was a problem, but a resolvable one. They folded the newspaper, rose, and walked towards the chemist on Market Hill.

Lawrence tapped his fingers across an empty table in the lounge and stared across the hallway for signs of life. He'd adopted a strategic position near the door, taking advantage of the view into the market room where the evening's gathering would take place. Lawrence had checked the meeting arrangements with Minnie Panks earlier, and she'd dispensed the information without asking any questions. Violet had been right. Minnie lacked natural curiosity in the same way that Lawrence lacked patience. The wait for seven o'clock seemed interminable, and Lawrence glanced at his watch. It was approaching ten minutes to the hour. He might have reasonably expected some signs of life by now, but he was still the only person downstairs. Lawrence began to wonder if there had been a cancellation.

His eyes grew heavy and unfocused as he waited. Boredom set in and he leaned on the table with his chin propped up on his hand trying to remain alert. Then, without warning, the front door swung open, and a group of men milled towards the market room, their voices gruff and low. Lawrence recognised some of the men from previous evenings at The Crown. Their faces were solemn and bore none of the jollity of the crowd of young men from the previous night. They filed into the market room and sat upon the wooden chairs waiting, in virtual silence, for the meeting to begin.

Lawrence remained seated, hoping that they would not shut the door, but after the last man entered it swung back muffling the sound of the speakers. He got to his feet and picked up a discarded newspaper which he pretended to read while loitering in the hall. When the coast was clear, he pushed the door open an extra inch, creating a partial view of the room without revealing his position. Lawrence leaned nonchalantly against the wall in case anyone else arrived and wondered what he was doing.

After a few moments, Harry Aldrich made his way to the front of the room and coughed. He was wearing a black sash, and a similar black-edged apron to the one Lawrence had seen in the cupboard the previous night. Aldrich made a sign that Lawrence didn't understand and gestured for quiet before pulling a piece of paper from his apron pocket.

"Bow your heads for Robert Moore," he said. "Brothers. Will you join me in recognising the dedicated and zealous service of our friend Robert Moore – a dear friend cut down in his prime in a wanton act of murder. Brother Moore rendered valuable assistance with fundraising in his capacity as deputy treasurer. He has been a loyal and faithful member of this lodge and is held by his brethren in high esteem. We, his friends, lament his loss. Amen."

A murmured 'Amen' followed from the seated men.

Harry Aldrich continued. "It is our sad duty to assign his position to another, and in these circumstances, we may accept proposals outside of an annual general meeting. Yes, George?"

George Fairweather, who had been sitting ramrod straight, stood up. "I have a proposal," he growled.

"Go on?"

"I propose we find the filthy cur who killed him and string them up in the market place."

Harry sighed. "It's neither the time nor place to have this conversation," he said.

"But what are they doing about it?" demanded another man at the back of the room. He rose to his feet to make the point and glared at his friend on the right-hand side who reluctantly joined him. One by one, every man stood.

Harry turned towards Arthur Thompson, who was sitting with Joseph Pope in the first row. "What's the latest news, Arthur?" he asked.

Arthur Thompson joined Harry and faced the hostile crowd. "There was an examination of Brother Moore's body as you know, and there will be an inquest here on Tuesday afternoon. There is no doubt that he drowned..."

"He didn't drown, someone murdered him," said the man at the back.

"As I was about to confirm before you interrupted," said Arthur. "Though there is room for doubt, both the surgeon and coroner report bruises and cuts to Robert Moore's head. More specifically, there were finger marks to the side of his neck; marks that may have been caused if someone held his head beneath the water."

There was a shocked silence, followed by a shuffle of chair legs as the men returned to their seats. Arthur continued. "Though Robert's death is common knowledge, I appreciate that the details are new and I'm sorry to give such a graphic description of his final hours. He did not deserve to die so horribly."

"He did not deserve to die at all. What are they doing to catch his killer?" George Fairweather was still standing in the middle of the room, eyes blazing with fury.

Harry and Arthur exchanged glances. "The authorities are conducting a thorough investigation. They are doing the best they can."

"Which isn't much from what I've seen," muttered Joseph Pope. He was sitting, legs apart, hunched over his ample belly with a rare frown across his face.

"No," agreed Arthur. "So far, there has been little progress. I would have hoped for more."

"Someone is going to get away with murder," said George Fairweather pulling off his sash. He hurled it to the floor. "I won't mourn him until they've caught his killer," he snarled.

Harry opened his mouth to speak, but Lawrence had already spotted what he suspected would be his best opportunity. He strode into the market room, past the stony-faced men and towards a startled Harry Aldrich. Turning to face the group, Lawrence held up his hand for silence. "Be careful what you wish for," he said, dramatically. "For the murderer of Robert Moore is a member of your organisation."

"No!" Joseph Pope eased himself from his chair. "That cannot be. We are good men, charitable and kind. You have seen the work we do."

"Nevertheless, one of you is a killer, and he has killed more than once."

There was an explosion of angry voices as the men protested their innocence.

"Leave this meeting at once," said Harry Aldrich in a controlled voice, barely containing his fury. "How dare you come in here and insult the memory of our friend."

"I dare because whoever killed Robert Moore also killed a young girl. And not just her – there have been others, the names of which you will learn in due course. And make no mistake, I will find this killer. Consider my words tonight. Think about what happened to your friend. Then look around this room and ask how well you know your neighbour. Where was he on the night that Robert Moore died? Cast your mind back twenty years. Could he have killed Fanny Nunn?"

"Fanny Nunn killed herself." George Fairweather snapped out of the almost catatonic state into which he had fallen upon hearing Lawrence's words.

"How do you know?" asked a man at the back. "You didn't even live in Diss back then."

"Stop." Harry Aldrich snapped, his anger in full flow. "Don't entertain this fantasy. We are brothers. Do not cast suspicion upon each other." He turned to Lawrence. "Do as I say and leave."

"Yes. Get out." The man at the back stood and made his way towards Lawrence, his friend trailing in his wake.

"I'm going," said Lawrence lunging for the exit. He sidestepped the large man and grasped the door handle, then left, taking the stairs two at a time. He reached his room and sat on the edge of the bed, deep in thought. It had been a good night's work. He had undoubtedly lost some friends and a great deal of goodwill, but he had made an impact, and something was sure to come of it.

Five minutes later, he reached for his wallet and found it absent. He patted his jacket pocket and checked his coat, but to no avail. The wallet was missing. He wondered where it could be, and just as he began to panic, he remembered. The last place he'd used it was in the lounge. He'd been counting cash while killing time waiting for the Oddfellows to arrive. The wallet must still be on the table. Lawrence crept downstairs, and as he reached the bottom step, a low murmur emanated from beyond the closed door of the market room. To Lawrence's relief, he saw the familiar shape of his wallet on the table and grabbed it, turning back towards the stairs. But directly in his eyeline was the portly form of Joseph Pope hunched by the market room door and breathing laboriously.

"Can I help?" asked Lawrence, hoping that Pope wasn't as antagonistic as the other Oddfellows.

Joseph raised his head to reveal a florid face crowned by sweat-streaked hair. He uncurled himself and fanned his face with a chubby hand. "Quite well, thank you," he muttered. "It's just a combination of this damnable business and a touch of indigestion. I felt quite faint for a moment ."

"You should get some air," said Lawrence.

"Yes, I will." Joseph shuffled towards the front door and stumbled over the tattered doormat.

"I'll join you," said Lawrence, concerned. Pope's face was ashen, and he looked as if he was about to pass out.

A light breeze graced the April evening, and Joseph Pope raised his face towards the wind. "That's better," he said.

"I'm sorry about your friend," said Lawrence. "And I'm even sorrier to be the bearer of bad news regarding his connection to the Oddfellows."

"Robert was a fine man," said Pope. "I have known him all my life. It's hard to believe he has gone. And when you said it might be one of us..."

"Was that the moment you felt unwell?"

"Yes. It was. The thought of it. Those men are my brothers."

"Including Harry Aldrich?"

"Of course. Why ever not?"

"No reason," said Lawrence. "Except that he is in charge. Sometimes that distinction creates barriers to friendship."

"There are no barriers, I can assure you," said Pope. "We respect each other equally, and that applies regardless of our standing in the town."

"What do you mean?"

"Well, George is a blacksmith and works with his hands. I am a teller in the bank and Harry owns a thriving auctioneering business. Yet we are all close friends."

"Is it true that Aldrich takes on house clearances."

"Yes. A fair few."

"He must see some interesting things?"

"I daresay. And some dull ones too. Some of the furniture is in such poor condition that it's only fit for firewood."

"And personal possessions?"

"He takes them too and sorts them into items of value. Anything else ends up on the rubbish heap. He auctions all the valuable stuff."

"Including books?"

"I expect so. I don't know."

"And you believe him trustworthy."

"I would stake my life on it," said Pope, firmly. "I'm not sure what you are driving at, but you have picked the wrong man in Harry. He is a committed Methodist, and honourable in all his dealings. Now please excuse me. I feel better and will return to my friends now," he continued, emphasising the word 'friends' as he turned and re-entered the hotel.

Lawrence was about to follow him when thoughts of Violet stopped him in his tracks. He would give anything to discuss the events of the evening with her. She didn't need to comment to keep him on track. A nod of her head or an occasional word of sage advice was good enough, and his instinct would pick up from there. He missed her, and the thought of going back to an empty room was too depressing to contemplate. He decided, instead, to walk to Scole and prevail upon Michael for companionship and a bed for the night.

CHAPTER THIRTY EIGHT

Testing for Arsenic

Monday, May 27, 1895

Once Michael overcame the surprise of Lawrence's unexpected visit, he greeted him warmly and welcomed him with a large glass of port and a good supper. Michael abandoned his plan to write to his brother that evening. Instead, they sat talking into the small hours about the case, speculating whether Violet had arrived in Overstrand yet. Michael had already offered his spare room to a friend, but his sofa was available. Lawrence accepted it and slept surprisingly well, waking at daybreak. He joined Michael at the table, and they breakfasted on eggs and bacon before Lawrence returned to Diss. The sky was cloudless, and despite the early hour, the sun's rays were fierce. Lawrence was perspiring heavily by the time he returned to The Crown.

He strolled through the hallway, almost bumping into George Panks who shot him a withering look. Unabashed, Lawrence climbed the stairs removing his jacket as he went, relieved to be free of the heavy clothing. He poured a jug of water into the blue and white porcelain basin, splashed his face, and towelled it dry. The cold, refreshing water made him feel thirsty, and Lawrence reached for the smaller drinking vessel by his bedside table then poured himself a drink. He raised the scratched glass to his lips then stopped at the sight of a hair floating in the liquid above a fine layer of sediment. He fished out the offending object and wiped it on his trouser leg before stopping to consider the implications of what he had just seen. A hair in a glass was unfortunate, but the fine white sediment below it was something else again. He sniffed the water. It was odourless and colourless. But for the presence of the stray hair, he wouldn't have looked twice at the contents. He swirled the water around and rechecked it. The substance had very nearly dissolved. For a moment, the temptation to put his finger in the liquid and taste it was overwhelming, but common sense prevailed. Instead, he sat down on the bed, trying to organise his thoughts. Yesterday, he had deliberately and provocatively set out to display his suspicions publicly. Today, he had found a strange substance in his drinking water. The connection between the two things was unavoidable, and he wasn't about to take a chance.

He emptied the contents of his glass into the white ceramic jug and thrust the empty drinking vessel deep into the pocket of his trousers. Draping his coat over the water jug, he set off downstairs to find the helpfully insouciant Minnie Panks. Ten minutes later, he had gained enough information to know that Mr Gostling the chemist would be at his home in Linden House. Lawrence walked the length of Denmark Street and entered Gostling's driveway at a lick of speed.

Linden House was a handsome property set well back from the road. Lawrence climbed a small set of steps to reach the doorway located beneath a balustraded balcony. He rang the bell, and a young servant girl greeted him. She waved him through the door and left him alone in the spacious hallway while she went to fetch her master. Lawrence began to feel uncomfortable as he waited. It was one thing asking for an opinion in a drug store, but quite another invading a gentleman's home. He needn't have worried. Thomas Gostling grasped the potential severity of the situation as soon as he had finished speaking.

"You've come to the right place," said Gostling, reaching for the jug. "I'm almost retired, you know. But I have a small laboratory in the back of the house and more than enough equipment to conduct a Marsh test."

"Marsh test?" echoed Lawrence.

"Yes," said Thomas Gostling, leading him through a corridor and into a room that smelled of sulphur. "It's as good a detector of arsenic as it was when they convicted Marie Lafarge in the forties."

"If you say so," said Lawrence, feeling out of his depth.

"I'll tell you how it works if you like," said Gostling enthusiastically, reaching for a porcelain apparatus containing taps and tubes. He placed the device on top of a wooden table and carefully adjusted it.

"We need one of these," he said, unscrewing a jar. He reached for a small pair of tongs and extracted an even smaller piece of metal which he placed in one arm of the tube.

"What is it?" asked Lawrence.

"Zinc," said Gostling, "and this is sulphuric acid." He pointed to a cabinet, donned a pair of heavy gloves, and poured in the contents of the bottle. Now, let's take a sample from your jug," he continued, decanting a small amount into the other arm. "One stopper," he said, producing a rubber bung, "and a short wait." He stepped back and stared at the device.

"It doesn't seem to be doing much," said Lawrence.

"That's because you can't see through the porcelain," said the chemist. "But rest assured that hydrogen is now building up in the short arm." He made a vague gesture towards the apparatus. "Water?"

"Where?"

"I mean, would you like a glass of water as you were unable to drink yours earlier?"

Lawrence faltered, unsure whether to accept given his recent experience.

"It's perfectly safe."

"Yes, then," Lawrence muttered, feeling foolish.

Thomas Gostling poured a glass and smiled as he passed it to Lawrence.

"Thank you," said Lawrence, gulping it down.

A clock chimed from outside the room, and the chemist looked up. "Is that the time? I must get on," he said. "Now, for the clever bit." He struck a match, released a nozzle on the device and ignited the gas. Then he opened a small drawer beneath the desk, took out a piece of glass and placed it in the whitish flame. "Oh dear," he sighed as a brownish-black spot appeared. "Your suspicions were correct. There was arsenic in your water."

By the time Lawrence returned to The Crown, the full implications of his narrow escape had set in. His fingers shook as he untied his cravat, and he sat down slowly on the bed, thankful for the stray hair that had saved his life. By rights, Lawrence should have slept at The Crown the previous night and was in the habit of drinking water if woken up in the small hours. Had the arsenic been introduced before bedtime, which was likely, he could have gulped it down without seeing the contents. Lawrence shuddered at the thought of death by poison. He'd already witnessed the unendurable pain of a strychnine victim and would never forget seeing the dying spasms of the poisoner's target during one of his first cases as a newly promoted inspector. The memory would haunt him forever.

He bolstered his pillows and lay back, reclining against the bedstead while surveying the hotel room. The bedroom door was to his right and easily visible from the bed. It would be too risky for someone to interfere with his drinking water at night when he would be in the room. An intruder would be easy to see. In any case, he remembered drinking from the glass yesterday morning. The contamination must have occurred in the afternoon or early evening. It was most likely after he announced his suspicions to the Oddfellows which implied their involvement. Equally, a member of the Panks family or their servants could have doctored his water. The keys were available from the recessed area of the hallway, and the front door to The Crown was open from early morning to late evening. Anyone could have walked in off the street, which opened up the possibility of further suspects. While musing upon that thought, Lawrence fell asleep.

He awoke to a pang of hunger, and his stomach growled in response. He hadn't eaten since breakfast, and if he didn't shake a leg, he would miss dinner too. Lawrence stood and walked towards the dressing table where he picked up a comb and ran it through his hair. His reflection stared back, and he didn't like what he saw. The spray of grey at his temples had extended towards his ears. Faint vertical lines on his forehead suggested a perpetually worried man. He raised his eyebrows and watched the lines disappear, wishing that the change was permanent. It had been several months since he had last called upon his barber, and his hair needed a good cut. All in all, he did not feel his usual impeccably-groomed self.

As he turned away from the mirror, he spied a glint of metal on the floorboards near the bed. Lawrence peered more closely in case he had imagined it, but there was something on the floor. He walked towards the bed and stooped down, closing his hand over the object. Adrenaline coursed through his body as he opened his hand. In his palm, was an object which looked like a chunk of metal but was a cufflink with a symbol etched on top. The last time Lawrence had seen a similar symbol was inside the cupboard at the back of The Crown Hotel. It was a close match to one of the medallions from what he remembered, but Lawrence was by no means certain. He would have to go back and check, which might prove difficult in the middle of the evening. Patience was not his strongest virtue, but he was going to have to wait. In the meantime, he was starving. Gritting his teeth in frustration, Lawrence made his way to the dining room.

Dinner was not a memorable meal, and Lawrence would have struggled to describe what he had eaten if asked. His concentration was lacking, and impatience overrode every other emotion as he waited for the evening to pass. Lawrence wasted an hour walking the streets, and at ten o'clock, returned to his room, making an unsuccessful attempt to sleep on top of the bedclothes. Eventually, he gave up and decided it was late enough to risk a visit downstairs. The hallway was empty, and the doors to the public areas shut, so he slunk towards the counter and removed the bunch of keys. The back of The Crown was dark and still. Lawrence located the lantern that he had borrowed on his earlier walk and stowed by the rear door. He ignited it and made for the cupboard again, encountering no one this time, feline or human. Once again, the cupboard door opened easily, and this time the lantern cast a powerful illumination over the contents of the closet.

Lawrence located the Oddfellows jewels on the middle shelf where he had last seen the symbol. The little pile gleamed in the beam of the lantern as he compared them to the cufflink. He had been right. One of the icons was identical. But something beneath the jewels was different. Propped up against the shelf immediately below was a burlap sack tied with a rough rope that he did not recognise. Lawrence stared at it, trying to remember. But the bag occupied the spot on which he had spilt wax so it could not have been there the night before. Lawrence untied the rope and pulled out the contents. First, he retrieved a dark grey jacket in reasonable condition for a garment of its kind. Then, he rummaged inside again and removed a flat cap and a pair of trousers. A halfpenny fell out of the trouser pocket, startling Lawrence as it rolled across the floor. Something white protruded from the other trouser pocket.

Inch by inch, he tugged at it until he was holding what looked like a small furry animal. He held it aloft and saw an all too familiar wire and spring arrangement. The object he held was a long, full, white beard. Suddenly he realised what he was seeing. The outfit and beard fitted the description that William Miller had given of the man by Moyse's bookstall. The man who had asked him to find the Bible and who was responsible for many deaths. The man who had come perilously close to poisoning Lawrence earlier that day. He dropped the disguise and turned the sack inside out. There, at the bottom, was a bundle of invoices bearing the mark of Aldrich's auctioneers. With shaking hands, Lawrence replaced the clothes and papers in the sack and set off for the police station.

CHAPTER THIRTY-NINE

A Mysterious Note

Tuesday, May 28, 1895

Lawrence whistled as he descended the stairs of The Crown Hotel for the second time that morning. He'd delivered the burlap sack to the police house late on Monday night, anticipating a lacklustre response. Instead, the constable had listened intently. Mr Gostling, the chemist, had been summoned to the police house shortly after breakfast to give an account of the Marsh test conducted the previous day. Then, the constable had sent for his inspector who regarded the sack solemnly, promising to question Harry Aldrich at the earliest opportunity. Lawrence had only given scant details of his suspicions. The facts surrounding the burial club deaths were too disorderly to make public. But he was making progress. As soon as he gained irrefutable proof of financial wrong-doing, he would present the evidence to the authorities. Lawrence decided to spend the rest of the day cross-referencing his records.

As he reached the foot of the stairs, the formidable shape of George Panks loomed before him. The worst of his embarrassment about the late-night feeding foray had passed, and Lawrence greeted him with a cheery 'Hello'.

Panks scowled. "When are you leaving?" he growled.

"I haven't decided," said Lawrence, taken aback at the man's tone. George Panks' attitude had changed from the tolerance of a simpleton to outright hostility.

"I suggest you decide soon," he said. "You are not welcome here."

"Why?" asked Lawrence, perplexed. He was sure he hadn't caused any further offence to his host since the affair with the pie.

"The arrest of Harry Aldrich this morning is why. The poor fellow is in the police house because of some cock and bull story that you cooked up. Aldrich is a good man, Harpham. And a good customer of this hotel."

"So it's about money, is it?" asked Lawrence. "Worried there might not be any more meetings held here? Is that why you risked the life of one of your guests?"

"What are you talking about?"

"Poison," said Lawrence. "I don't know who you've been speaking to, but I was nearly killed in your hotel yesterday. I've since found incriminating evidence of Harry Aldrich's involvement. So I suggest you consider your position, before condemning mine."

George Panks continued to glare at Lawrence, but stepped away and allowed him to pass. As Lawrence made for the front door, Minnie Panks breezed past, oblivious to her father's mood.

"I've got a letter for you, Mr Harpham," she said, bustling towards the counter. "I would have delivered it earlier, but Father sent me to the butchers, and I clean forgot. Here." She thrust two envelopes towards him.

"Ah. A telegram from Violet," he said, looking at the markings on the envelope. "Hello, what's this?"

The second envelope was white and written in a chunky, almost childish hand with the words 'Private & Confidential' inscribed at the top. Intrigued, Lawrence slipped Violet's telegram into his trouser pocket and slit open the envelope. He read the slip of paper inside. 'Come to the reading rooms at The Diss Express as soon as you receive my note.' Lawrence turned the page over. The reverse was blank.

"Who gave you this?" he asked, showing it to Minnie.

"Nobody," she replied, not troubling to read the page. "I found it on the doorstep this morning."

"When?"

"About seven o'clock."

"Hmmm," he said vaguely, reaching for the door, not sure what to make of the letter. He supposed that it must have come from young

Charles, the compositor, but quite what he wanted with Lawrence was a mystery. If the message been for Violet, he would have understood. Charles had taken quite a shine to her since her help with his handwriting problems. But the letter was explicitly intended for Lawrence and therefore a puzzle.

Lawrence hastened straight for the printworks and was there within ten minutes, hoping it was not another waste of his time. He was keen to get back to his notes and produce a timeline of evidence that might satisfy the constabulary. He pushed the wooden door, but it did not open. Turning the handle did not remedy the problem, and it was clear that the door was locked. Lawrence walked down the side of the building and to the rear where he remembered seeing another door on his previous visit. Sure enough, he could tell from a distance that the rear door was ajar. He pushed it open and walked inside. The small rear lobby led to the open door of the reading room. Lawrence peered inside, but the room was empty. He went to the front of the building, through the compositor's office and into the entrance with the long counter. The printworks were bafflingly devoid of human life. He returned to the rear again, wondering whether he was being taken for a fool by the letter writer. It could be a punishment for his part in the arrest of Harry Aldrich. After all, Harry was one of the town's most esteemed inhabitants. Lawrence was only too aware of the strength of feeling against him from his earlier encounter with Panks.

He returned to the reading room, deciding to use his time wisely by consulting the archived newspapers while the place was empty. But as he glanced across the room, his eye was drawn towards another envelope. It had been propped up against a book in the middle of the table and marked, 'private'. On the front of the envelope written in a familiar childish scrawl, was 'For the attention of Lawrence Harpham'.

CHAPTER FORTY

Derailed

Monday, May 27, 1895

The train journey that should have taken Violet no more than four hours had begun badly and rapidly turned into the worst travel experience of her life. The steam engine had pulled out of Diss station and gone no more than a few miles before grinding to a halt on the tracks. After a long delay, a harassed conductor informed the passengers that the boiler was faulty and would need repairing. Another hour passed before they were finally underway. The engine limped on a while longer until they reached the outskirts of Norwich. Then disaster struck as an explosion ripped through the front of the train. Time stood still. The windows imploded from the force of the blast and shards of glass spiked across the forwardmost carriages. Violet joined the other passengers as they scrambled onto the tracks in a disorderly mass.

Outside, the scene was chaotic. Two boilermen, dragged from the front of the train by their colleagues, lay bleeding on the grass. Another man slumped by the side of the locomotive was beyond help. The engine lay broken and still, pipes and metal spilling from the front of the boiler. A young mother sobbed frantically, and her frightened children huddled by her side while an elderly lady tried to console them. The woman continued screaming, caught in an unending cycle of hysteria until a wiry, dark-haired man slapped her on the cheek.

"How dare you, sir," bellowed a white moustached man, in colonial attire.

The young man ignored him and shook his head before kneeling by one of the injured boiler men. He cradled the man's head and made a clumsy attempt to dress his wounds, working in silence. The slap had done the trick, and the young woman had stopped crying. She rocked backwards and forwards on a grassy mound, arms cradled around her children. Their sobs quietened as they leaned into their mother. Violet joined the young man and offered her help. He nodded his acceptance, and she explained that she was an experienced first aider. He introduced himself as Maurice.

One of the fallen boiler men had suffered a deep gash to his upper arm, from which blood spurted in a pulsing stream. Violet asked Maurice to remove his belt to use as a tourniquet. He unbuckled it without speaking, and Violet applied it to the injured arm. The bleeding slowed to a trickle, and the boiler man's complexion gradually changed from grey to pink. Violet loosened his shirt and made a thorough check. He'd suffered cuts and bruises from the flying metal but was not in any immediate danger.

His companion had been less fortunate. Though initially seeming in better health, he was now flagging. He'd walked from the train unaided, according to Maurice, and had appeared uninjured. But now, he breathed in rasping gulps and beads of sweat dotted his brow. Violet felt for his pulse. It was slow. She rested her head on his chest and listened to his rattling lungs.

"This man needs urgent medical help," she whispered.

"I'll go," said Maurice, and he set off towards a hamlet in the distance.

Violet was still sitting next to the boiler man an hour later. As dusk had fallen, the temperature dropped. The injured man clung to her hand as his body shivered in shock. Some passengers had taken their chances and made for the hamlet, but Violet remained with the stricken men. She was not alone. The train crew had stayed behind, helping anyone unable to walk, including elderly passengers, a middle-aged man with a walking stick, and two young children.

Pins and needles spiked through Violet's legs which she feared would turn to cramp. Just when she thought she would have to get up and walk around to relieve the discomfort, she saw the glow of lanterns in the distance. Moments later, Maurice appeared with two other men.

"Help is coming," he said. "There will be enough carts to take you to Norwich."

He was as good as his word, and the transport arrived within moments. The injured went first, and Violet rode with them, staying until they arrived at the hospital. She watched as medical staff assisted them into the emergency wards, wondering what she would do for a bed. But as she walked away, a nurse ran up to her and guided her back into the hospital where she gave her a thorough examination. Typically, Violet had given no thought to herself.

At first, Violet had protested but realised that she would be less of a nuisance if she agreed. And when the nurse removed her coat, there were swathes of dried blood on her dress. Violet had sustained wounds of her own and not noticed the pain in her bid to aid the more seriously injured. The nurse dressed her cuts and grazes then offered Violet a bed. Both knew it was not necessary, but Violet would be comfortable on the ward, even if only for a few hours. As it happened, she didn't leave until the next morning.

Tuesday, May 28, 1895

Violet located her luggage at Norwich station where her rescuers had left it the previous night. It was still early when she boarded the Cromer train. The trip was quicker and safer than the journey from Diss, and she pulled into the station well before lunchtime taking her carpetbag while leaving her suitcase in the conductor's care. Violet continued the short trip to Overstrand by carriage as the sun blazed high in the sky on a perfect May day. She walked to the centre of the village pondering whether to stay or return to Bury on the evening train.

Violet strolled down the high street intending to go to the Cottons' house on Gunton Terrace but determined to make the most of the balmy weather she took a detour instead. Turning into the Londs, she walked past the flint cottages, stopping to peer through an ornate wooden gate where vibrant violet wisteria crowded the wall. The pretty gardens burgeoned with spring flowers.

At the end of Pauls Lane, she saw a fisherman crouching by a net at the top of the cliff with a large-eyed needle in his hand. Beside him was a wooden bucket containing seawater in which freshly caught crabs clawed at the surface. A second bucket contained the still bodies of previously boiled crustaceans. Violet asked the fisherman if he would mind her bag, and he nodded his assent. She left it by the side of the buckets, free to explore the beach without the burden of luggage.

Violet removed her shoes and stockings and made her way across the sand, avoiding the pebbles. The tide was halfway out, leaving little pools of seaweed and shellfish in its wake. Violet walked to the water's edge letting the sea lap against her ankles and inhaled the salty odour. Her senses were alive with the sound and smell of the sea; yesterday's accident already a distant memory. Life was transient, she thought, easily lost. It took an experience like the train explosion to appreciate life and the good health she enjoyed. Violet paddled for ten minutes then found a dry spot towards the cliffs and let her feet dry in the sun. Brushing the sand from her toes, she put her shoes on and headed back. By the time Violet climbed to the top, the fisherman had repaired his net and was dressing crabs on a little wooden trestle table. She retrieved her suitcase, and the fisherman suggested she might enjoy a small crab for lunch. Violet accepted gratefully, remembering how much she'd enjoyed them during her stay with Lord and Lady Battersea. She located a nearby seat and began to eat the crab, but a wave of nausea came from nowhere, and she could not finish. Disappointed, Violet left the uneaten crab by the side of the path where seagulls soon disposed of it. With a churning stomach, she returned up Pauls Lane and towards Gunton Terrace.

Amelia Cotton was sweeping the pathway outside number four when Violet approached. She regarded Violet quizzically before recognition dawned, and she greeted her warmly.

They exchanged small talk and Violet began the tricky task of explaining the purpose of her visit.

"So, are you suggesting that my father's Bible belonged to a murderer?" asked Amelia, misunderstanding the Bible's provenance.

"No," said Violet. "The man who sold it was the victim. Someone killed him."

"After my father received the Bible."

"Yes. A few months later."

"But, what has it got to do with Father?"

"Nothing," said Violet. "It is a coincidence. But I have reason to believe that the Bible might contain a document which the murderer went to great lengths to recover."

"Father never spoke of any such thing," said Amelia doubtfully.

"He may not have understood the significance. Have you kept the Bible?" asked Violet.

"I have, as it happens," said Amelia. "Mother gave it to my husband, George, as a keepsake."

"May I see it?"

"If you wish."

Violet followed Amelia into her kitchen and waited at the table while the younger woman went upstairs. She returned with the Bible and set it down on the table, anxiously hovering as Violet opened the front page. The bookstall stamp and inscription were as Violet remembered. She flicked through the pages of the black-bound book, checking for a letter or document, but the Bible was empty. She turned to the final page, checked the binding and pressed the cover. The lining was intact and undisturbed.

"I didn't think you would find anything," said Amelia, "If there ever was a letter, it is long gone."

Violet put the book on the table, trying not to feel too deflated. She'd known that finding the confession was an unlikely prospect, but one worth checking.

"Thank you anyway," said Violet. "It was kind, especially as..."

Violet stopped in her tracks as she glanced at the Bible again. There was one place she hadn't yet checked. She stood the book on end and scrutinized the spine. The cover fitted neatly around the pages with no visible gap. Violet splayed it open, and the space between the spine and cover gaped just enough for her to insert the tip of her index finger. She could feel a slight difference in the lining of the spine and dragged her nail along the inside. Something moved, and she tried again, inching an object up the spine until the tip of a curved piece of paper emerged.

"What is it?" asked Amelia, eyes wide.

Violet pinched the tube of paper and pulled it out, unfurling the document across the table.

"Oh no," she said, colour draining from her face. "It can't be."

"Can't be what?" asked Amelia, but Violet was already rushing out of the door. Time was short, and she had an urgent telegram to send before the post office closed.

CHAPTER FORTY ONE

At Muskett's Staithe

Lawrence picked up the envelope and examined it. The anonymity of the writing evoked the stomach-churning memories he'd felt when he'd received Catherine's crests. But whatever the envelope contained, it couldn't be that. Nobody from Bury Saint Edmunds knew that he was working in Diss. Well, nobody apart from his domestic, Annie, who he trusted implicitly. There were no further clues on the back of the envelope, and he opened it gingerly, revealing a newspaper cutting dated December 8, 1877. The clipping was from the *Bury Free Press* and detailed Fanny Nunn's inquest. The article was familiar. Lawrence had already seen it during his research. But the snippet in his hand was a fraction of the original piece, and someone had underlined a paragraph in blue ink. It read:

There's thirty pounds of money in this little bag. You will find it in my Ulster coat pocket tomorrow morning 20 yards from Mr Muskett's staithe in the mere under the weeping willow.

Carefully written beneath in the same childish writing as the original note, was the figure nine. It was drawn next to a depiction of a clock face, with a half-moon scribbled below.

Lawrence sighed as he leaned against the table with the note in his hand. The whole thing left him feeling like a participant in a parlour game. The picture was an unsubtle clue to time, and the presence of the moon indicated that he should be somewhere at nine o'clock at night. Judging by the reference to Mr Muskett's staithe, it was an instruction to meet underneath the willow tree at the appointed hour. But it was silly and dramatic, like a theatre performance. And not a very good one at that. Lawrence felt too old to participate in a purposeless charade, and yet, he was still curious. What might he find there? And would it be a risk if he didn't arrive at the requested hour? He mulled it over for another ten minutes, vacillating between obeying instructions or ignoring the note. If he decided to go, should he take a companion or set off alone. He even contemplated asking for Michael's opinion, but the long walk to Frenze church deterred him. Not to mention the embarrassment of Michael knowing he had given credence to the note. In the end, curiosity got the better of reason, and he decided to go by himself. The risks were low. It would still be light at nine o'clock, and he had no cause for concern about his safety now that Harry Aldrich was in police custody.

Making the decision made him feel more comfortable, and he left the printworks for The Crown Hotel. Once there, he spent the rest of the day arranging records. Satisfied with his progress, and confident that he could prove his suspicions, he broke for supper. Then finding it unusually quiet, he read the paper in the lounge until quarter to nine. Earlier that day, it had occurred to Lawrence that he had no idea where to find Mr Muskett's staithe. As usual, he broached the subject with Minnie Panks. And obligingly, she not only shared the location but told him what a staithe was without him having to go through the indignity of asking.

Feeling better prepared, Lawrence set off towards the mere, looking out for a large willow tree near to Muskett's landing stage. He saw it as soon as he approached the mere and, as Lawrence drew closer, it was apparent that the rickety structure required repair.

Lawrence loitered beneath the willow and ran a hand over its ancient bark. Shrouded within its golden leaved boughs, he realised that he was almost invisible to anyone passing. Whoever had summoned him here, must have understood the cloaking effect of the willow and thus hoped for privacy. The thought made Lawrence nervous and he walked towards the water's edge and picked up a small rock which he placed in his pocket, for protection. Nine o'clock came and went, and nobody appeared, and at five minutes past the hour, Lawrence wandered away from the mere. As he reached the footpath, he almost collided with Joseph Pope, Arthur Thompson and George Fairweather.

"Good evening," said Joseph. "Which of us are you arranging to arrest today?"

"It wasn't like that," sighed Lawrence. He hadn't expected anyone to welcome him with open arms, but the overt hostility came as a surprise.

George Fairweather glared at him. "I'm going," he growled. "The air smells bad around here." He stalked off without looking back.

Joseph Pope tipped his hat and forced a smile. "Enjoy the rest of your evening," he said sarcastically. "Are you joining me, Arthur?"

"Later," said Arthur, holding his hand up. He waited until the men were distant shadows.

"Sorry," he shrugged. "They are still upset about Harry."

"But you're not?" asked Lawrence.

"Only because I'm sure that he will soon be a free man. I don't hold you entirely responsible," he continued. "Are the fish biting well?"

"I beg your pardon?"

"It's ten past nine and getting dark," he said, snapping open his pocket watch. "Why else would you be by the mere?"

His question caught Lawrence off guard. "I'm waiting for someone," he said, without thinking.

"I'll keep you company if you like?"

"No." Lawrence immediately regretted the force of his refusal and the suspicion it might generate.

"Are you sure?"

"Quite sure."

"Pity," said Arthur. "I've nothing better to do."

Lawrence watched him stride away, waiting until he was sure that he was alone. Then he returned to his place beneath the willow deciding to wait for another half an hour before giving it up as a bad job.

A slight breeze rustled through the leaves as he stood in semi-darkness concealed from the sight of any passer-by. Gently lapping water punctuated the silence and Lawrence shifted his weight from one leg to the other as the evening cooled. A branch snapped underfoot as Lawrence eased towards the edge of the willow, then another, until enlightenment dawned. Lawrence was standing on grass, so why could he hear footsteps? The sound was coming from someone else. He tensed, barely

227

breathing, listening for a clue to the direction of the noise, but the only sound was the high-pitched yowl of a passing fox. He must be hearing things. The failing light was making him nervous, and he was getting cold.

He decided to give it another five minutes then retreat to The Crown for a quick bedtime brandy. His mouth watered at the thought. Lawrence pulled his collar up and thrust his hands into his pockets. His fingers connected with Violet's telegram, discarded earlier in his haste to identify the letter writer. He retrieved it and opened the envelope, straining to read in the poor light. It was no good. The words swam in a blurry mess on the page. He patted his inner pocket and found the tin he always carried containing a candle stub and matches. Then he struck a match, lit the candle and examined the telegram. It was a brief and concise warning. And as the words registered in his mind, Lawrence heard the unmistakable crunch of footsteps behind him. He had no time to draw breath, let alone move before he felt the cold metal edge of a knife against his neck.

CHAPTER FORTY TWO

Unmasked

"I wouldn't move if I were you," said a familiar voice, as the sharp-bladed weapon pressed into his carotid artery.

"I wasn't planning to," Lawrence retorted.

"I suppose you recognise my voice?"

"Yes. It's quite distinctive. Are you going to tell me the point of this charade?"

Lawrence winced as the knife dug deeper and he felt a drop of blood well against the blade and trickle down his neck.

"Careful. This waistcoat is new."

"Then I would say that you wasted your money," said his assailant, chuckling at the play on words.

"Are you going to tell me why we are here?"

"If that's how you want to spend the last few minutes of your life, then by all means. What would you like to know?"

"Let's start with Amy Sullivan, shall we? What was she to you?"

"Amy Sullivan." The man sighed wistfully as he drawled her name in elongated vowels. "What a woman."

"But you never married her?"

"Why would I? I didn't love her."

"Yet she loved you."

"You probably find that difficult to understand. I was a handsome young buck in my day. Amy's adoration was useful. But I didn't need a wife. I needed a partner."

"Partner in crime?"

"Precisely."

"And it was all about money?"

"Now, Harpham. That's rather offensive. The money was a useful extra, but it was all about power."

Lawrence snorted. "Power," he exclaimed, momentarily forgetting the knife against his throat. "You killed women and children. They were easy targets."

"Not power in the crude way you describe. And I killed full-grown men too. It was about possessing the power of life or death."

Lawrence shuddered at the excitement in his captor's voice, betraying naked passion at the thought of murder.

"Have you ever seen anyone drown?" The man closed his eyes as if accessing a favourite memory. "The pleasure of watching is exquisite, but nothing surpasses the act. I can make the end quick or prolong it indefinitely. The power, the thrill..."

"But why?"

"Because I like it."

"And Fanny Nunn. Was she just another victim?" asked Lawrence, discreetly sliding his hands in his pockets.

"Fanny Nunn was an interfering busybody," hissed the man. "Always poking her nose into matters that did not concern her."

"Tell me more."

The man expelled a sigh and Lawrence recoiled at the warm breath as it brushed the back of his neck.

"Sit down," the man commanded.

Lawrence lowered himself to a seated position beneath the willow and looked up at his assailant.

"Won't you join me?" he asked.

"Hardly," said the man, running his thumb along the edge of the knife. "Move so much as a finger, and I will cut your tongue out. Stay still, and I'll tell you a story."

Lawrence sat quietly and waited for the man to begin.

"My mother killed my father," said Joseph Pope casually. "And I was quite happy to go along with it. We were poor, you see – had nothing. Father was sick and didn't work. He was a useless waster.

I was sixteen when Father died. Mother and I discussed it first, both agreeing that my meagre income could support two of us, but not three. Father was ten years older than she and as weak as a kitten by the time we killed him. He didn't struggle when she put the pillow over his head. Nobody questioned his death. Nobody cared. And then we remembered that he had been paying into the burial club. Not only did my earnings go further, but we received a little more than the cost of the funeral. It was a good Christmas that year. For once, there was food on the table." Joseph paced as he spoke, keeping a watchful eye above Lawrence's head.

"The following year, Mother had a fall. She lingered for a week, then died. A terrible accident, they said. It wasn't anything of the kind. I pushed her down the stairs. Fortunately, she never regained consciousness. Waiting until thirteen months after Father's death gave me time to pay a year's worth of insurance premiums on her life. It was a much better return on investment than the pitiful offerings of the burial club. Then I met Amy."

"How?"

"She nursed my mother in her final weeks," said Joseph. "Amy was lonely and liked to talk, which was irritating to begin with until I realised how useful her village tittle-tattle could be. One day she told me that Hannah Rampling had been complaining about her sick child, wishing that it would die so she could have the burial club money. Amy deplored her sentiments, but all I could see was the flaw in her logic. Hannah Rampling wouldn't get the money, you see. Children under eight are uninsurable. But it put me in mind of a scheme for use outside the confines of the burial club payments, so I insured the life of a sick child. I had no relationship with the boy. He belonged to one of the parishioners, but the insurer accepted me as the parent, and I waited for him to die. The child had a wasting disease and did not take long to succumb. The insurers asked few questions, and I profited handsomely, but Amy discovered the insurance papers, and started to pry."

"I'm surprised you didn't kill her too?" said Lawrence, staring at Pope from his seated position.

Joseph's lip curled. "Why would I kill her when she could be useful? No. I courted her and made love to her until she became devoted to me. I gave her little gifts from my profits. She did not mind the deception when it only amounted to fraud."

"But that did not last?"

"No. There's only so many times one can fool an insurance company. In any case, sickness is unreliable. Illness does not always lead to death, and when it does, the timing may not work. As it happened, a solution arrived courtesy of Amy, who had been speaking to Hannah Rampling again. Hannah had too many children to feed and wasn't attached to any of them. I asked Amy to suggest to her that the demise of one might be to the advantage of the rest. At first, Amy baulked at the scheme, so I withdrew my affections. Within a week, she'd come crawling back, prepared to do my bidding. Amy agreed to act as my agent in the strictest confidence, never revealing my involvement. And under my guidance, she encouraged Hannah to invest a little money into the burial club. Nine months later, she had paid enough to guarantee death benefits, and we set to work on the second part of the plan."

"Which was?"

"The death of one of her children, of course. She chose one of her sons. He was not a pleasant child, though it would not have mattered if he was. But Billy Rampling was particularly obnoxious. He was rude, foul-mouthed and the sort of boy who pulled wings of flies for fun. His mother sent him down to the river on Amy's instructions, and I killed him there. His death was the first at my hands since Mother, and the most satisfying. Nothing has ever compared to the thrill of holding him under the water and watching the air bubbles disperse. The shudder of his final breath, the moment that life became extinct. The power of it, Harpham. The sheer, unadulterated power."

"Steady on," said Lawrence, sarcastically.

Pope frowned at the interruption to his recollections. "You will soon find out what it's like to be on the other end of that power," he snapped. "Now, where was I? Oh yes. The Rampling child. I left him in the river, and they found him later that day. The surgeon examined him and declared him drowned. His mother had the burial club money, as planned, with a bit for me and a bit for Amy. And that's how it began. A combination of insurance and burial club frauds. Sometimes with the cooperation of the parent or the spouse, and sometimes on my own initiative. It has been very lucrative, Harpham."

"And nobody ever knew?"

"No. Amy was a nurse with easy access to the weak and vulnerable, none of whom knew about me. Well, not until that interfering creature Fanny Nunn stuck her nose in."

"So, she was blackmailing you." Had he not been in fear of his life, Lawrence would have relished the thought. He and Violet had guessed as much.

"I was discussing a proposition with Amy one day, which Fanny Nunn overheard," said Joseph. "Fortunately, I was standing in the lea of the building, and she could not see me. She heard the conversation and saw Amy but didn't understand the consequences of what she had witnessed at the time. Later, they found old man Goode in the hay barn with his head smashed in, and she remembered the conversation and understood our intentions."

"His death was not an accident, then?"

"Quite the contrary. I fully intended to smother Goode, but he fell from the hayloft and hit his head on the stone step. It looked exactly like an accident to anyone except Fanny Nunn, who had heard us discussing Goode earlier. Luckily, she was greedy and resorted to blackmail instead of telling the authorities. She visited Amy and asked for thirty pounds. We could easily have spared it, but she would have always been there, waiting for another opportunity to make money. She had to go. Amy summoned her to the staithe to collect her ill-gotten gains, and I tossed her into the mere, knowing that she could not swim."

"Nobody saw you?"

"Not a soul. It has always been that way. Nobody knew of my involvement – nobody even guessed that the deaths were anything other than natural. I am just Joseph, large and jovial, a friend to all. Even if the good people of Diss knew there was a murderer in their midst, I am the last person they would suspect. Which is why I won't get caught when I kill you."

"What makes you think I haven't told someone where to find me?"

"I made you wait, didn't I? There was a reason for that. Passing with Fairweather and Thompson allowed me to watch you. Of course, I didn't expect you to leave your position under the willow. I picked it precisely to hide you from view. And the quick chat established that nobody else was nearby. I caught up with Fairweather, waited for Thompson and entered my house while they watched, before doubling back. All in ten minutes and leaving me with an excellent alibi."

"Tell me about Moyse," said Lawrence, ignoring the glee in Joseph Pope's voice.

"Ah, yes. A far greater problem than Fanny Nunn, it turned out, but providence has always smiled upon me. Moyse had a secret. A secret that did not endear him to his brother-in-law. I don't even know what it was, but it didn't matter. William Jackson was intolerant of anything that Moyse had to say. He received a letter about Amy's blasted confession to which he cannot have attached any credence. I know this because he screwed it up in a ball which fortuitously dropped to the floor of The Crown Hotel as I was passing. I shudder to think what would have happened if it had fallen into the wrong hands. I needed to act quickly."

"And you went to Liverpool."

"I did. But not on impulse. I pondered the matter overnight, weighing up the risk and considering if there was an alternative course of action. There was none. The man was a danger and disposal of the confession was essential."

"So, you went to Liverpool in disguise?"

"As you found out. It was quite a shock when I realised that you knew."

"I don't recall talking about it."

"You didn't. I found a journal in your room. I was always going to introduce arsenic into your water. But the act gave me even greater pleasure once I read through your notes and realised the extent of your knowledge. You had accumulated an alarming amount of information, including reference to my disguise."

"How did you do it?"

"Do what?"

"Doctor my water with arsenic. It's necessary to sign a poison register and even then, chemists colour the poison. There was the barest trace of sediment in the glass. I nearly missed it."

"The arsenic came from an old tin of rat poison," said Joseph Pope. "It has been in my possession for many years and is as effective now as it ever was. I use it sparingly, though," he continued. "Varied murders are less likely to look suspicious."

"Returning to Moyse," said Lawrence. "I don't understand why he died."

"Neither do I, to be frank. In hindsight, it was the perfect solution to my problem, but I did not set off to harm Moyse. There was no danger to me without Amy's confession. Nobody knew who had written it. It was clear that she had not named me, and if she had signed it, it would have been evident in the letter that Jackson received. But I did not know if there were any other means of identification within the confession. And if Moyse returned to Diss one day with the letter, there was a chance that someone might recognise the handwriting. My sole intention was to locate the letter and destroy it, and I employed Miller for that purpose. How he made such a meal of it, I cannot imagine."

"Frustration and panic," said Lawrence. "He could not locate the confession, nor the Bible in which it lay."

"He didn't look hard enough. Moyse kept his book stock at his dwelling. I questioned one of his boys."

"You overlooked one thing, though."

"What?"

"He ran a bookstall, the sole purpose of which was to make money."

"And?"

"He'd sold the Bible. It wasn't there to find."

"I don't believe it." Joseph Pope spluttered with incredulity. "Why would he sell the very book that contained the confession he was so disturbed about finding."

"I doubt very much that he did. Books littered his house, and he employed several assistants at the bookstall, all of whom had access. He may not have even been aware that it was missing."

"How do you know?" Joseph spat the words angrily. Lawrence considered his reply. Joseph Pope was a cold-blooded, conscienceless killer from whom he would be lucky to escape. If he said too much, it might implicate Violet. And if he saw the telegram in his pocket, it would cement her fate.

"You'll never know," he said coldly, with a recalcitrant expression on his face.

"Tell me." Pope knelt behind Lawrence and pulled his head back by his hair, tracing the blade of his knife down Lawrence's thorax.

Lawrence clenched his fists, trying to prevent his body from shaking too hard. Sweat ran in rivulets down his temples. He was starting to panic about his weak position and vulnerability to the whims of a multiple murderer.

"I said tell me," hissed Pope. "Or I will cut you." He moved the knife up to Lawrence's face and placed the tip at the top of his cheek. "An eye or your tongue?" he asked. "Choose."

Lawrence slowly unclenched his right fist as another drop of sweat trickled from his brow. His hand moved undetected towards his coat pocket.

"Eye or tongue, eye or tongue," said Pope in a sing-song voice as he moved the knife from cheek to lip all the time pulling Lawrence's hair tighter with his free hand.

"Oops, slipped," said Pope, as the knife cut the skin between Lawrence's lip and nose. A trickle of blood seeped into his mouth. Lawrence licked his lips, feeling sick at the metallic taste. But it focused his mind. Joseph Pope was going to kill him, and if he didn't act soon, it would be too late.

In one swift move, he plunged his hand into his coat pocket, grabbed the rock he had collected earlier and thrust his hand behind his shoulder, connecting with Pope's jawbone. Pope howled in pain and dropped the knife. Lawrence rolled to one side, searching for Pope in the shadows as he scrambled to his feet. Daylight was long gone, but he could see the dim outline of Pope a few yards ahead of him. The portly killer was on one knee clutching his head. A twig snapped as Lawrence moved forward and Pope jerked his head up, piggy eyes meeting Lawrence's stare. He snatched at something on the ground before him, and Lawrence held back realising that Pope had located the fallen knife. Joseph Pope got unsteadily to his feet, holding the blade in front. He waved it towards Lawrence.

"Don't be a fool," snarled Lawrence. "I can outrun you. Put the knife down."

"Alright," said Pope, placing the knife on the ground directly in front.

"Step away," commanded Lawrence.

Pope took one pace backwards and waited. Lawrence moved forwards uncertainly, suspicious at the speed of Pope's capitulation. But Pope was a safe distance away and Lawrence knew he had time to swoop for the knife even if the killer came at him. But as Lawrence knelt and reached out, he felt a crack against his temple and dropped to his knees. The last thing he saw before the world went black, was the same bloodied rock he'd used on Pope a few minutes before.

CHAPTER FORTY THREE

Submerged

Lawrence woke to the sound of grunting as a noise like a truffle pig disturbed his slumber. His face was wet and cold and a searing pain shot through his head. He shivered, wondering whether he was in the grip of a nightmare. Then the grunting started again, and he felt something brush against his face – something like grass. He inhaled a mossy smell and realised that he was close to the ground and his body was moving. Rough hands clutched his ankles, dragging him onto a muddy path, as his arms followed uselessly behind. He coughed and inhaled a mouthful of dirt then twisted his head to orientate himself. A pale moon hung high in the sky illuminating a body of water to the front. It was the mere. He was inches from the riverbank. The grunting stopped, and his feet were released as a shape loomed ahead, kicking him over to face the night sky. Joseph Pope stood above him, brandishing the knife.

"Ah. You're awake. Good," said Pope, a cruel smile etched across his face. "I would hate you to miss your death."

Lawrence planted his hands behind him and tried to heave himself up.

"No, you don't," hissed Pope. "Not this time." He took the knife and plunged it into Lawrence's forearm. Lawrence felt strangely detached from the scream that exploded from his chest, piercing the silent night.

Pulling himself together, he sat up and lunged towards Pope with his uninjured arm.

Pope grimaced then aimed a boot at Lawrence connecting with his stomach. Lawrence flailed, trying to catch his breath, but it wouldn't come. Gasping like a landed trout, he gulped at the air, but it was futile. Lawrence lay winded, the air kicked from his lungs as Pope grabbed his ankles again, pulling him towards the water. As they reached the edge of the mere, Pope stepped to one side, kicked Lawrence until he lay horizontally along the bank, then rolled him into the water. As Lawrence felt the freezing liquid seep through his suit, he raised his head in shock and took a deep breath, finally inflating his lungs. But Pope was waiting. Standing on the edge , he raised his boot and slammed it onto Lawrence's skull. Lawrence thrashed beneath the water as Pope ground his face into the gravelly bottom. Sediment streamed down his throat and into his eyes, and his lungs screamed for air. He shook his head, but the water sapped his strength, and he could not escape Pope's hobnailed boot. He felt a bubble escape from his lips, then another. It was all over. He couldn't hang on. Just as the blackness began to overwhelm him, his head seemed to float weightlessly to the surface. The boot was gone. A pair of arms pulled him from the mere and dragged him to safety.

"Hold on, Harpham," said a voice. Lawrence stared through blurry eyes. Suddenly, multiple lanterns illuminated the edge of the mere.

"Out of the way," another man continued, pushing him to a seated position and slapping his back. He coughed as a lungful of water sloshed from his mouth.

"Here," said a man he didn't recognise, covering him with a blanket.

"What happened?" Lawrence croaked, recovering his faculties.

"I heard you cry out," said a familiar voice. "I wasn't about to let you suffer the same fate as Fanny Nunn."

Lawrence looked up into the concerned eyes of Harry Aldrich.

"They've let you go?"

Aldrich nodded.

"Pope left evidence in your shop, I suppose?"

"I expect so."

"Where is he?" Lawrence looked around in alarm.

"There." Harry Aldrich pointed to an object in the mere that looked like a floating log.

"Is he dead?"

Aldrich nodded. "I heard you cry out, opened my window and saw you in the mere, just like I saw Fanny all those years ago. But I wasn't going to let the same thing happen again. I roused my neighbours, and we ran down to the water. Pope was standing there with a maniacal expression on his face. We pulled him off, but he ran towards Muskett's staithe. The steps were rotten. He fell and hit his head on a post. Pope is dead, Mr Harpham. Drowned. It is all over."

CHAPTER FORTY FOUR

No Reprieve

Tuesday, June 4, 1895

A clock ticked loudly in the premises of Harpham and Smith Private Investigators in Bury Saint Edmunds. The occupants of the room stared wordlessly at the timepiece, barely breathing. They watched as the second hand circumvented the clock face twice and both jumped when the clock chimed the hour.

"That's it, then," said Lawrence Harpham, turning towards his companion who occupied the desk to his side.

Violet nodded. "I thought William Miller might get reprieved."

"I didn't," said Lawrence. "Uncle Fred sent a telegram yesterday. He was not expecting leniency."

"Do you think Miller saw his family before he died?"

"I should think so," said Lawrence, looking at the clock again. "It's usually the way."

Lawrence and Violet were in their office half an hour earlier than usual. Each had decided, without conferring, that they would mark the hour of William Miller's execution at their desks. On any less sombre occasion, seeing Violet for a few extra minutes would have pleased Lawrence no end. She had not been herself lately, disappearing at odd hours and looking sickly and pale. On several occasions, she had started to say something and stopped herself mid-flow. Recently, they had spoken of little other than work-related matters, and he was beginning to think that he might have offended her. Yet Violet was still a source of considerable strength to him. Especially the day before when another anonymous envelope had arrived. They both saw it at the same time, but Violet had snatched it from the doormat and set light to it, dropping the burning remains in the empty fireplace. Lawrence had protested, desperate to know what was under the sealed flap, but Violet had gently told him that it was the only way to save his sanity. And she'd been right. The letter had not blackened his mood nor opened tender wounds. Catherine occupied a more modest part of his feelings, commensurate with her absence from his life. Violet, on the other hand, was beginning to take up an increasing number of his thoughts. His concern over her recent demeanour and insularity had caused him to request that she join him in the abbey grounds at lunchtime. It was time he acknowledged her importance and showed her how much he cared. Perhaps then, she would feel able to confide in him.

"Did you get the letters," he asked, breaking from his reverie.

Violet nodded. "They arrived last night. Please thank your uncle."

"I will. Did you find anything worthwhile?"

"Oh, yes. Take a look at this."

Violet handed Lawrence a long blue envelope affixed with a New Zealand postage stamp. Uncle Fred, an avid reader of *the Liverpool Mercury*, had seen notice of an auction to sell the effects of the late Edward Moyse. His nephew had kept most of his personal items, but Uncle Fred had purchased a small cabinet, inside which was a bundle of letters tied with string.

"I've seen this before," said Lawrence, slipping one of the letters from the envelope. "I recognise the name." He pointed to the neat signature at the bottom of the document.

"James Dunleavey wrote the majority of the letters," said Violet. "They confirm what I suspected."

Lawrence reread the message and felt none the wiser by the time he reached the end. "He says he has had a successful trip and will return home within the month," said Lawrence. "He trusts that Moyse is well and hopes that he is not lonely. The content is trivial."

Violet passed him another letter. "Try this one."

"Much of the same," said Lawrence. "Idle chatter."

"Don't you find it rather intimate?"

Lawrence knitted his brow as he scrutinised the pages. "It is somewhat," he conceded. "Perhaps Dunleavey was a relative."

Violet raised her eyebrow half an inch.

"You're not suggesting..."

She passed him another envelope, this time white and square. The Scole address was typewritten, and the letter inside bore the date, 1887. The formally written missive contained a thinly veiled warning from the Hobart branch of the Plymouth Brethren. Moyse should not approach the Norfolk Brethren sects who were now aware of his behaviour. The letter referenced a scandalous relationship and Moyse's subsequent voyage back to Blighty.

Lawrence squirmed in his chair. "I see," he managed.

"You see? Is that all? Why are you not angry at their treatment of him?" Violet demanded. "That poor man. He cannot help his feelings or choose who he loves. They destroyed his life when they banished him from New Zealand. Look through the rest of the letters when you get a chance," she continued. "Before the incident, Moyse was a highly regarded evangelist. He made huge personal sacrifices to spread God's word. But not content to expel him from the Antipodes, these so-called men of God conspired to ruin his life in England."

"So, the stranger who approached William Jackson was from New Zealand?"

"Or Tasmania. It could have been either. But, yes. That is my best guess. William Jackson could not bear what his brother-in-law was and sent him away. Poor Edward went to Liverpool where nobody knew him in the hope of privacy so he could continue his life without scandal."

"Only to be murdered." Lawrence steepled his hands and considered the transience of life. "We should make the most of every moment," he said, gazing towards Violet. She was unjudgmental and compassionate. What more could a man want in a partner? "We need to talk," he said, voice brimming with emotion.

As Violet opened her mouth to speak, the doorbell jangled, and an elegant young lady closed her parasol and came into the room.

Lawrence turned hot and cold as he met Loveday's eyes.

"Are you pleased to see me?" she gushed. "We had such a lovely time in Liverpool, that I thought I would look you up."

Violet stared at Loveday open-mouthed, closing her eyes as if in pain. Swallowing hard, she got to her feet, cleared the letters from Lawrence's desk and stowed them in her drawer. Nodding silently at Loveday, Violet left the office with her head bowed. Lawrence watched in stunned silence as she disappeared from the Butter Market and made her way towards the railway station.

THE END

Thank you for reading The Scole Confession. I hope you liked it. If you want to find out more about my books, here are some ways to stay updated:

Join my mailing list or visit my website
https://jacquelinebeardwriter.com/

Like my Facebook page
https://www.facebook.com/LawrenceHarpham/

If you have a moment, I would be grateful if you could leave a quick review of The Scole Confession online. Honest reviews are very much appreciated and are useful to other readers.

Author Note: The Scole Confession combines the real-life murder of Edward Moyse in Liverpool with the unsolved drowning of Fanny Nunn in Diss. Edward Moyse is a real person and was an evangelist in Tasmania. He returned to England after becoming the subject of a scandalous relationship. As usual, many characters in The Scole Confession existed. Some are creations of the author's imagination.

Printed in Great Britain
by Amazon